The Art of

Straightening Nails

A Story of Triumph Over Adversity

Randy Judd

Paperback ISBN: 9798431566318

Hardcover ISBN: 9798434865364

Author Contact: *randy.judd@randyjuddauthor.com*

Facebook Page: *Randy Judd, Author*

Author Website: www.randyjuddauthor.com

This is a work of fiction. Names, characters, businesses, events, and incidents are the products of the author's imagination. Any resemblance to actual persons, living or dead, or actual events is purely coincidental.

Chapter 1

*H*e couldn't deny it. The fear was real!

While hugging close to the outside of the one-story bungalow, Robert was hoping his stealth moves would help him escape into the night. Slinking around the corner, he then peered back around to see if the something was still behind him. He imagined he could discern shapes in the darkness at the other corner of the house ... he imagined. He wasn't sure, but he thought he could see part of a cheek, or was it a forehead, or ... nothing. As he stared into the night, suddenly there was a flash and instantly, a bullet shattered the stucco only inches from his face. He recoiled into his hiding place, the echo of the gunshot still reverberating across the night. Robert turned and ran. He wanted to look back, but dared not.

The pursued man ran quickly, but also cautiously, into the dark woods beyond the house. He was cautious because of the trepidation he felt about running into a limb or tripping over a stump amongst the trees.

In an instant, the unseen being that had been following him was now somewhere in the trees before him. Robert stopped, not sure whether to proceed or retreat. Everything was quiet. The only sound he could discern was his own breathing. Whatever it was, it was surely closing in on him, silently. Robert knelt, then lay powerless amongst the leaves, unsure of his next move.

Robert lay in bed for a few minutes, his heart still racing. Though this dream may have been disturbing to some, it didn't concern Robert much. He had gotten used to it.

A column of light pierced the slight opening in the curtain. As he watched the dust particles stir randomly in the light beam as though they were stars in a galaxy, he thought about the dream, and how it did indeed frustrate him. Though not always the same, this recurring dream always had common elements. In the dream, he was always being followed, but could never see *what* was following him. In the dream, the thing trailing him always remained some distance behind him yet was trying to hurt him. Some things were always different in the dreams. The location in the dream was seldom the same. The method of attack varied, bullets, arrows, rocks, mud, even darts. To say it was recurring was not to say it happened often. The dreams had started in high school and had occurred maybe a dozen times since. Robert had learned to expect the dreams on the night before big occasions or big decisions: graduations, marriage, promotions, awards. He could not interpret the dream but felt as if it had something to do with his successes and something not wanting him to succeed. The dream often caused him to wake with doubt about the upcoming event. He knew why he had the dream *this* time.

As he lay in a Hilton Garden Inn near the Bay in San Diego, he knew it was about the car.

The purchase of the Jaguar F-Type S had been somewhat spontaneous, at least spontaneous by the standard that Robert had set. For Robert to purchase any car meant studying out the decision for many months. For example, when he last bought an SUV for the family, he spent hours on the web looking at reviews and message boards to make sure he was making the right decision. This approach had served him well although it caused much frustration for his wife and kids. They couldn't understand why he couldn't just go to the showroom, drive a car, and say, "*Yes, I'll take it*". He couldn't understand it either. He knew it was a little strange and almost compulsive, but it worked for him. And if his reluctance were some sort of psychological problem that he could pay two-hundred dollars an hour to have diagnosed, in the end how did his problem hurt anyone?

Yes, this purchase had been different. When he got an unexpected bonus, he looked around at his circumstances in life and gave himself a little permission to be spontaneous. At forty-eight years old, he didn't seem to fit the profile of someone having a reason for a mid-life crisis; He loved his wife dearly. He had a job that left him feeling fulfilled. He was secure financially—although not wealthy by most measures. He abhorred debt and so owed nothing except his mortgage. So, with the encouragement of his sweetheart—who never thought he rewarded himself enough for all his hard work—Robert had begun looking for an impractical car to purchase. He had first seen a Jaguar F-Type S in a parking lot weeks before and imagined what it how it would feel to have a sports car. The convertible could be a fun diversion and he could keep it stored, hidden away as a kept mistress, where he could drive it when he needed a distraction, when his stress was reaching a zenith.

Although he had given himself permission to buy a sports car, he certainly couldn't justify buying a new one. Robert searched online until he found the perfect one for his specifications. The car had to have very low miles, be one or two years old—so someone else had taken the depreciation—and it had to be a very conservative color. He refused to even look at colors of red or yellow, as these colors would draw attention to him and would no doubt cause tongues to wag about his impending mid-life crisis.

Within two weeks, he had found his car online at a dealership in San Diego and, after making arrangements with the dealership, flew from Little Rock with a certified check for fifty-six thousand dollars and change. He purchased his Dark Sapphire Blue (deep blue was his wife's favorite color) Jaguar on a Tuesday morning and immediately drove off the lot and back toward his sanity in Arkansas.

Yes, the dream had been in response to the car. As usual, *something* didn't want him to succeed.

As Robert's car surged up the freeway on-ramp, it pleased him to feel the power of his new toy. He knew that the roadster's three-hundred-eighty horsepower V-8 engine would get him into traffic quickly, and it did. He didn't know if he would ever know the top speed of the car, but he knew it would go faster than he ever needed to go.

After a bathroom stop in Oceanside, he zipped up the on-ramp, eager to check out the zero-to-sixty in three point nine seconds as the literature promoted.

Several miles north of town, he reviewed the expanse of Camp Pendleton, a Marine Corps base to the East of Interstate five. He had spent a brief time on base, not in the military, but working for a civilian contractor. During the week he was there, he felt validated in his decision to never join the military. He had great respect for the men and women who had given part—and sometimes all—of their lives to serve their country, but his personality was full of defiance; the kind of defiance the Marines might not have appreciated.

To the west of I-5 was the Pacific Ocean. Today was a gorgeous day to be driving his new toy. There had not been any fog that morning (or if there had, it had burned off early). The high temperature was going to be around eighty, and he was already above freeway speed—cruising with the top down—his bald head slathered with sunscreen.

Between the freeway and the ocean, were fields of produce. As he looked closer, he decided the crop of the waist-high green plants with bright red dots was tomatoes. With his culinary background, he decided the tomatoes were probably Romas, but this far away, he couldn't possibly be sure.

On the edge of the field, parked off the road, were ancient farm trucks with flat beds and spotted with rust. As his eyes traced the rows of the fields—while periodically glancing back at the road ahead of him—he could pick out the workers. Families of migrant workers slogged their way between the rows. The men and some of the women worked in the rows while a few mothers stayed near the trucks with the children. The children played games in the dirt around the trucks. These families would pick the tomatoes for a few days or weeks before moving to the next crop. They were all Hispanic and were no doubt undocumented immigrants, especially this close to the border. Robert smiled as he thought about the politically correct words *undocumented immigrants*. Most people just called them *illegals*. Their presence in the country had recently been causing a heated political debate. On one side of the debate was a human rights issue, on the other side was an economic and legal issue, and the truth lay somewhere muddled in between.

Robert couldn't help but ask himself what he would do in that type of circumstance. What would he be if he had been born into a third world country with little chance of improving life for himself and his family? At first, he thought he would go about getting a better life for his family legally, but what if he couldn't get into this country? Could he really look at his kids in adverse poverty and let it remain that way, or could he find a way to get into a better place and work hard for his family to be better off? *He knew the answer.*

Now as he drove along in his new roadster, he again felt a twinge of guilt he had felt often in his life: guilt for having had success that others hadn't, guilt for having money that his parents never knew, guilt for living in circumstances that these workers may never have.

Through his work in the restaurant industry, Robert had worked with many immigrants. He hadn't hired them because they were cheaper to employ. He paid them well, and they worked hard for him. They would work as many hours as they could and rarely complained. He listened to their stories and knew of their sacrifice and love for their families. *Yes, he knew his answer.*

As the fields of tomatoes shrank in his rearview mirror, Robert was aware of the kinship he felt with these workers; a kinship born almost fifty years before, when he had been the little boy near the back of the truck playing in the dirt while his family labored in the field

Chapter 2

No, Robert wasn't Hispanic. Fifty years ago, it wasn't Mexicans that did this work but the poor roaming—mostly White— nomads of North America. His dad had told him the people referred to them as 'fruit tramps' and they followed the harvest from town to town.

When Robert Bolls Rhodes was born, it was an oppressively hot August day in 1961, and just hours before he was born, his mom and family were picking cotton. His mother, Olivia, had gone into the field that morning although she was a full nine months pregnant. Having had other pregnancies, she knew the signs of the impending birth and recognized she probably couldn't finish out the day. A little before the workers broke for lunch, she went into labor. The foreman's wife loaded Olivia in the back of her tan '55 Ford Fairlane and took her to the nearest hospital in Elk City.

When Robert's father, Larry, requested to go to the hospital with Olivia, the foreman replied, "You can't do any good there, and you can sure do a lot of good here, so get back to work."

So, Larry and his two kids continued working, knowing they had debts to pay, and that they didn't have the financial security to risk being fired. Their hearts, though, were with Mom.

At the hospital, Olivia had never felt so alone. Her husband and children were still in the field, and any other relatives were hundreds of miles away in the Ozark Mountains of Arkansas. When she first arrived, the hospital staff efficiently wheeled her into the maternity ward. The efficiency of Olivia's care, however, seemed to turn when she heard the nurse mumble to the doctor something about 'fruit tramps'. Through her eight hours of labor, Olivia seldom saw the doctor, and the nurses seemed inconvenienced by her. Olivia had never felt so alone as she did during those hours.

Fortunately, her other children were both born during the winter, so the family was back home in Arkansas, in between seasons. She had been pregnant four times before. Her first and third pregnancies had ended in miscarriage and stillbirth, yet she felt passionately that they were her children, and her deep-seated religious views gave her hope that she would one day see them again. She experienced her first live birth when she was just eighteen. In the hills of Arkansas, that wasn't too unusual. The birth gave her a large baby boy, which she named William and whom everyone immediately called *Will*. Just over three years later, she gave birth to a smaller baby girl born almost a month premature. Olivia wondered for quite a while if the premature little girl would soon join the two others she had already lost. The wrinkled little pink thing was in and out of the hospital for much of the first year of her life. Olivia was always overprotective of this child. They named their only daughter Louise, but as nicknames stick, they mostly knew her as *Lou*.

After Lou was born, the doctors at the hospital in Clinton told Olivia that she shouldn't have any more children as the chance of miscarriage was almost certain. So Larry and Olivia were content with their two children. They loved them dearly and thought their family was complete—at least for the next seven years.

One afternoon, as Larry was coming in from working in the garden, Olivia very guardedly said, "I might need to go see Dr. Lindon soon."

"Oh, and why's that?" Larry responded with an uncommitted tone. He didn't stop immediately to look at her, but instead went to the water bucket, which she had drawn a few minutes earlier from the well outside the back door. As he ladled it out, he released a sigh because the water was cool, pure, and refreshing.

Physically, Larry was an average-looking man. He stood about five feet and eight inches tall, with thinning brown hair and an average build. Although he was only in his late forties, his time in the sun had taken a toll on his skin, marking it with lines—roadmaps on his face.

"I am pretty late on my cycle," she said hesitantly as she ran her gingham apron through her calloused fingers.

Larry wiped his mouth. He looked off into the distance, deep in thought, and said, "Why that can't be. I mean, the doctor said we shouldn't …, and we've been pretty careful …."

"Halloween night, remember?" She prompted, "the kids were out trick or treating … and we were home …"

"Doing a little trick or treating for ourselves?" Larry said while grinning mischievously and pinching at her dress teasingly.

Olivia blushed. "Anyway, the timing works out about right."

Larry was quiet, reflective, and after a few minutes said, "If the good Lord wants us to have another child, then we'll do everything we can to welcome it. We'll all make sure to treat you like a queen so you can have that young-un."

Olivia began to weep softly. "I don't know if I can go through the pain of losing another one, Larry. I just don't think I can do it."

Larry pulled her close and held her as he had many times before and comforted her. "Well, let's not get the cart before the horse. Let's wait and see what the doctor says. Yeah, I'll go with you, and we'll see … together."

Although Larry was being strong for his wife as he often had to be, inside he had his doubts about what would happen if she were pregnant. He couldn't help but wonder how it would affect going out on the road next spring to work the crops. The Rhodes lived at their house in Arkansas during the winter, accruing debt at the feed store, the market, and other stores in the nearby town of Clinton. Then in late spring, the Rhodes loaded up and hit the road to become fruit tramps again and make enough to pay off their debts. They again returned in the fall to the Ozarks to start the cycle over again. An interruption in this pattern could be devastating financially, and creditors were not generally very forgiving.

The next day, the doctor confirmed that Olivia was indeed pregnant. The baby would be born in late July or even early August. Olivia would be fully pregnant in the sultry heat of a summer in Arkansas, or Illinois, or Indiana or Kansas, or ….

Immediately, Larry started making alternate plans for work so the family wouldn't have to go on the road. Larry had worked many jobs during his life. It had only been in the last five years that the Rhodes had been performing the fruit tramp routine. They started because it seemed a fun way of spending the summer while the kids were out of school. He knew they would also get to see different parts of the country. Indeed, even though most looked down on the Rhodes kids in most places they visited, Will and Lou had seen more of the country than most of the children of that era. During most of his life, Larry had worked mostly in timber. Sometimes he worked in the woods felling the trees and sometimes in the lumber yards cutting them. Working in timber was where he felt most at home. It didn't take long for him to line up work for the spring.

The Rhodes planned on staying home that summer and making a home for the new baby. The kids, especially Lou, were dedicated to help with Mom's chores so she could rest, not taking unnecessary chances with this much wanted child.

The Ozark winter slowly relinquished to spring as Olivia's belly proudly showed the impending birth. As the pregnancy progressed, Olivia felt very confident in her ability to carry this baby to full term. Looking out the kitchen window of her tiny four room rented house, she felt very content with what life was offering her. She could see her two healthy kids climbing over the fence at the yard's edge on their way to the stock pond to fish. Mom saw Lou leading the way, carrying a bouquet of wild daisies she had just picked. Will carried the fishing pole and tackle. He had a stick to turnover rocks and look for snakes. The new addition to their family would just make Olivia's life even better. The little one was very active in her womb, kicking and turning, giving Olivia no need to fear for its health. She treasured the thought of not being out on the road this year. She had planned on telling Larry very soon that she didn't want to go on the road again, ever. She planned on telling him, but those plans changed abruptly when he came home early from the woods.

It was unusual for Larry to get home before six or seven in the evening, so she felt a pang of unease when she saw his rusty pickup turn down the clay-packed driveway a little after lunch. Wiping her hands on her apron, she walked across the porch and down the steps to meet him. She walked with hesitancy toward the truck. After slamming the truck door, he rested his elbows on the fender. Approaching him, she remained silent—expecting the worst, but hoping for the best.

He spoke first. "Well, there's no easy way to say it. They laid me off."

The words hit hard. She had to catch her breath, then after a few seconds could only muster, "But why?"

"The boss said the timber business has been slow and he can't make ends meet, so he let all of us go, effective today."

This moment was not much different from other times Larry and Olivia had endured during their financially challenged marriage. After fifteen economically distressed years, this scene was not totally abnormal. Instead of saying anything more, she walked gingerly toward him and they held each other, leaning against the family pickup truck. As they did, they could hear the kids giggling at the pond. The baby kicked inside its mom.

A week passed after Larry had been given the news. He found Olivia behind the house, doing the laundry. Her washing machine was a Maytag Model J Wringer washer. They bought it used two years before. Since the purchase, it rested on the back porch of their house. To do laundry, Olivia was required to get water from the well, heat it, and pour it into the washer. The washer was then plugged in and allowed to agitate for a period. After which, she drained all the water and filled the washer with clean rinse water. After sufficient rinsing, she took the clothing out individually and ran it through the wringers—being very careful not to get her fingers in the rollers. She then hung the clothes on a line so they could dry in the fresh Ozark air. Larry thought nothing smelled quite as nice as freshly washed sheets cleaned in this manner.

As Larry approached, he threw down his cigarette—which had been dangling from the corner of his lip—then rubbed it deep into the dirt with the toe of his work boot. "I talked to Bob Stoker today at Hal's Market."

"Did he know of any jobs around?" Olivia asked without missing a beat in her washing, wringing, and hanging symphony.

"Nothing around here." Larry hesitated. "But he said the cotton is about ready to be worked in Oklahoma, over near Wadsworth." Larry finished, knowing his words would land hard in Olivia's ears.

After a little time, Olivia responded, "Larry, we just can't. I'm eight months pregnant. Wadsworth would be an eleven or twelve-hour drive, and that's if the truck would even make it. We could get over there and find out there is no work to be had. It's happened to us before."

"I know," said Larry, "but I could go by myself. Bob said his cousin could guarantee a job for me. Besides, I'm not finding nothing 'round here. And you know we need the money."

Olivia couldn't argue with him. The money in timber was not as good as they had been used to earning when the whole family worked the fields in the past summers. They still had the substantial debt they had incurred the previous winter. "Let me sleep on it, Lar. I just need some time to think."

They said nothing more until in the middle of the night, when Larry returned from the outhouse. In the summer, the thirty-yard trip in the woods wasn't bad, but in the dead of winter, it was a trip everyone dreaded. This night was warm.

As Larry slipped quietly back into bed, he could see by the light of the full moon coming through the open window that Olivia was awake. "Are you ok, Hun?" Larry whispered.

"I've been thinking," she said. "If you can make some money working in the cotton, then the kids could help you and make even more. We could get out of debt even sooner."

"Oh, I could never leave you here alone, Sweetie. What if something happened? I could never forgive myself." His reply had measured desperation.

"Then maybe I'll come too. We could make a bed in the back of the pickup for when I get tired. Who knows, I might even feel up to weedin' some cotton myself." Olivia could see the great hesitation in Larry's brow. "Look, Lar, I'm already eight months along. I've got a strong, determined little one inside of me. I just feel as if everything is going to be ok. Sometimes, a family must make tough choices."

Chapter 3

So the Rhodes family ended up in the cotton fields of Wadsworth in the southwest part of Oklahoma. The whole family worked between the rows right up until the time when the foreman's wife took Olivia to the hospital in the back of the '55 Ford Fairlane.

Later that day, the foreman's heart softened. Whether by his own accord or the fact that his wife came back from the hospital and gave him a tongue lashing didn't really matter. Larry and the kids loaded in their pickup and headed for town.

Of course, in 1960, they didn't allow fathers in the delivery rooms and when Larry arrived, Olivia was already starting to deliver. With nothing to do to help, he sat down in an overly warm waiting room, purchased a five cent Nehi grape soda from the chest cooler and waited.

The Rhodes kids were so excited for the new baby that they pooled their nickels and pennies and walked by themselves to the town square to find a present for the new little brother or sister at the Ben Franklin five and dime. Since they didn't know which it would be, they chose a present that would be appropriate for either a boy or a girl, a new yellow baby blanket. It cost thirty-five cents, almost all they had.

When the children arrived back at the hospital, their dad was not there. A nurse in a starched white dress and hat led them to where their mom and dad were. Dad was standing beside his bride, with his hand under her head.

Olivia saw her two children sheepishly enter the room. "Come on in," she said, "and meet your new baby brother."

Will smiled with approval. Lou frowned at first, then smiled bigger than all of them when she saw the new little baby scrunched up next to Mom.

They named him Robert Bolls Rhodes, and Olivia was determined he would only be called Robert and not Robbie or Rob. Her other two kids had nicknames, but she was resolute this one wouldn't. Though only a few minutes old, Robert was already greatly loved, and he already shared part of his family's debt.

Olivia convalesced in the hospital for three days. Since the weeds between the cotton wouldn't wait, Larry and the kids returned to the fields the next day. They worked harder and longer to make up for the time they missed on the day of Robert's birth.

On the evening of the third day, the family went back to the hospital—as they had done each evening. This time, they knew they would get to bring the rest of the Rhodes family back with them. As the nurses prepared Mom to leave, another nurse directed Dad into a room to sign the discharge papers. As Larry signed the papers, paying very little attention to what they wrote on them, the door opened and shut behind him. Larry was unaware of the unknown visitors in the room, but as he glanced up, it surprised him to see a man in a suit and a sheriff's deputy.

"Mr. Rhodes," the suited man said. He was a little man, about fifty years old. His hair was thin and slicked straight back, held down by the use of some Brylcreem. Even though he wore a suit, Larry could tell it was old and threadworm. "I am Wilbur Fenway, the accounts administrator here at the hospital." Wilbur laid a paper in front of Larry. "How did you plan on paying this bill today?"

Larry looked at the paper and was shocked when he saw an amount equal to a month's pay. "Well, sir," Larry said, "I always pay my debts. I'll just have to send you some each month until it's paid."

"I'm afraid that will not do, Mr. Rhodes. Every year, we get some of you people in here to work the cotton, and you leave town owing us. Usually, we never collect and never see our money. When you go back to Alabama or wherever you're from, we have no reasonable expectation of ever getting paid."

Larry—belittled by the term *you people*—scrambled for something to say, then quickly responded, "Well, don't you have some kind of charity care here at the hospital? Some way of taking care of those who don't have much?"

"Oh, we do," Wilber replied, "but we reserve that for the good people who live around these parts, not for vagabonds."

Larry felt put down again by the label. Larry was a good man, an honest man, but this guy in the suit didn't know him and had no way of knowing his character. Humiliated, Larry muttered, "But I don't have that much money right now."

For the first time, the deputy spoke. He was a large man, over six feet tall. He was probably in his early forties and had the stern look of one who delighted in being the authority figure. "Mr. Rhodes, what we have here is a situation that must be resolved before you can leave these parts." For a moment, Larry thought he was going to be arrested. "I have a motion from the judge that says you cannot leave this area until the debt is paid. You may travel anywhere in this county or any of the five adjoining counties, but you may not leave until we discharge this debt. Otherwise, we'll issue a warrant for your arrest." Larry

17

didn't know what to think. In a way, he *was* being incarcerated, just in a jail that was the size of six counties.

So much for due process, Larry thought.

"But my wife and kids …?" Larry asked, confused.

"Oh, you're not under any constraints while you're here. You can move around freely, find a place to live, shop, and so on. You just can't leave the area until you've paid your debt," the deputy explained.

As Larry finished signing the papers, it humiliated him, having been labeled as one who wouldn't pay his debts. Many months later, he thought about how he had never seen any court orders or papers from a judge. As many times in his life, his lack of formal education had been a burden for Larry. He felt even worse thinking they had gotten one over on the poor 'fruit tramp'. He dreaded telling his sweetheart that they could not immediately return to her little rented home in the Ozarks and that the new baby boy would spend his first couple of years playing in the red dirt of western Oklahoma.

The next day, Larry returned to the fields chopping cotton. They called it *chopping cotton*, but in mid-summer, the workers were actually chopping weeds between the rows of cotton using no more than a hoe or, occasionally, a scythe. The actual picking of cotton didn't occur until fall and into early winter when the plants were dead, and the bolls of cotton released more easily.

So, Larry had a job until they completely harvested the cotton near the end of the year. The Rhodes family looked to move from their temporary cotton field quarters to something more substantial. Through word of mouth, they heard of a small grocery store and gas station along Route 66 that needed a manager. The salary was minimal, but included living quarters in the rear of the store. Olivia could manage the store while Larry worked in the fields. It was a perfect fit for the family.

Gas-rite Gas and Groceries was a typical roadside gas station for the days before the interstate came through. The building itself was made of cement. In front hung a solid awning shading the two gas pumps. One of the pumps dispensed *regular* gas, and the other dispensed *Ethyl.* Ethyl was short for *tetraethyl lead* that was added to the gasoline to increase the octane and prevent the engines from knocking. Ethyl Gasoline was distinguished from Regular because it had a red tint added during manufacturing. Ethyl became obsolete when they introduced the no lead laws of the 1970s.

Inside the store itself, there was not much to choose—just sundries that someone buying gas might buy. There were some car repair material, small snacks, a few groceries such as bread, milk and meat. Items resting on the counter ranged from road maps to men's combs.

In the corner sat a chest-type Coca-Cola machine. After putting the nickel in, a customer slid the neck of the bottle along tracks until the cold beverage reached the mechanism that would allow it to be pulled straight up and removed.

Behind the store sat five cabins for daily rentals. After a visitor registered at the counter of the store, they gave them a key to one of the rooms in back. The rooms were very basic: a bed, nightstand, table and chair. Each room did have its own bathroom, though. The rooms cost three dollars per night to rent.

In the days before Interstate 40, Route 66 was the primary thoroughfare across Oklahoma. The historic highway was the main road from Chicago to Los Angeles. The cars on the highway raced by just 30 feet from the front edge of the market. Three or four times per hour, the hum of the car's tires on the pavement would lower in pitch, signaling that a car was slowing down. As it left the highway, the sound would change from a hum to a grind, drudging across the gravel and pulling up to the pump. Whoever was attending the station—Larry, Olivia, or sometimes the older children—would approach the car and get the gas order: "Fill 'er up," or "a couple of dollars' worth, please." While the twenty-three cent per gallon gas was pumping, the attendant washed the windows, checked the oil, and even the air in the tires if requested. The customer then paid with a few bills and drove out, often leaving dust and spitting a few pieces of gravel as they did.

The family settled in and adapted easily. Larry headed out to work each morning—except Sunday—before sunrise. The kids stayed home with mom. They did chores, helped in the store, but mostly played, explored, and did the things a child should do. Lou stayed around her mom a lot and helped tend to little Robert. Sometimes, Will helped by tending to cars that stopped for gas, but mostly he enjoyed exploring the area around the store. He sat for hours watching the cars go by and wondered where the travelers were from or where they were going.

As fall came, the two older children enrolled in school, which was only about a mile away, an easy walk. The kids made friends. Larry's job in the cotton wasn't bad, and Olivia enjoyed the time in the store tending to customers and little Robert. By their best calculations, Larry figured it would take about two years to pay the hospital bill. The Rhodes made the best of the situation and decided to call this place home until they could get back to the Ozarks. Life had seldom taken the turns the Rhodes would have wanted, but they had learned to enjoy the unexpected turns instead of kicking against them.

After the cotton was all stripped from the plants, Larry found a new job helping build a new dam nearby. This was the first *real* job the family ever remembered Dad having; a job that didn't have an end, which wouldn't have him thinking about his next move. Olivia enjoyed the security of seeing him go out the door every morning with a lunch pail in his hand and a hardhat on his head.

All in all, Oklahoma wasn't bad for the Rhodes clan. Even though Robert only had glancing memories of living there, he sometimes wondered if his life would have turned out differently if they had stayed there. He wondered how different his life would have been and if he could've kept the pleasant experiences and avoided the bad events, he would later deal with.

On an overcast day in February 1962, Larry Rhodes walked into the Elk City hospital and went straight into Wilbur Fenway's office as he had done every month for the last eighteen months, but this time Larry handed him the last payment. Wilbur, appearing to be wearing the same suit he had worn in the previous visits, looked at the cash for a minute and started writing out a receipt. When Wilbur wrote the words—*Paid in Full*—Larry felt proud.

Wilbur handed the receipt to Larry, then offered his hand. "Mr. Rhodes," he said, "you have been diligent in your effort to pay this debt as dependable as clockwork. You haven't been late on a payment in eighteen months. In fact, you have paid more than the required amount each month." Mr. Fenway got quiet as if he were almost choking up. "I misjudged you, Mr. Rhodes. I would be proud to have you as a neighbor and member of our community … if you wanted to stay."

Larry took the receipt and—as if measuring his response—paused for a moment, stroked his chin and said, "Mr. Fenway, just because people ain't had a lot of breaks in life … just because they don't have much education or parents who leave them an inheritance, doesn't make them bad people. I try hard to be an honest man. I ain't never had any savings to speak of, but I've always paid my debts when I owed them."

Larry was speaking in a slow, respectful manner but not cowering. He had a point that he wanted to make. "You've held my family—in a manner of speaking—captive here for eighteen months.

"Although we've met some great folks here and could've made a go of it under different circumstances, I am afraid I would always feel the way I felt in your office a year and a half ago—shamed, humiliated, and dishonored.

"I will take my family back to Arkansas, and with them I will take my pride and dignity, but please remember us when you have another family standing in front of you that needs a little help."

"I will, Larry," Wilbur said sheepishly.

As Larry turned to leave, Wilbur lifted the cash he had just been given and extended it back toward Larry, saying, "Mr. Rhodes, take this money as my gift to you to help you get on your way."

Larry turned back and looked at Wilbur awkwardly. "I can't take that money. It wouldn't be right. It was part of my debt."

Thinking quickly and with a twinkle in his eye, Wilbur asked, "Did I mention that the hospital has a policy that if you pay a bill off early, they give a rebate in the amount of the last payment? It's … uh … um, our way of rewarding people who pay early."

Larry looked at him for a few seconds and—discerning the goodness of the man in the tattered suit—reluctantly took the money and quietly said, "That's a good policy."

"You're a good man, Larry Rhodes, and don't forget it. A man's value is not determined by the size of his bank account."

The two men shook hands and, putting their free hands on the other one's shoulder, almost embraced.

"Thank you," Larry said. "The money will certainly help."

"Good Luck," Wilbur finally replied.

It took a couple of months to get everything in order to leave. It was with some apprehension that the family left Oklahoma on a gorgeous spring morning in April 1962. A year and a half to a pre-teen can seem forever and the kids had made good friends and loved their school. They had wonderful memories of Arkansas too and looked forward to getting back to their cousins and grandparents. Mom and the kids loaded up in a recently purchased blue and white 1957 Chevy Nomad and Dad followed in the old rusty pickup truck. They headed for their familiar rented home in Arkansas. The older kids thought it was quite a treat to take turns riding with Dad in the truck. Aside from having a flat tire just outside of Oklahoma City, the trip was uneventful, and they arrived at their cousin's house in Dover, Arkansas shortly before bedtime. It was a grand reunion as they all sat around eating cornbread and buttermilk, reminiscing and making fresh memories. The next morning, they finished the trip in less than two hours. It felt great to be back home.

Randy Judd

Chapter 4

It's hard to say for sure whether he was hungry before he saw the *In-N-Out Burger* just off the freeway in Corona, but as soon as it came into view, Robert signaled and veered the Jaguar toward the off ramp. The restaurant chain was one of his favorite fast-food stops, and since there were none back home in Arkansas, Robert wanted to make sure he got one of their classic burgers before leaving California. The restaurant was really quite an operation. It was very simple. All that it offered were burgers, fries, soda and shakes, and yet every *In-N-Out Burger* he saw had a line to the door. He parked his new roadster away from the building and other cars so he wouldn't get door dings in the blue metallic paint. He strolled across the parking lot, noticing how good it felt to stretch his legs. The cramped space in his cockpit would take a little getting used to.

As he opened the restaurant's door, he could see the familiar simplicity of the décor and smelled the wonderful scent of their hot fries. As suspected, there was a line, but it gave him time to decide exactly how he would have his anticipated burger. Would he have two or three burgers or just have one and eat it very slowly to savor the flavor? Robert was pleased with the way that sounded, *savor the flavor* and thought it should be someone's slogan, and no doubt it already was. He placed his simple order for a combo meal, got his Diet Coke at the fountain, found a seat, and waited for his number to be called. When they called seventy-seven, he felt a twinge of excitement as if he had just won at bingo.

While sitting at the little booth trying to *savor the flavor*, he noticed an Asian family directly in front of him. The family was about as typical as they could be—mom, dad, a boy about five years old and a girl about three. The boy was trying desperately to get his mom's attention by blowing air on her hair through his straw. She kept swatting at her head as if a fly were on it. The boy was giggling at his mom without her being aware. The little girl was having a rough moment. She was pouting as if some life-altering episode had just occurred; the boy taking her seat or her hamburger mistakenly having pickles on it (and she hates pickles). As Robert watched her, she saw him staring at her and buried her head bashfully in her mother's lap.

Robert loved kids. He always had. As a teenager, he used to love playing with his nieces and nephews. He delighted in joking with them and making them laugh, but most of all, he loved their innocence. The bad things in life had not spurned them yet. He would have enjoyed making friends with these kids, maybe by making a penny appear from behind their ears and watching them giggle with delight. The days were gone when a man could readily talk to kids, even with the parents present. If the parents were to catch him smiling at their children, they would no doubt pull them closer and tell them not to look at the stranger. Robert completely understood and would do the same with his kids. It was a shame but a necessity of life in the twenty-first century. Because of the proliferation of pedophiles and abductions (or at least the wider reporting of such things), parent warned their children early about the realities of evil.

Robert was thankful he had been allowed to live an unblemished life as a toddler and preschooler, for those years—as his innocence—would pass very quickly.

~*~

As the Rhodes pulled up to their old home place, it disappointed them to see how decrepit it looked. The yard was overgrown with vegetation, the dirt driveway was mostly mud and a cow had broken through the nearby fence and was actually standing on the porch staring at them.

The house didn't belong to the Rhodes family, although they had lived in it, on and off, for several years. The house actually belonged to a local merchant, Hal Springer. They always knew they could come back to *Hal's Place* because no one else would consider living in the run-down shack. Hal didn't even charge them rent. He let their family live there in exchange for feeding and tending to the cattle that grazed in the field next to the house. To the Rhodes, it was their home in the hills.

The house consisted of four rooms: the front room (which had a potbellied stove against the center of the back wall), two bedrooms and a kitchen. The house had electricity but no running water or phone. Even in the Ozarks in the early 1960s, most homes already had running water. The Rhodes were the last of a breed, true hillbillies. They drew the water from a well a few steps from the back kitchen door. Between the kitchen door and the well was an uncovered back porch. A covered porch ran the entire length of the front of the house with steps down into the yard. In front of the house, hidden in weeds, was a storm cellar—as old as the house—which had never been used except for storage. It was a dark and mysterious abyss, with spider webs and a musty smell.

The Rhodes would rather face a tornado than go in there in the middle of the night. Behind the house, rested chicken coops and a pen for small livestock. A space for a large garden was nestled beside the house.

Although located on a main road, the isolated house sat back from the road about two hundred yards. Making the homestead even more isolated was having no neighbor within a mile. Overgrown and under used fields bordered both sides of the house, each twenty acres or more. They used one for grazing cattle. The original owners had strategically placed a small pond in the center. They designated the body of water for quenching the thirst of the cattle and providing fishing opportunities for the children. Long since abandoned, they had once used the field on the opposite side for crops. The hard soil bent plow blades and tripped the pulling mules. The house sat in front of dense Ozark hardwoods that quickly dropped into a hollow.

Several sounds lived around the house. Wind hissed as it swirled through the trees even with the gentlest breeze. The livestock mooed, clucked, and oinked. The children laughed, screamed, and yelled. During the day, though, the house could be extremely quiet. When the winds were still, the kids were quiet, the animals slept, a person could almost hear their heartbeat. Most of the time, no traffic could be heard. If a car did travel down the road, they could hear it for several miles before it arrived. One would think that nighttime would be the quietest, but this wasn't necessarily so. Amongst the brush and trees around the house, the crickets, katydids and other insects were joined by bullfrogs, owls and howling dogs in a magnificent symphony that could almost be deafening to a visitor—but lulled the locals into blissful sleep.

Larry spent the first two weeks home driving his pickup to different neighbors' houses, spreading the word that he was back in town and was looking for work. He hung around *Hal's Market* and talked to the various farmers and ranchers who came in to get supplies or sell their goods. There was no *Help Wanted* section of the newspaper because … there was no newspaper so finding a job was largely done by word of mouth. Larry Rhodes had a reputation for being a very dependable and hard worker. If he did have one downfall, it was his tendency to get bored with a job and job-hop from one employer to another. Locals immediately offered him day jobs when someone had a task that could be completed in a day or two, but Larry wanted a more substantial job that could sustain his family for a longer, more secure period.

One sultry afternoon at the market, Larry sat cross-legged on the porch, whittling an old piece of birch with his worn pocketknife. He heard a familiar voice coming toward him. Raising his eyes, it pleased him to see Howard Simpson walking toward him at a hurried pace. Along with most men in the hills, Howard wore faded denim overalls. The various holes were a result of assorted jobs he did daily. He donned a full head of wavy dark hair—which he combed occasionally. Sweat darkened the collar of his shirt.

"Larry, you old coon dog." Howard delightfully greeted him. "I heard you were back around these parts, so I had to come find you. What you been up to?"

Larry reached out to shake his hand, but Howard pulled him close and gave him a hug—pounding his back so hard it almost knocked the breath out of his friend.

"Oh, you know how it is, Howard. I never know what life's going to throw at me. We've been out in Oklahoma for a couple of years paying off a debt. Life's always a surprise when you're an old fruit tramp like me."

"Larry, you stop talking that way. You know I've never considered you anything less than a hero and certainly not any kind of tramp."

Larry and Howard met in the early 1940s when they enlisted for World War II. Neither man had great aspirations of fighting the Germans or Japanese, but they also saw their chances of getting drafted increase and decided to enlist instead. They assigned the young men to do basic training in Fort Robinson, Arkansas. On the first day of training, they assigned the two strangers to bunks beside each other and were fortunate to stay by each other throughout most of their tenure in the war.

They joined the Marines and—being uneducated Arkansas hillbillies—were assigned to the infantry, where they did the grunt work and the fighting for the more educated and trained troops. The men were involved in battle many times amid MacArthur's Pacific Campaign—stops such as the Philippines, the Solomon Islands, and Guadalcanal.

It was in Guadalcanal that Larry and Howard saw their friendship welded in a trust and love that would last a lifetime.

One night during one of the bloodiest battles of the war, the two crouched in a muddy foxhole as they had done many times in the past two years. These were terrifying times, but somehow the routine had become familiar. The two were always able to avoid personal trauma while internalizing the terrors of war. The enemy shelling had been constant most of the day but as night came, the sky remained lit by the explosions surrounding them. The typhoon-like rain pelted them and created a pool up past their ankles within their foxhole. The downpour was a white sheet in the flashes of mortar explosions.

A command came from the captain a few holes over. Larry heard it clearly. "Stay down new rounds coming." But apparently Howard heard something different, something about "coming". Without hesitation, Howard climbed out of the foxhole and—crouching—started running toward the captain's voice. Larry screamed at him, but his voice was muffled by Howard's adrenaline and the explosive sounds of thundering rain and munitions. Larry impulsively climbed out of the foxhole—his feet slipping with every sought-out foothold. Once out of the hole, he chased Howard across the battlefield. As Howard slowed to get his bearings, Larry struck him with the full force of his weight and pushed him into a nearby foxhole occupied by the captain who had been watching the episode. Falling flailing to the bottom of the foxhole, a deafening explosion produced mud and rocks which pounded in on the three men. As they were able to gather their wits, they peered out of the hole to see that a grenade had landed at the exact spot where Larry had tackled Howard. There was no doubt to all three men that Larry had saved the soldier's life. Larry carried the remnants of that act with him for the rest of his life. Shrapnel had penetrated Larry's leg as he dove behind Howard in the foxhole.

They discharged Larry after he spent a month in a hospital in Guam. The Marines awarded him a Purple Heart for his injuries. There was a rumor of a medal for his heroics. Later, he heard that they had put aside the application for this medal as bureaucrats pushed through the submission for a Pennsylvania senator's son instead.

Larry returned home to the Ozarks, and several months later, Howard returned. Howard never forgot the heroic thing Larry did and never let anyone else forget it, either. For a while, they revered Larry as a hero in the small towns that dotted that part of the hills. But time and life went on, and few people referred to it anymore—except Howard.

Howard had married well. Elizabeth Simpson came from a well-to-do family in Harrison. She dressed in fine clothes she had bought on shopping trips to Little Rock or Memphis. She smelled of perfumed talcum powder and hair spray. Elizabeth's dad owned a small textile factory and was a ruthless man to his employees. She had learned well from her father and was a ruthless woman to Howard. Howard thought he loved her, so he put up with her spitefulness all these years. Larry did not mesh well with Elizabeth and tried to avoid her at all costs.

With his hero sitting on the front porch of the market, Howard knew it was his time to try to repay him.

"So, what kind of work are you doing now, Larry?"

"Actually," Larry said sheepishly, "since we've been back, I haven't found much. Oh, a little bit here and there, but nothing to support a family."

Howard got a gleam in his eye, and his entire face smiled. Maybe his time of repayment had come. "I'm starting up a sawmill in Van Buren County. My wife's uncle died last year and left it to me."

"How is Elizabeth?" Larry said with propriety, hoping somehow the answer would be 'passed away'.

"She's still the same. Hasn't changed a lick," Howard responded. "As I was saying, I have inherited a mill. I haven't started it up before now because I didn't have the right people to help me run it, but there is no doubt that you could do it, with all your experience in the timber."

"I would love to come work for you, Howard." The thought of working with his old friend delighted Larry.

"Not working for me, Larry, working with me! I've been thinking about this since I heard you were back in these parts. I want you to be my partner."

Larry couldn't reconcile what he was hearing. "Howard, I can't help run a business. I ain't got the education."

"I'll handle the bookwork stuff, and you handle the yard. I've seen you, Larry. You have a knack for getting the most out of men. They look up to you and work hard for you. With my book learning and your people skills, we could make a mint!"

Larry had to sit back down. The wind almost knocked out of him a second time—only this time, not literally. Life had not given him many opportunities. This plan sounded too good to be true. He couldn't wait to return home to tell his bride.

Randy Judd

Chapter 5

The two friends became partners, and the partnership worked as well as a successful marriage. As they had previously discussed, Howard ran the office, got the contracts, and sold the lumber. Larry directed the production, the timber, and the people. Within six months, the old mill was turning a miniscule profit for the two men to split. On the hood of an old Buick, they painted the words *H&L Mill* and hung it above the entrance. The mill was booming, and life looked promising for the Rhodes family.

By this time, Olivia and the children were settling into comfortable routines. Will and Lou rode the bus every day to school, and little Robert grew. His memories of his early childhood were all good. As a toddler, he stayed near mom's skirt as she did her daily chores.

As he grew, he slowly gained more independence, and his mother allowed him to roam. The little boy enjoyed exploring the sights and sounds of the yard around the house. He chased chickens with no intent of catching them, but just for the joy of seeing them run. Robert didn't own many store-bought toys, but he did have more than his siblings had ever had and certainly more than his parents when they were kids. He relished in playing with his toy pickup truck, constructing roads through the dirt all over the driveway. As Dad's sawmill got more successful, Robert was allowed to buy little green army men when the family went into Clinton. Robert sometimes got consumed with battling all day in the front yard with his pretend platoon. On occasion, the older kids would leave saying goodbye to Robert warring in the front yard and return with him still fighting the battle. He often assigned one of his little green men to be his dad, fighting the Japanese at Guadalcanal—another man always represented Howard. Sometimes Will played with Robert, but he soon became bored with his pre-school mentality and would head off to do teenage activities. But most of the time—as a matter of fact, most of his growing-up years—were spent alone. There were some other boys his age who lived a few miles away. Sometimes, the moms would get together, and Robert could play for a few hours with other boys, but he really didn't know what to do or how to interact, so he was anxious to get back to the familiarity of his army men.

Summer was the highlight of the year for Robert because it meant his big brother and sister would be home every day and they might let him tag along on their adventures. May first was an important day every year. That was the day mom let the children go barefoot. The shoes would stay off all summer except for putting them on occasionally to go to church or the doctor's office.

Just because it was summer didn't mean the kids were playing all day without responsibility. The older kids had to work to help earn money. Will worked at the mill or in the various alfalfa fields hauling hay. Lou shared in the house and garden work with her mom. Robert was too young to do any of this work, but he knew the play times would end someday, so he enjoyed his current status even more.

The highlight of the children's summers was when Mom and Dad loaded the family in the pickup and went swimming—down the mountain—in Beaver Creek. The creek wasn't a very large body of water. In most places, a person could wade across it, but in certain places it settled in deep, dark pools that remained cool even in those blistering days of July and August. The swimming hole could accommodate fifteen or twenty people to swim in, but most times a single family or group of kids occupied it. Tied to a large granddaddy birch tree that grew tight to the bank was a rope swing—the focal point of the swimming hole

Robert didn't cause much trouble for the most part. He didn't throw tantrums or whine much. He did cry when he something disappointed him, but even then, it was normally a gentle heart wrenching sob. He was a tender-hearted boy. This touched Olivia's heart, and she would usually relinquish to the child. Robert didn't take advantage because he loved his mother and didn't want to disappoint her.

Sometimes, though, he could be mischievous. Mischief for a four-year-old is not always cute, though. In fact, it can have tragic outcomes. As most little boys do, Robert found great sport in looking under rocks for bugs. He lifted rock after rock to see what kind of treasure he could find. One day as Will was walking out to the well to get some water for his mom, he heard a little whimper coming from the front yard. Rounding the corner, he could see his little brother looking down at his hand with an overturned rock at his feet.

"What's the matter, little guy?" William asked.

"I think a stupid snake bit me," Robert replied.

"Oh, I don't think so. If a snake bit you, I think you would know it."

As his older brother approached, he was immediately distressed at what he saw. Robert was holding his hand—two little blood dots on his wrist. Will looked at where the rock had been. Though it was crawling hastily away, Will knew the pale-yellow snake with brown bands was a poisonous copperhead.

William swooped the lad up and ran to the house. Their family had always heard about snakebites, but no one they knew had ever actually been bitten. The family had to make some quick decisions. The Rhodes didn't have a phone, so they had to drive five miles to *Hal's Market* to make a call. The market was the opposite way of the nearest hospital in Clinton. They assumed the doctor would tell them to go to the hospital anyway, so they headed straight to town. The trip that normally took forty-five minutes was shortened as the family car threw gravel and left a cloud of dust—speeding over country roads. Olivia held tight to the now scared, crying Robert.

After being in the waiting room for an hour, the doctor came to deliver the news to the parents.

Dr. Salvage was a young doctor who looked as though he had recently started practicing. The physician had tight brown curls that were prematurely showing gray. He spoke with a slow Arkansas drawl, which made the Rhodes happy to know he might be a local boy who had done well. They hoped he would be nice to them.

"The little boy? Robert or Robbie or Bobby?" The doctor asked, searching for what they called him.

"Robert," Larry responded. "Robert, no nicknames."

"Sure, … Robert. As you may or may not know, Mr. and Mrs. Rhodes, copperhead bites are rarely fatal. In an adult, they can cause a lot of pain and often some tissue damage if the venom is not stopped. Now, that's in an adult." The doctor paused long enough to hear Olivia take a quick deep breath and see her squeeze Larry's hand tighter.

"But in a child," The doctor continued, "in a child, it can be much more serious. We don't have an anti-venom for the copperhead, so we just have to hope we can extract all the poison. We honestly don't think we got it all from your boy."

Larry felt Olivia slip as her knees buckled, so he squeezed tighter to hold her up.

"The little boy is showing some signs of poisoning, his breathing is slowing, and his heartbeat is erratic. We've got him sedated, so he is not in any pain, but now we'll just have to wait. There's not much else we can do at this point."

"Can we see him, Doc?" Larry asked.

Olivia and Larry cautiously walked in, but as soon as Olivia saw the little boy with all his tubes, IVs, and bandages, she lost her composure. She sobbed as she stood beside the bed, her little boy unaware she was there.

Larry reached around her waist and pulled her close. She turned toward her husband, threw her arms around his neck, and cried.

"I thought it was bad when I lost the other babies," she said, "but I didn't even get a chance to know them. This little guy is my buddy. I don't know how I can go on if …."

"He'll be all right," Larry said, not sure if he believed it himself. "He is a strong little boy, and defiant. He'll fight that ole snake venom somehow."

That night seemed never-ending. The doctor went home with the promise of returning early in the morning or even earlier if the nurse called him. They all would know more in the morning.

The next morning, after the doctor had visited Robert, he reported to Larry and Olivia. "I'm pleased to say his breathing and heart rate are pretty good. I'm going to go ahead and take him out of sedation, and we'll see at that stage how bad the pain is."

Larry and Olivia were relieved to hear this news but apprehensive to know that their little boy might soon be in pain.

After about an hour, the nurse came out. "I have a little boy in there who is asking for his mom and dad."

The parents leaped up and hurried into his room. The little boy—though still somewhat sedated—smiled at them. They showered him with affection.

"I want to go home," Robert said groggily, "so I can kill that stupid snake."

This caused his parents to smile.

Later that day, the doctor let Robert go home, still amazed that the boy had absolutely no repercussions from the bite.

As the doctor was releasing him, he said to the parents, "This is one fortunate little boy. The good Lord must have something in store for him."

Robert would hear similar statements other times in the years to come.

Even Robert could tell that life was looking up for the former poverty-stricken family. He noticed his parents saying yes to more things he wanted. One vivid memory Robert had was the day his mom and dad went mysteriously to town and came home a few hours later with a nearly new Ford F-100 pickup. The Rhodes family had arrived!

A big part of the children's growing up experience was 'going to town'. With the town of Clinton just 45 miles away, it was the closest thing to a big city that the Rhodes children knew. Less than one thousand people populated the town, but it had all the amenities that were normally found in a small Arkansas county seat. The town square surrounded the county courthouse, which—it seemed by some unwritten law somewhere—had to be the largest building in the county. The Van Buren County Courthouse was a magnificent building to Robert. He was both amused by its grandeur and awed by the mysterious events that transpired inside. Around the outside, a dozen seated men in overalls whittled as their women shopped. Lining all four sides of the town square were usual stores: Ben Franklin Five and Dime, JC Penny and other clothing stores, a theater, a market, a feed store, barber and beauty shop, and other various retail establishments. This was the retail hub of the county. Offices—those of lawyers, accountants and title officers—were just off the square down the side streets.

For the most part, the family only went to town one time per week—Saturday morning. This day was the shopping and social event of the week. Families from all the outlying areas crowded the town square to spend part of their day. After the Rhodes parked the pickup on the square, the kids jumped out of the back and ran their separate ways to meet up with friends or spend their nickels and dimes they had accumulated. Even though Robert was told to stay close to his parents, it wasn't long before he got tired of following his mom's errands. Something would catch his eye, and he would be off on his own. No one worried too much about his solitude because the town was small, and if he felt insecure, he knew he could find his dad whittling and sharing war stories at the courthouse.

On a cooling fall day as the family was returning from town, Larry drove a different route. As he reached a crest in the road, he pulled over to the side. He instructed everyone to get out next to a beautiful pasture bordering the road. The clearing was about twenty acres, with a stock pond and a small stream running through. There was a small, deliberate grove of oak trees nuzzled next to the reflective pond.

"What's up Daddy-o?" Lou inquired, using her best pre-teen lingo.

"I wanted you all to see this," Larry replied.

They all walked to the barbed wire fence surrounding the property. They looked, expecting to see something in the field, maybe some kind of animal.

"I don't get it, Lar," Olivia said.

"I used to pass this piece of land while working in some timber up Morton Hollow," Larry started. "That was probably fifteen years ago. William had just been born, and I wondered what kind of life I could give my new family. I found out who the owner was, but the price was far too much for me to come up with. After that, I came to hate this piece of land. I would avoid it or look the other way as I drove by."

The family wondered why he would stop today then.

"This land represented all that I couldn't do for my family. It made me struggle inside to know if all I ever would be was a *fruit tramp*. Over time, I realized that it wasn't the land that was the problem. The field was just a pretty piece of property with a stream that lined the road. So, I didn't hold a grudge against the property.

"I *did* hold a grudge, though, at the hand life dealt me. You know I didn't get much of a formal education and didn't have parents that could leave me an inheritance. I guessed I would never amount to much.

"Now, for the first time in my life, I feel I am amounting to something. The mill is going great, and Howard and I are talking about expansion."

"Larry, you were a success in our books a long time ago and we are really proud of all you've been able to do for the family," Olivia said lovingly. She looked at the sky, then the kids and finished. "But it's getting cold, and the sun will be down soon, so we'd better go."

"This is gonna be ours," Larry said solemnly.

At first Olivia thought he was speaking yearningly, but there wasn't the desperation that accompanies yearning. "What do you mean, Lar?"

"I put a down payment on the place yesterday." Larry revealed.

There was an awkward silence as everyone looked at each other, then a burst of yelling, screaming and laughter. "What do you mean? I mean … how? What?"

"I have been putting money aside every week to save up for it. I finally got enough for a down payment. In another year, it will be ours. Then we'll get a loan to build a house on it. Olivia, we'll have our own house!"

Olivia wanted to ask if they could afford it, what the payments would be, and so on, but at that point, she didn't care. The thought of having a house overjoyed her.

"Can you believe it, Olivia?" Larry asked gleefully. "You'll have your own place with running water and indoor plumbing and shutters. The kids will have a tree swing and a room of their own."

At fifty years old, Larry was going to own a home for the first time in his life.

As they got back on the road, Olivia reflected on the day in Clinton and how it had all ended. Robert snuggled up next to his siblings in the bed of the pickup and fell asleep under a wool army blanket, dreaming of the Ben Franklin store.

Later, Robert reflected on Clinton as being the true Mayberry of his life. Everything about it matched the *TVLand* town. It was an innocent little town, and, in some ways, it represented the innocence of Robert's early childhood. A few years later, a tornado tore through town, destroying much of the town's innocence, coincidently, about the same time as Robert was experiencing storms of his own.

Randy Judd

Chapter 6

As he approached Barstow, Robert was trying to make an ad hoc decision. The Jaguar's GPS was telling him to turn on to I-40, which would be the most direct way to Arkansas. If he ignored the pleasant voice in his dash, he would be staying on I-15 and heading toward Las Vegas. Going by way of Las Vegas was certainly not the quickest way back to Arkansas, but Robert thought since he was celebrating his new car anyway, he might as well take a little more exciting return trip. He chose to ignore the voice in the dash, and she quickly chastised him and recalculated the route.

Less than two hours later, he turned off at the Tropicana exit. He purposely didn't choose a hotel on the strip. The activity of the Las Vegas strip, with its mesmerizing lights and moving tide of tourists, was fun for a while, but he enjoyed getting away from the clamor at the end and retreat to a nice desert setting. He pulled into the Courtyard Inn in Green Valley. Robert had only visited Vegas a few times, and he knew he would rather stay in a hotel that was familiar to him. Robert was comfortable with familiarity. Adventure was definitely in his personality repertoire, but eventually, he always returned to familiar.

After checking in at the hotel and putting his overnight bag in the room, he sat behind the wheel of his new toy and headed for the lights.

At the MGM, Robert gave his roadster keys to the valet. He then walked toward the Bellagio. The walk took a couple of hours as he strolled and gracefully avoided the people who were making no effort to avoid him.

Gambling didn't tempt Robert. Robert had taken many gambles in his life, but nothing that was monitored by the gaming commission. He wasn't averse to dropping whatever change he had in his pocket into the closest slot machine on the way out of the casino, but that was the extent of his involvement.

To Robert, money was almost sacred—not that he worshipped it or was stingy with it. He just felt a certain stewardship over it. There was no doubt where these feelings came from. Years of not having any extra money made him careful of how he spent it. His parents had both gone through the depression era and had talked about it enough to scare Robert—just a little—into thinking it could happen again. Because of this, he made sure to hang on to what he had. These feelings made it even harder to reconcile that he had just bought a nearly new Jaguar.

As he walked the strip that night, he couldn't help but think of the excesses all around him. The casinos were beyond extravagant. In the last decade, the trend was to blow up perfectly sound buildings and replace them with newer, more superior, more lavish ones. The fountains were the biggest, the lights were the most brilliant, and the shops in the malls presented the most expensive offerings. For fun, Robert walked into *Versace* and looked at the clothing. A pair of women's boots was priced at twelve hundred dollars. A purse was fifteen. A simple pair of jeans, eight hundred. It amused him to see the staff of the store seemingly looking down on him as he shopped wearing his *Old Navy* jeans and T-shirt, but it did not intimidate him. He knew the people working in the shops could probably not even afford the wares they were pitching. Robert even approached one of the staff who was standing near the men's shoes and mischievously asked, "How does it feel watching these spoiled rich snobs coming in all day and buying clothes that good people such as you and me can't afford and wouldn't buy even if we could?"

The worker spontaneously smiled, but knowing he had to get back in to character as if he were at a Disney theme park, simply replied, "It pays my rent."

Ten years earlier, Las Vegas started marketing itself as a family destination. In the end, they were only fooling themselves, though. The city fathers recently gave up the charade, realizing no one was buying that gambling, alcohol, and strippers equaled family entertainment.

Vegas also displayed a myriad of contrasts. The biggest one was the city itself. Founded originally by Mormon settlers, it was now the vice capital of the world nicknamed *Sin City*. The city was also a contrast because it was located in one of the driest parts of the United States, yet was opulent with its use of water, from fountains to lush greenery.

Robert also found a contrast in the people that populated the strip. There were high rollers and celebrities that flew in on private jets and occupied lush suites. These modern aristocrats could spend a hundred thousand dollars in one weekend. In contrast, the casinos were dotted with people who were spending their last dollars trying to buy a dream until they got their next government assistance check. Robert witnessed a lady pushing a sleeping baby with her foot as she moved from machine to machine. The majority of the people, though, were somewhere in between. He realized that there were many people walking the strip without being greatly affected. They were able to walk with their families as if they were having a day at the park. The ability to be unaffected was quite a talent, Robert thought. He remembered a few lines from a poem by Stephanie Waas that he had read in a college literature class:

Relaxing by the waters nice,
Her feet dangling above it,
She cherished her father's advice,
To be in the world, but not of it.

As Robert walked on the sidewalk, he was careful to avoid the day workers who sporadically tried to give flyers of local strip clubs. The cards were almost pornographic themselves. He wisely avoided them.

As with past visits to Las Vegas, a couple of hours in the chaos were all he needed. He headed back to the MGM Grand and exchanged his ticket to retrieve his car—covertly slipping the valet five dollars as if it were an illegal transaction. That night, as he drove back to his hotel, Robert reflected again on the decadence that surrounded the strip—yet many people were able to rise above it even while having it all around them. He was sure most people on the strip that night were good, honest, hardworking people who were just out for a weekend on the town. He also knew that many vices—more damaging and degrading vices—were manifesting themselves behind closed doors all around him.

In the end, it wasn't about what he experienced, but how he responded to his experiences that made his life what it was.

He arose early the next morning and drove toward Hoover Dam. Robert knew that Hoover Dam was more permanent and would never be blown up just for the sake of replacing it with a newer, more sparkly dam. Besides, the curvy roads would be entertaining in his mostly new sports car.

The Rhodes family derived great joy from planning their new home. They talked about how great it would feel not having to go out in the middle of the night to use the outhouse. As she washed the dishes, Olivia daydreamed about how she would decorate the yard. Yellow flowers everywhere—she had always been drawn to yellow flowers.

His thoughts of the future caused Larry to work even harder to make the sawmill a success. He visited the forests to inspect the trees being cut. He worked beside his men back at the mill and taught them how to be efficient. Although Larry was not a large man, he was incredibly strong. His biceps were massive trunks formed from all his manual labor. Even later in life, Robert marveled at how toned his father's muscles had remained.

Howard paid Larry a weekly paycheck and told him they were close to pulling more profit that they could continue to split monthly. Larry started getting dreams of paying the land off early and building their home sooner.

As the chill of winter chivalrously welcomed the warmth of spring, the hopes for the dream house gave way to realistic plans. Larry and Olivia had drawn, erased, and redrew their ideas on the back of a brown paper bag—the blueprints of their dream.

At the mill, diesel or electric ran most equipment, but they had one old steam boiler that Howard's uncle had used when he started the mill thirty years before. Everyone referred to the boiler as Ol' Bessie, named after the uncle's wife. Ol' Bessie was temperamental. She would go for weeks running efficiently, and then need work day after day.

Randy Judd

On a transitional day in April, the wind blew stiffly and the gray clouds stared ominously down on the mill. Larry was helping his men pull boards off the conveyor belt, then stacking them. He noticed Howard going into the shed where Ol' Bessie was. The action was not unusual because everyone took their turns in enticing her to run just a little better, or at least a little longer.

In an instant, the shed was disintegrated by a deafening explosion—Howard was still inside! Fragments of the building rained down on Larry and his men almost fifty feet away. Most men instinctively ran away from the sound and took cover, but Larry's instincts forced him *toward* the explosion.

As Larry neared the destruction, the reality of the situation set in. Ol' Bessie had blown up and, in the process, destroyed the shed and all that was in it. Under a slab of wood—previously part of a wall—he could see Howard's arm jutting out. With the last of the small debris settling down to earth, Larry lifted the piece covering Howard. As he lifted the wood, he wasn't prepared for what he saw. The left side of the man's body was ripped and bloody, his arm was attached only by a thin strand of muscle. The left side of his face was practically missing. There was no doubt about it—Howard was dead. Larry had saved him in Guadalcanal, halfway around the world, but there was no hope of saving his dear friend now that they were back home.

As the workers approached the scene, they found Larry cradling Howard as a baby against his chest—sobbing at the loss of his buddy.

The family held the funeral three days later in a cemetery across from *Hal's Market,* where the men had reunited. By this time, the ominous clouds had turned to menacing rains. The casket was closed, so little Robert understood even less about the death, the funeral, and why he would never get to see 'Uncle Howard' again.

The next day, Larry reluctantly made his way to the sawmill. Larry had asked the workers not to come in for the rest of the week until he could get his sorts about him. Turning the ancient skeleton key in the door, he noticed the creak of the wood for the first time. It had never been this quiet at the mill before. The desk chair sat as a throne of a fallen king. He choked back tears as he stared at this chair that he had seen occupied by his friend so many times. He sat down across the desk from Howard's chair. He stared around, overwhelmed by the stacks of files. It reinforced a fact he had thought about ever since Howard died. Larry knew nothing about running the business. Howard never shared any of what he did, and Larry never had any desire to know. Larry doubted his own abilities, for good reason. He had less than five years of formal Ozark education, and though he was an intelligent man, his parent's circumstances never allowed him to go further in school.

Though he didn't know anything about how Howard conducted the business end of the mill, Larry was determined he could learn. At that moment, he became resolute to not let the men's dream die. It resolved him to carry on.

The following Monday, Larry started the mill up again. The workers needed the money, and Larry needed to be busy. As the men in the lumber yard took care of their responsibilities, Larry dug into the mountain of mail and paperwork. No matter how much he wanted to do the job, he couldn't make sense of most of the things before him. Though Larry didn't want to ask for help, he needed it and wasn't sure where to find it.

Knowing that the workers could operate the mill just fine, he left a little after ten o'clock and headed for Clinton. Walking past the whittlers, he headed into the courthouse, not exactly sure what he would find or to whom he should talk. He saw a placard on a large oak door that read *The Honorable Judge Marvin Spanks*. Larry knew Judge Spanks from a couple of years before when Howard and

Larry had cleared some trees from the Judge's land. Larry found him to be very easygoing and easy to talk to.

The large oak door creaked as it opened. The only person in the office was the clerk behind her desk. She was a small woman with gray hair. She looked so brittle she would break if she turned too quickly. She pulled her wispy gray hair back in a bun with dark bobby pins. She looked over her bifocals as her little prune lips asked with a drawl, "May I help you?"

"I was hoping to see the Judge." Larry stammered.

"Do you have an appointment?"

"No, I just wanted to talk to him, even just for a minute."

"Well, if you don't have an appointment, you ain't going to be seeing nobody," the secretary responded, proud of her stance.

"I can wait."

"No need, he ain't even here. He's in court."

Larry, needing to speak to someone immediately, did not bother trying to make an appointment. He turned and started toward the door, which was now opening. As he looked up, he saw the Judge coming in. When Judge Spanks saw Larry, a big smile developed across the judge's face as he recognized him.

The smile quickly turned solemn as the Judge remembered. "I heard about Howard, Larry. I am very sorry. My deepest sympathies."

"Thanks, Judge." Larry nodded. "Have you got just a minute?"

"I've got about thirty and Larry, they're all yours. Come on in my office." The judge put his arm around Larry and pulled him into chambers. Larry smiled at the clerk as he passed.

Behind closed doors, Larry explained his dilemma and summoned the judge's help.

"I have some great people, Larry, who I know would love to help you at a time such as this. They are good at what they do and probably will charge for their time, but they will treat you right." The judge pulled a legal pad out from his desk and started to write.

"Of course, I'll pay, Judge. What I'll pay will probably be a lot less than what I would lose if I didn't get help."

"I'm writing the name of an accountant, Richard Stark, and an attorney, Lloyd Baxter. Here are their phone numbers and their office addresses."

"Thanks so much, Judge."

"Listen, Larry. You can come to me anytime. My door is always open and call me Marv, ok?"

"Ok, Marv, and thanks so much for the leads," Larry graciously said.

Larry went immediately to both men's offices just off the town square. Unfortunately, neither man was available, but the secretaries assured him they would call.

He headed back toward the mill to finish up the day.

When Larry pulled up to the office of the sawmill, he saw a sight not welcome today—and most every other day. The black Cadillac Coupe Deville sitting at the office belonged to Elizabeth, Howard's widow. Larry and Elizabeth were oil and water, and things were better if he just avoided her. Larry couldn't remember how it started, but their relationship had never been cordial. It might have had something to do with the attention Larry got from Howard for being his hero and how his friend treated him. After all these years, Larry had gathered she was somehow jealous of him or had some hidden agenda. Whatever it was, she always seemed to take delight in Larry's failures. He assumed she was at the mill to pick up some of Howard's belongings. Instead of going to the office, he strolled over to the mill to help the men.

"She's been looking for you, Larry," one of the men yelled over the noise of the machinery.

"Who?" Larry asked, hoping they weren't talking about Elizabeth.

"The witch," the man replied, rolling his eyes toward the office.

Larry reluctantly walked the fifty feet to the office. No part of him wanted to deal with her at the moment. *Maybe she was having a soft moment and wanted them to console each other.* Larry doubted it.

Reluctantly, he stepped through the door. Elizabeth was flipping through some papers in the file cabinet. She looked up, not surprised it was Larry.

"Well, Larry. First day back and already playing hooky?" Her sarcasm cut him deep. *How dare she question his loyalty to the mill … and Howard.*

"I had to take care of some things in Clinton."

"Sit down, Larry. We need to talk." It was true they would eventually have to sort matters through. He had just hoped it would be later rather than sooner.

"Larry, you and Howard had a pretty good thing going here for a *sawmill*." She said 'sawmill' with quite a bit of disdain, as if it was beneath her. "The only reason I even put up with this old thing is that my uncle left it to me. I didn't want to have anything to do with it, but since Howard wallowed in it, I figured 'what's the harm? It will keep him away from home and out of my hair'."

Apparently, her mourning period was over. Larry found her attitude quite disrespectful, but wasn't surprised by it, so he continued his silence.

She continued, "but now that he is gone—God rest his soul—I really don't want to have anything to do with it."

Larry finally heard her say something agreeable. "That's ok with me Elizabeth, it may only be half mine, but I can run it by myself."

"Half yours? Larry, you don't have any ownership in this place, it was all Howard's. Actually, all mine. Everything is in my name."

"Maybe so, but we were partners. We split the profits right down the middle." Larry defended.

"He was just being nice to his pathetic, old war buddy, but there are no written agreements. Nothing is signed. Larry, you were no more than his worker."

Her words were as demeaning as she meant them to be. "Howard had a banknote with a lien against some of the newer equipment. When Daddy was in last week for the funeral, we came by and looked at this decrepit place. Daddy said the whole place with all of its equipment would barely cover the note itself. So, we're going to close the mill down, sell what we can, and I am going to pay off the note and forget about this place."

Larry sucked the air for the breath that had been forced from him. He stared at her, not even knowing how to respond. "But we were partners." He sounded like a defeated little boy.

"Today is the last day of this dirty old sawmill," she said victoriously.

After thinking for a minute and looking around as if to find the answer written on one of the walls, he spoke up. "I could buy you out!"

"Hah! Hardly. You ain't got a pot to piss in, Larry Rhodes. You don't own a house, land or even a horse. What are *you* going to put up for collateral? And don't go and try putting up that sorry piece of land you're trying to buy. Howard told me all about that."

Larry didn't have an answer. She was right. He had no wealth and his savings amounted to only a few hundred dollars put aside for the house. He walked out of the room, not knowing what else to say.

Randy Judd

Chapter 7

As he drove home, Larry moaned aloud in misery. What could be done? What had he done, letting himself get so far down the road of hope without realizing it would all come crashing down? He wasn't ready to give up yet. Tomorrow he would go see the judge and the accountant and the lawyer. Someone had to be able to help.

He had decided not to tell anyone yet. During the evening, he wore a cheerful face. The ruse didn't work on Olivia, though.

"Hard to go back today without Howard there?" Olivia asked as she lay her head down on the pillow and put her hand on his shoulder.

"You don't know the half of it, Olivia." Larry kissed her and turned over for sleep.

The next day, he left at his normal time, but a half mile down the road, he turned toward town instead of the mill. Luckily, he was able to get in to see all three men—first the lawyer, then the accountant and finally the judge. All three men told him he didn't have many options. There had been no written agreement. He couldn't validate the oral agreement, and the mill rightfully belonged to Elizabeth, anyway.

On the way home, he drove by the dream property again. What would happen now? Any thoughts beyond today were clouded in despair and uncertainty.

He drove toward the mill, but as he turned the corner a quarter mile away, he could see large trucks parked in the yard, and Elizabeth's helpers were already ravaging her interests in the enterprise. He made a U-turn and headed back to his house, his refuge. When Olivia saw him pull in, she felt the same pang she had felt several years before in a similar circumstance.

This time the news was much harder for Larry to relate. He cried—not a sobbing cry, but a gentle, hopeless cry—as he told her the story. Tears rolled down his cheek and fell to the floor. She held him tight wondering what this news would mean.

Outside, the children were all returning from the pond. Robert held two fish on a string, and Will helped him watch for snakes.

Even though Larry had been here before, this time the situation seemed much more hopeless—the despair much deeper. Maybe it was because he had let himself start to get a positive outlook on life. For the first time, he had allowed himself to feel as if he were more than just a fruit tramp. He had permitted himself to set goals and look to the future. He let his hopes expand to the kids and their future. He had made plans for an actual house that the family could own. How foolish of him to think things could be different.

Because of their financial obligations and debt, they had incurred—the tractor and the pickup—Larry did not have any time to waste. He had to find a job quickly. The obvious place to look for work was the other sawmills in the area, but there were two problems: first, Larry had not been on good terms with the owners because of the competitive nature of things. Larry had eaten crow before and was prepared to do it now for his family. Second, the other men from Larry and Howard's mill had already taken any available openings. Larry was right back where he was a few years before when he had met Howard in front of *Hal's Market*. In some ways, Larry wished that day had never occurred. He wondered if he would have been better off just being a laborer all this time. Then again, he had a great time working daily with his friend.

The money the Rhodes had set aside for the house would help them hold out for a month or so, but after that he wasn't sure what they would do. He and Olivia took a drive to talk to the owner of the land they were buying. They were six months into his twelve-month contract to buy the land. Jared Wilcox owned the land, and he was a strict businessman. He lived in town and didn't care a lot about his relationships with the hill folks. The sale of the land, which had been in his family for a hundred years, was purely for business. Mr. Wilcox had held no affection for the property.

Larry and Olivia went to talk to him about their impending financial situation, hoping to get some grace. Before they left home, Larry tried to read the contract he had signed, but couldn't make heads nor tails of the legalese.

They drove their new truck to Mr. Wilcox's real estate office in town. His office was located in a building that had once been a home and had been redesigned to house an office instead. Mr. Wilcox was the only attorney in his small office and only occasionally used a girl in town to file and type. Today wasn't one of those days. Mr. Wilcox was a large barrel-chested man who looked as though he hadn't seen a hard day's labor ever. He wore gray slacks with red suspenders and a shirt that had started as white, but over the years of sweat and wear was now a pale yellow.

After hearing Larry's dilemma, Mr. Wilcox placed the contract for the land—which he had previously pulled from his files—in front of him.

Without hesitation, the large man spoke. "Folks, plain and simple, I'm a businessman. When you folks came to me last year and inquired about the property, it got me thinking. I made the contract with you, but I have several properties around the counties, and it is about time I start unloading these. Now I don't want to get part of the way into it and then not get to finish."

"Surely a month or two won't hurt and then we can pick up from there," Larry pleaded.

"Normally you would be right," Wilcox continued. "It might be hard to find another buyer. After all, it sat there for all these years without any interest.

"But, coincidently, just yesterday, someone came inquiring about that property. I told them it was under contract, and they said if the contract somehow fell through, they would buy it with cash and pay twice what you had offered me."

Larry knew the games that some businessmen played and wondered if the story was true or if he fabricated it to see if somehow Larry could come up with the money after all. Larry, though, was unskilled at such negotiations, assumed the story was true, and pleaded his case. "Mr. Wilcox, sir, this land is going to be the site of our dream home. I've always been able to pay debts and come up with the money. Just give us two months, that's all we're asking."

"Larry, as I was saying before, this is not personal. I am, however, a businessman and I abide by the contracts I make. As I read the contract that you signed, it reads *'If buyer is thirty days late on any payment, the contract is deemed null and void and all funds previously paid are forfeited.'* If you are more than thirty days late—and as I look at the calendar, the clock starts ticking next Monday—I will have to cancel our deal and sell to this other party for cash."

Larry and Olivia got up and wandered almost aimlessly toward the door. Just before exiting, Larry turned toward Mr. Wilcox to ask a question. Larry wanted to test the man to see if he was making up 'the other party'.

"Mr. Wilcox," Larry started, "do you mind if I asked who the other party was that wants the property?"

"Not at all, Larry. I doubt that you would know her. She's from up around Harrison. Her name is Elizabeth Simpson."

Olivia gasped. Larry just sighed. *Thank you for the nail in my coffin, you witch*, Larry thought. There was not much conversation between the couple as their truck rattled back home—the sun setting on the horizon and apparently on their dreams.

Randy Judd

Chapter 8

They urgently needed to make some decisions regarding the money they had saved for their future house. They decided to use it to pay the land payment in hopes that Larry could get a job in time to not miss a payment. The downside of this was that if Larry didn't find work, they would have used the money and lost it all anyway, but they wanted to take a chance. Larry was able to find some sporadic day work, but it didn't provide the steady income he needed and was accustomed to making. As the days turned into weeks, Larry wore his distress in his face and carried it on his countenance. There was a need for action, yet he didn't have a way to act.

Larry and Olivia started to become late on their financial obligations. Three months into his unemployment, Robert saw two men come and drive Daddy's pickup away. Without a vehicle, Larry was even more hard-pressed to find work. He walked, hitchhiked, rode the family mule and even took the tractor—although it used too much gas for long trips—to get to a day job or talk to people about work. Several weeks later, the same men took the tractor.

On an early fall day while Larry was working in the garden digging some potatoes for Olivia to cook for supper, a government looking pickup truck pulled up into the driveway. A tall man, dressed in dungarees, got out and started toward the house with long strides. Thinking it was probably something bad and wanting to shield the children from much of the truth, Larry intercepted the man.

"Can I help you?" Larry questioned the stranger.

"I'm looking for Larry Rhodes. Is that you?" The stranger spoke in respectful terms.

"That's me alright, who are you?" Larry asked cautiously.

"I was over at the market, and they said you might be looking for work," the stranger continued. "My name is Barron Lawrence. I'm with the Arkansas State Highway Department."

"Why, that's right, Mr. Lawrence," Larry replied. "I've been looking for any kind of steady work. Have you got some?"

"Well, as a matter of fact, I do. We are building a new state road over by the town of Flat Rock over in Izzard County. There aren't a lot of workers over there, so I'm scouring the hills looking for people to come help us. The job will probably last about a year. They told me down at the market that you were a heck of a worker." Barron explained.

"It might sound good. I'm not sure how ready my family would be to move for a job that will only last a year." Larry challenged. The fact was that just a few years ago, the fruit tramp was moving much more often than that. He hoped those days were over, but would do what it took to support his family.

"Actually, Larry, what I am looking for are men that can live in work camps along the road. You would have to leave your family Monday through Friday, but you would come home every weekend. We would send a bus to pick all of you workers up early Monday morning, then bring you home Friday evening."

"When would it start?" Larry asked, obviously interested. He removed his cap and scratched his sweaty head.

"Whenever you could. The road work has already begun. I just need more workers."

The two men discussed more of the details. The pay wasn't as much as he had made with Howard, but it was much better than anything else he had seen around, plus they provided three meals a day and transportation.

Larry had a positive tone in his voice for the first time in a couple of months when he said, "I'll have to discuss it with my wife. I'm sure you understand since it will affect her so much. How do I get hold of you?"

"I tell you what, Larry," Barron outlined. "If you want the job, we'd love to have you. Just show up at Hal's Market at 5:30 on Monday morning. That is where the bus will be to take all the workers I've talked to around here. I don't need to know before that."

"Thank you for coming by, Mr. Lawrence. I appreciate the offer."

"I hope to see you on Monday, Larry."

The men parted and Larry stepped toward the house to tell his wife.

"Was that a creditor, Lar?" Olivia asked as she met him on the porch. She had been watching the two men talk from the front room window.

"Actually, just the opposite, Olivia. It might be the answers to our prayers." Larry answered Olivia, his voice full of hope.

As he explained the offer to Olivia, there was really no decision to be made. They needed the money, and this might allow them to keep the land. Of course, it would be difficult to have him gone during the week. The kids were getting bigger, and Will could do the harder work around the house. They would miss their dad, but the family would at least get to see him on weekends.

Though the Rhodes family were sporadic about attending church, they always tried to make it when they were humbled by great need or overwhelmed by gratitude. This was one of those weekends that they attended.

The First Baptist Church of Tilley was a wood-planked, one room church typical of that region. Outside, the cars parked on the gravel and grass, and churchgoers milled outside before the service. Church was not only a religious event but one of the key social events of the week. The women wore their nicest dresses; the men were generally in their best overalls, and the kids wore their shoes even in the summer. Everyone showed respect for the church and their Lord by wearing their Sunday-go-to-meetin' clothes.

The First Baptist Church of Tilley should have been called a non-denominational church because it was a melting pot of religious views. Worshippers attended more out of convenience than devotion. The Rhodes didn't consider themselves Baptists either. They never really considered themselves belonging to any one denomination. They attended whatever congregation which they felt comfortable.

The sermon was about the trials of Job. Larry reached for Olivia's hand, knowing they could relate. Just as Job had gotten deeper and deeper in despair, the Rhodes seemed to continually see doors shut on their opportunities. Larry always tried to be an optimist, but the events of the sawmill had wounded him deeply. He hoped this was just his refining fire.

Monday morning, Larry kissed his sweetheart and walked out the door at 4:00 a.m. to walk the five miles to the market. He hoped he could sleep on the bus. The gibbous moon gave enough light for the man to maneuver the road, although he probably knew the road well enough after many years of living there. Larry hoped he could meet someone with whom he could catch a ride with on Mondays. He also counted on buying a cheap family car within a few weeks, so Olivia wouldn't have to be stranded while he was gone. By the time the kids woke up, Larry was already sharing war stories with the men on the bus.

Slowly, things at the Rhodes' home started to return to normal. The kids, who previously had to do without new school clothes, were able to get a new pair of shoes each and one new set of store-bought school clothes. Olivia was a talented seamstress and was able to provide nice clothes for her children. It wasn't unusual to hear the rhythmic hum of the Singer treadle sewing machine late into the night. Larry was able to buy a used '54 Country Squire station wagon from a co-worker for three-hundred dollars, so Olivia had transportation while Larry was away.

The family missed their dad, but as they got used to the routine, it seemed tolerable. Since the bus came by their house anyway, Larry was able to convince the bus driver just to stop long enough to pick him up each Monday. This way Larry could sleep a little later, not having to go to the store. "If you're not here, I don't stop," the driver had warned. Larry was always there because the family needed the money.

Larry and Olivia were able to make another land payment which kept Elizabeth at bay.

As the fall days got colder, and the hardwoods in the Rhodes' yard began to turn brilliant orange, yellow and red, everything finally seemed back in order at *Hal's Place.*

There was a chill of an approaching storm the morning Olivia asked Lou to stay home with her. Mom had woken that morning with a pain at the bottom of her belly. Even though Robert was old enough to take care of himself, Olivia felt better about having Lou home to help out so she could rest. By midmorning, Olivia felt as if her discomfort was something more serious than a bellyache. Olivia sent Lou to the Palmer's house—a mile down the road—to see if someone could come over to help.

By early afternoon, Olivia was in the back of the Palmer's station wagon being driven to the hospital in Harrison. They had made arrangements for an aunt to come over to the house later and watch the kids.

As Lou watched the car leave the driveway, she was frightened. This put the twelve-year-old girl in a position of adulthood where she did not want to be. Although her mother had told her not to worry, she couldn't help but be concerned as the car vanished under the dust, driving toward town. She wanted her daddy there beside her, but he was away, and she didn't know if he would return to help take care of them until Friday.

Even though Robert was only five, he still was acutely aware of the gravity of the situation. This was apparent when he turned to his sister and asked, "Is Mom dead?"

Lou tried to control her emotions for Robert's sake. "Of course not, Honey. She's just sick."

"Remember when you got a tummy ache and had to stay in bed all day?"

Robert nodded—his big blue eyes swirled with tears.

"Mommy's just got a big tummy ache, and the doctor has to fix her." Lou explained as she bit her lip so as not to sob.

It wasn't until the next morning that anyone could contact Larry, there were no phones in the camp. Neighbors got hold of the State Highway Department and talked to secretaries, who left the message for supervisors who told Larry first thing the next morning. Larry made a collect call to a cousin that lived about thirty miles from where the road crew was working. The cousin came immediately and drove the anxious husband to the hospital.

Olivia's surgery had been difficult. The appendix had become very inflamed by the time she arrived at the hospital. The surgeon was able to remove it through a five-inch incision in her abdomen. Larry stayed by her side for the first three days of her seven-day hospital stay. He then returned home to the kids to help them recover also.

Although it was fun to stay at their cousins' house, the children were glad to come back to their own rooms and looked forward to being reunited with Mom.

As the children snuggled in for their first night back, Larry stoked the fire and sat in the big easy chair and pondered.

Here we are again, he worried. The highway department had told him they would hold his job for him, but the doctor told him Olivia would be convalescing at home for a month or so. He could ask the help of neighbors and friends but Larry wasn't one to accept help. He had already received more help and felt obligated to more people than he wanted. The hospital had not calculated the final bill, but he knew they would be paying on it for years. He was grateful he was not back in Oklahoma. The Harrison hospital would let him work out a payment plan without holding him hostage.

As William walked through the front room to get a drink of water, he noticed Larry was sitting in the light of a lamp. The boy asked, "What are you smiling at Dad?"

Larry hadn't realized that he was wearing a slight grin at the hopelessness of his situation. "Nothing Will, just a joke the doctor told me." Larry lied.

A psychologist might have called it an anxiety attack or a mental breakdown, but Larry didn't have a therapist. He just knew he had reached the end of his rope. The land would be lost. The dream house was gone. He honestly did not know what the family was going to do.

In the days before Johnson's Great Society, there was little help from the government. A county commodities truck came around once a month and let the poor folks take some food: cheese, flour, powdered milk, but that was about all they would receive from any form of government. Bankruptcy wouldn't help.

The only debt that could be dismissed was the hospital bill. They had already lost the truck and the tractor and would soon lose the land. The only assets Larry had left were sleeping in the other room and in the hospital in Harrison.

He sat in that chair most of the night letting the same thoughts spin in his head repeatedly. How does a person manage to get out of this fix over and over again? He cursed his father for not being anything more than an Arkansas timber worker. Why couldn't he have gone to school and got a good job and left Larry and his siblings an inheritance? As he thought this, he thought about his own children saying the same thing to him. It made him feel heartbroken. How does this cycle of poverty get broken? Or can it be?

Chapter 9

In the morning, the school kids got themselves ready and Robert sat on his daddy's lap. Will came into the room and asked his dad, "Can I talk to you, Daddy?"

"Of course, Will. Sit down. Mom is going to be just fine," Larry said preemptively.

"Oh, I know. It's not that. It's school." William corrected. Will had never been a very successful student. They had held him back a grade, and he still did not quite keep up with his classmates. Olivia and Larry had met with his teachers countless times to try to help him. They weren't much help except to encourage him. Olivia had only finished eighth grade and Larry not even that. Later in life, Robert contemplated that under different circumstances, his father could have been an engineer. He thought Larry was very smart, just was never allowed the opportunity to develop any skills.

"The teacher talked to me again yesterday and said I am not keeping up with the rest of the kids. She wants to talk to y'all about putting me back in the tenth grade again." Larry could hear the embarrassment in his son's voice.

"Son, you don't have to be embarrassed around me. I am very proud of you. You are becoming a wonderful man. You have so many qualities that I would love to have. You are a great worker, and you always see things through till the end. You are a great older brother. You're kind to your brother and sister. They couldn't have a better example."

"Thanks, Dad," Will said, his eyes starting to tear up. They did not discourage tears in the Rhodes home, not even for the boys. Will was already taller than his father and at least fifty pounds heavier. "I just don't know if I want to do school anymore."

In the Ozarks of the fifties and sixties, dropping out of school did not have much social stigma attached. Barely fifty percent of the students continued to graduation. Larry and Olivia knew that education was the best way out of the poverty for their family. They also were realistic about their firstborn son's ability and knew that he would be more likely to make good as a laborer than an intellectual.

Dad put his hand on his son's shoulder. "Go on back to school and tell your teacher we'll talk about things once mom is home from the hospital." In his brain, Larry wanted to push his son as Larry's drill sergeant had pushed him so many years ago, but he also remembered the humiliation he felt and didn't want to be the instigator of that same feeling in his son. In his heart, he wanted Will to be the best he could be at whatever he ended up pursuing.

Larry visited the hospital the next day, and he and Olivia talked about all the issues and decisions that faced them. Olivia wanted to take the blame for the new situation in their life, but Larry wouldn't let her. They were a team and there wasn't any blame to be had. They reluctantly decided to not put any more money into the Wilcox property. It was a hard decision and yet an easy one. They would eventually have to make that decision, but sooner would be better than throwing money at it they didn't have. Besides, even if they followed through the last months and finished paying for it, the chance they would be able to build on it was remote. Larry had checked the possibility of finishing the payments and then selling the land, but the land around the area was not selling very quickly. There was only one buyer he could think of that would possibly buy it, but she probably wouldn't want to purchase it now since it wouldn't lead to his demise.

A few days after they released Olivia from the hospital, Will came into the room where his parents sat watching *Lassie* on a small black-and-white TV. When a commercial came on and their eyes and bodies were relaxed for the break, Will sheepishly asked his parents, "Dad, did you tell Mom about school?"

Larry and Olivia had talked about it in the hospital. Although it hurt to allow their son to quit school, the decision was as inevitable as selling the land had been.

His dad answered, "Son, we know you've tried hard to do well in school. Each of us is blessed with unique gifts at birth. Life blesses some with book smarts, some with the gift of kindness, some with the gift of reasoning, some with the gift of helping others."

Olivia added, "But none of us have all the gifts. Book learnin' might not be one of your strengths, but I know you have a lot to offer this world. We hope you find them somehow."

Dad continued, "So yeah, we'll let you drop out. But you've got to be a productive member of society. I won't put up with you just lying around." Larry regretted saying this and even caught a little chastising eye from his wife. Will wasn't one just to lie around. He was a hard-working, industrious young man, the same as his dad.

"But I know you won't," he quickly corrected. "You're a wonderful son and a good man. You'll do what's right."

Now there were to be two Rhodes men looking for work. At least the odds were a little better for the family.

In the days after Olivia got home, the decisions swirled around Larry's head as though he was in some *Alice in Wonderland* fantasy. He made a few efforts to talk to people about work, but they were the same people with the same answers. He couldn't go back to the Highway Department because of his need to be home every night. By the time Olivia was all healed the highway department project would almost be done. He drove to Clinton one day to inquire about jobs. The thirty-two miles each way was certainly doable, but by the end of the day, Larry had surmised that this small town had no more to offer than the hills around his house.

A few weeks before, a friend had mentioned the possibility of looking in Russellville, a town of about twelve thousand people a couple of hours to the south. Russellville was the county seat of Pope County. Two events happened almost simultaneously to reshape the town. Seven years before, they had built a new dam on the Arkansas River near Russellville. The backup of water created Lake Dardanelle, a very large lake that filled all the surrounding farmlands and meandered its way around the green hills. About the same time, they constructed Interstate 40 so that it skirted the edge of the town as a tangent to a circle. With the added transportation access, the town had begun to be a destination for manufacturing and commerce.

On his first Monday of deliverance, Will carried a sack lunch out to the station wagon, tossed it in the back seat and got in the front passenger seat beside his dad. The men had both taken baths the night before and Olivia had laid out clean dungarees and shirts for them. Will and his dad were going to spend the day looking around Russellville for work. Since it was a two-hour drive each way, they had warned Olivia that if they found a need, they would sleep that night in the back of the wagon and look on Tuesday as well.

It didn't take long for Larry to realize that they could probably find the jobs they needed in this up-and-coming town. They went to the unemployment office and found a bulletin board with dozens of papers attached with flat silver thumbtacks. Larry wet his short yellow pencil with his tongue as he began to write down names of companies and addresses. While many of the openings required skilled labor and education, many were for common laborers and paid as much as two or three dollars per hour, over twice the minimum wage. The Rhodes men were most attracted to the manufacturing jobs, which were abundant—chicken processing, canneries, lumber yards, and furniture manufacturing were all present on the board.

At the first place they stopped, The International Shoe Factory, the men were told that the factory wasn't currently hiring, but to check back in a week or so because business was booming.

Next, they went to the River Valley Furniture Factory. The men were told to fill out a simple application and then were led to a room where they interviewed together. The interviewer said there were immediate job openings if the men could start to work the next day. The pay was two dollars per hour, with increases after sixty days. They told the lady that was doing the interviews that they hadn't planned on finding a job so fast and were unprepared to make a decision.

"I won't hold it open, so if you want it, you need to get back to me before the next guy does," she told them.

As the men got back in the car, Larry spoke first. "Wow, I didn't expect to find something so fast. I hope these jobs will be open if we decide to move down here."

They drove to a little city park and pulled the car up under a fifty-year-old oak whose leaves had fallen off at least a month before. They stayed in the warm

75

car to eat their lunch. The bologna and saltines that Olivia had packed were delicious to the simple men.

Will interrupted the silence. "Dad, I've been thinking. Is there any way I could take the furniture job and stay down here?"

Larry hadn't even entertained the idea before, so now he had to process the scenarios before he could give a suitable response. He chewed attentively as he listened to his son.

"I feel as though we need to be down here," Will said. "It feels good, it feels right. It appears there is nothing back on the mountain for our family. I bet I could find a boarding house or somewhere to stay until the family could move down."

Larry really couldn't find anything wrong with Will's plan. His son had shown a lot of maturity before, so he was sure he could trust him. Larry responded to his son, "You're a man now. I think we can do it." Larry jostled his son's hair and—in that moment—his son became his peer.

They headed back to the furniture factory, where Will went in on his own and accepted the job. He also found out there was indeed a boarding house up the street that was close enough to walk. They were able to get Will into *Mrs. Johansson's Boarding House for Men*. Larry paid the first week up front, with the agreement that Will would pay Mrs. Johansson eight dollars each week as he got paid. The men then went to downtown Russellville and bought the younger man some simple toiletries and a change of clothes so he could rotate.

Larry stayed that night in Will's room at the boarding house. It was a very simple room with a twin sized bed, a chest of drawers, and a closet. There was a common bathroom down the hall.

"No more cold trips to the outhouse in the middle of the night for you, Will." Larry joked.

"What's that?" William said, pointing to a radiator against the window.

"That's where your room gets heat. It's called a radiator, remember the one in our car?" Larry answered.

"You mean I've got heat in my bedroom? Wow!" Will's eyes brightened.

"Yeah, you're living the high life now," his dad told him.

The next morning, when Dad dropped his son off at the gate of the factory, they both realized it was a moment that neither had prepared for. These times are meant to be prepared for and thought out: A mother prepares herself for her child's first day of school. Parents prepare themselves for their daughter's approaching wedding. But they had not prepared for the current moment.

"So, I'll bring the rest of the family down Saturday with all your stuff. Mrs. Johansson will sell you a sack lunch every day for fifty cents and you get your other two meals as part of the board."

"I know, Daddy." Will's voice trailed off, obviously hurting from his sense of the moment. "I'm kind of scared".

"I know how you feel, son. When I went off to the war, I didn't know what to expect. I didn't know how hard it would be. I didn't know if the other fellows would accept me." Larry tried to give solace to his son. "Now, I'm not trying to downplay the hurt, boy, but I'm pretty sure you'll come back alive and without any shrapnel in your leg."

William raised his eyes without raising his head. He smiled.

"Now I've found it's best in these cases just to do it quickly, so go on to work, son. I love you." Dad quickly patted his son's back.

"I love you too, Dad." Will walked precariously toward the factory. After he looked back and saw his dad's encouraging smile, his step had a new confidence.

Larry choked back the tears and carefully wiped the ones that had already escaped. Maybe it's better when you don't prepare for times like these.

A new chapter was starting for William, Larry, and the whole Rhodes family.

Chapter 10

The desert of Arizona was different from anything Robert had experienced in Arkansas. As he sped across the barren wasteland on I-40, he took delight in knowing that this road was the same road that passed near his home in Russellville. There were several things about the desert that he enjoyed. He loved being able to see forever without the obstruction of trees. The only vegetation in this part of the world didn't grow high enough to block any view. Some of the flora of the terrain was beautiful in its own way. The vast horizon gave him a sense of freedom. No claustrophobia to be felt here. As his car crested over some of the small hills on the freeway, he could see mountains forty or fifty miles away. That, to him, was amazing.

While growing up, his world had been small. Except for having been born in Oklahoma, Robert was twelve before ever leaving Arkansas. He didn't see the ocean until he was out of high school and didn't ride an airplane till in his twenties. It was incredible to him that now, at forty-eight, he had been in ten foreign countries and all but two states.

Even though he was deep in the desert, he was delighted to see he had a powerful signal on his cell phone. He decided to call his sweetheart and see what was happening at home. His wife was his favorite diversion. Whenever he needed his spirits lifted, he could count on her. If he had a choice of anyone to be around or talk to, it would be his wife. Reviewing all the places he had been in his life, he was still sure that by his wife's side was his favorite place to be.

To some people, the desert represents barren loneliness, but there had been many times in his life when Robert preferred to be alone.

It surprised Olivia when she heard the news that Will didn't return with his dad. Her sad reaction softened, but was still present after an hour. Just last week, her son was in school. Tonight, her son was living in another town, working as a man. Her thoughts could not allow her to accept the fact that her firstborn was on his own, at least temporarily.

Larry and Olivia sat up late into the night, discussing plausible scenarios. They finally determined that they would start getting all their affairs in order so that when Olivia's convalescence was over, the family could move to Russellville. Will would stay with Mrs. Johansson and save all the money he could so that they could find a house to rent by the time the family moved. Larry would continue to work day jobs and go to Russellville about once a week to secure employment.

At first, the men at the factory made fun of Will's awkward country ways. Eventually, though, his humility, kind heart, and hard work won over his fellow workers. The men even invited him to go out with them after work to the local clubs. The boy declined, though, feeling his obligation to save every cent for the family. Besides, he wasn't yet old enough to get in most of them.

At night, Will thought of his family; his sister Lou, who Will protected, and baby brother, Robert, who always had a hug for him. Most of all, he thought of his parents—the hard-working couple who were such a good example to him. Will also missed the crickets, katydids and other insects which were joined by bullfrogs, owls and howling dogs in a magnificent symphony back home in the Ozarks.

On his third weekly trip to the town, Larry found an employer, which didn't require an immediate start. Axtell Lumber Company was opening a new line which wouldn't be complete and running for another three weeks, perfect timing for the move. He hoped the move would be a chance for him to try his hand in another industry, but his skills were an easy sell for the lumber mill. This mill was nothing like the one he and Howard had operated. It spread out over at least ten acres, with about half of it covered with freshly cut logs stacked like giant toothpicks in triangular piles. Trucks with logs came in one gate as trucks with boards left another. It was not just a mill, but more of a lumber factory. Although it was intimidating, Larry knew he could feel right at home and adjust easily.

As Olivia's doctor-imposed rest ended, she accompanied her husband to the town for a couple of days to look for a house to rent. The children's protests were not enough to allow them to go also, so the Rhodes kids had to stay at their cousins. Will was just getting off work as his parents pulled up. Olivia was able to restrain herself from running up and hugging and kissing him in front of his coworkers, but as soon as the boy saw his mom, he dropped his black metal lunchbox and ran down to meet her. He hugged her, picked her up, and spun her around. He was clearly not embarrassed.

Later, they all sat at the boarding room table talking about what the next move would be. Mrs. Johansson got the local newspaper, *The Courier Democrat,* and they spread out the classifieds on the table looking for houses to rent. Larry and Olivia used the boarding house phone to call a few of the numbers to get directions and set up times to meet with the owners the following day.

Saying goodbye that evening was not as hard as before. The future had a little more defined view and they would all be together in just a couple of weeks.

The first week of January 1966, the Rhodes family arrived in Russellville with a borrowed pickup truck and car overloaded with family belongings. They pulled in front of the house that would be their home for who knew how long. The house was much nicer than *Hal's Place*, but not as nice as the one they had planned for their land in the hills. The rental house was a freshly painted, white wooden house. Olivia thought the house was smiling at them as they approached. It had four rooms—a living room, kitchen, and two bedrooms like their mountain home. This house, though, had running water and a bathroom, which everyone was excited about. Behind the house was a large area for a garden. Also, one outbuilding, a chicken coop, sat at the very back of the property. Although the house was in the country on a dirt road, it sat just five miles from town. This dirt road—Skyline Drive—was much busier than their former road had been. The drive was the principal thoroughfare for folks in the outlying areas to get to town. Every few minutes, the dust would get kicked up by a vehicle speeding down the road. Just as that dust settled, they could hear the roar of another vehicle approaching. There was nothing across the dirt road but trees. There were no houses to be seen in any direction along the other side. During the day, these woods would become a source of exploration for Robert, but during the evening, the dark woods were ominous.

The house sat fifty feet back at the southwest corner of an acre of cleared land. Because of its placement on the land, it was also fifty feet away from its nearest neighbor, a similar frame house just across the fence. There was a well-worn hole in the fence which allowed the two neighbor families easy access. Between the two houses lurked a storm cellar—similar to the one at *Hal's*

Place—which was never used and seldom opened. Other houses were randomly scattered within walking distance.

Olivia wasn't sure if she would enjoy having neighbors so close. She would have to wait and see. It excited the kids when they first saw the proximity of the neighbors, hoping there were kids their age.

When the Rhodes arrived, the house was immediately ready to be occupied. Will had checked out of the boarding house a week earlier and stayed at the new house without heat or furniture. They turned on the power the day before their arrival and a truck delivered butane for the tank out back. The Rhodes paid fifty dollars per month for the house and, with running water, they felt as if they were royalty.

As everything was getting settled inside the house, five-year-old Robert began exploring the outside to see what treasures the acre had to offer. It took him quite a while to explore the trees, weeds, and especially the chicken coop. He looked back into the dark crawl space under the house but didn't dare go there. The small abyss was high enough to get into, but the thoughts of what lay inside stirred Robert's fear.

He settled down on the cement front porch, hanging his legs over the edge. His feet did not reach the ground below. He held in his hand a large stick that served as his pretend weapon while he explored. Robert glanced at the neighboring house and saw a figure by the opening in the fence. As he looked closer, he could see it was a boy. The boy was older than Robert, but not by many years. His clothes were dirty and his hair unkempt. At first, Robert was kind of startled by the boy just standing there. The boy had a bashful smile, which relieved Robert. The two boys exchanged timid waves, then the older boy entered through the hole in the fence.

"What's your name?" the older boy asked, now having the confidence of owning the neighborhood.

"Robert."

"I'm Ricky. I live over there," he said, pointing to the house across the fence.

"Oh."

"Where did you move from?" Ricky inquired, fully in control of the conversation.

"Up in the hills," Robert replied, still unsure of himself.

"So, you're a hillbilly!?" Ricky's voice started to take on a tone of sarcasm.

"Ain't that something? A real live hillbilly. Well, you're probably not used to seeing things like toilets and cars and stuff like that, are you? Did your family bring your moonshine still with you? I'd love to have some of your white lightning. Are your parents cousins?" Ricky laughed, quite proud of his comedic prowess.

Robert didn't understand sarcasm and the boy's questions came so fast he didn't know which one or how to answer. All he could muster was, "huh?"

"You sure *are* a hillbilly." Ricky felt triumphant.

This interaction was uncharted territory for Robert. He had very little experience interacting with kids his own age. He rarely met someone new and was poorly versed in any social or conversational graces. He wasn't really shy, just inexperienced.

He thought for a few seconds and came up with an awe-inspiring question.

"How old are you?"

"I'm eight. How about you?"

"I'm five, but I'll be six in the summer." Robert felt as though he was gaining speed.

"I'll be nine in August. My whole name is Richard James Goodman but they call me Ricky. What's yours?" Ricky asked.

"Robert Bolls Rhodes," he said with pride.

"That's a funny name," Ricky said, deflating the other boy's pride.

The boys sat beside each other quietly for a few minutes. The silence became awkward for Robert, and he wished this boy—Ricky—would leave. Soon Olivia came out and saw the two boys sitting on the porch.

"Oh, Robert, you've already found a friend," Olivia said. Then directed herself to the older boy. "What's your name?"

"Ricky Goodman, ma'am," Ricky responded with not a trace of his former sarcasm.

"And such a gentleman," she said, impressed.

Robert may have only been five, but there was something about Ricky that already made him uncomfortable. The way he changed attitude when Mom came out struck Robert as odd.

In a matter of minutes and a series of questions, Olivia knew all about Ricky's family. There were three boys, ranging in age from eight to sixteen. Almost a perfect age fit for her own kids. They lived with their mother, Martha, and stepfather Verl. Robert didn't even know what a stepfather was. The word seemed funny. He would ask his mom later.

Although Olivia learned the basics from young Ricky, she soon learned much more about the family next door. The Goodmans had lived in their house since Ricky was a baby. Martha had divorced Ricky's father while she was still pregnant. Martha worked at a chicken processing plant on the other side of the neighboring town of Dardanelle. She labored there amongst the blood, guts, and feathers. She was a thin lady whose diet consisted mostly of Tab Cola and Marlboros. As a chain smoker, as soon as one cigarette burned down to her fingertips, she would use the butt to light another. She had long ago given up on her three boys and now let them run unsupervised. Although she was good at yelling obscenities at them, she didn't have the energy to discipline. The oldest boy was Joel. He was sixteen and already had a criminal record with the juvenile courts. The next boy was Ernie. He wasn't inclined to commit a crime, at least not yet. At thirteen, he was already acutely aware of his interest in girls. Ricky had come along quite unexpectedly for Martha. She couldn't even say for sure who his father was, so she just went with the easiest explanation.

Martha met her current husband, Verl, at the chicken plant. He was a chicken truck driver. After a quick courtship, they were married, and he moved in with her—much to the dismay of the boys. He was a heavy drinker and dangerous when he was drunk. Verl made no effort to get acquainted with the boys. He had no kids of his own and didn't really want hers either.

The Goodman house was always in disarray, both inside and out. Piles of clothes replaced dressers, and they washed dishes on an *as needed* basis. The house's septic tank was in front of their house, which welcomed all visitors with a hostile stench.

The Rhodes may have been a good, hardworking, loving family, and if that were true, the Goodmans were their antithesis.

Even though there was a three-year difference in age, the two young boys found enough similar interests to start playing together. Further exploration of the houses near the new Rhodes home didn't produce any boys his own age, so Robert conceded that eight-year-old Ricky would have to do.

The Monday following the big move, Larry and Will left early for their prospective jobs. By this time, Will had settled into his job and had made many friends of the mostly older men. The older men took Will under their wings and taught him the ways and methods of making cheap assembly line furniture.

Larry's first day at work was uneventful. He had to perform all the first day's tasks, filling out the paperwork, touring the mill, finding out where he would be working. It wasn't until after lunch that he even started actually working. His job was to pull the bad boards off the two by four line as they flew by on the belt. It was hard work for the man in his early fifties, but mountain life had made him strong, and he appreciated hard work.

Olivia, with Robert in tow, took Lou to her school to get registered. Gardner Junior High was a one level building which sat on South Arkansas Avenue adjacent to the three-story High School. For the Rhodes teenager, it was foreboding. Her school in the Ozarks had only two buildings, one for first through sixth grade and one for seventh through twelfth. Olivia accompanied Lou to the registration office of the Junior High and enrolled her in seventh grade. With a hug and kiss on the head—which embarrassed Lou—Mom left the girl to start at her new school.

Lou—being the most gregarious of the Rhodes children—was excited at the new opportunity. By the end of the week, friends surrounded Lou.

Olivia and Larry had decided that Olivia should stay home with Robert until he started school the next school year. With both Will and Larry working, they thought they could make ends meet and pay off some of the debt they had incurred. Aside from the gigantic hospital bill, they had also incurred debt in buying vehicles. Most of the furniture they had at *Hal's Place* belonged to the owner of the house, so they didn't bring much with them. Olivia and Larry used the next weekend to buy some furniture for their new residence. They couldn't resist the smooth salesman and ended up leaving with more than they really needed and bought it all on credit.

For the most part, Robert played by himself as he had while he was in the hills, but some days Ricky Goodman would wander over after the school bus dropped him off. He and Robert would explore together or play with Robert's army men.

The Rhodes family settled easily into their new life in Russellville. The first spring in the new surroundings was uneventful for the family. Even though each of them had adjustments to make, they generally made them smoothly. This was not to say there were no challenges, though. Lou was growing up a little too fast for Olivia. Mom thought her daughter was a little too flirtatious for her age. Mother and daughter often fought over her choice of clothing. Will was making the adjustment to adulthood quickly. He had bought a near-new 1965 Chevelle and was talking about moving out on his own. Robert—on the other hand—was basically the same boy, just in a different environment.

Chapter 11

With the arrival of summer, the dynamics of the Rhodes family began to change. Instead of just turning his paycheck over to his parents, Will started paying them rent. The rest of his money was being eaten up by his car and running around with his new friends. Larry saw the writing on the wall that his oldest son's cocoon was opening and he would soon feel the need to spread his wings and fly. Lou knew that if she were to have any spending money, she would need to get jobs as well. Lou—with her outgoing personality—was soon hired to work the walk-up window at the new Tastee-Freeze. At thirteen years old, she had already developed the savvy needed to persuade adults, especially if the adult happened to be male.

Larry and Olivia's finances were still very tight and made tighter with some news Olivia shared one day upon Larry's return from work.

With no preface, Olivia bore the bad news. "Lar, we got a registered letter today from a court up in Harrison."

Larry stopped to listen.

"It seems there is a court judgment against us for the medical bills. It says they are going to start garnishing your paycheck."

"How much?" Larry asked. After Olivia handed him the letter, he saw the amount and said despondently, "Well, that's only going to leave about twenty-five dollars a week to bring home." He sat down, feeling hit again.

His wife had been thinking about the situation since she had returned from the mailbox. She spoke up and laid out her plan. "Larry, I can get a job at night. Then when you get home from the mill, I can go to work and you can stay with Robert."

"I don't want you to have to work at night," he said compassionately. "There must be another way."

"Larry, you've been working really hard to support this family. You enjoy your new job. I don't want you to do anything that might jeopardize your ability to keep the job at Axtell."

She was right. Larry did enjoy his new job at the mill. His foreman had immediately noticed his work ethic. He had been relocated to different places along the line and had performed well at every position. There were rumblings about a promotion for him.

"What kind of job do you think you could get?" Larry asked reluctantly.

Olivia was obviously ready for the question. "I was looking through the paper this afternoon. There is a job for a night waitress at the *Poultry Palace* on the other side of town. You know that chicken and biscuit restaurant? I walked next door to Martha's and used her phone to call the place. They said the job was four nights per week. The pay is just tips, but they said some of the waitresses make ten to fifteen dollars a night."

"Hun, you've never waitressed before." Her husband protested.

"Oh, how hard could it be Lar? I've worked in cotton fields and potato fields and picked tomatoes in hundred-degree heat. I've raised three kids and put up with you all these years, you old coot," she responded.

"I know you're tough, doll. I bet you could do anything you put your mind to. I don't know—that place is kind of a dive. What about all the riffraff that might come in and bother you?" Larry asked protectively.

"As you said, I'm tough. Don't worry, it's not that bad," she said trying to comfort and win his approval.

"Well, if you want to check it out, I guess it wouldn't hurt." Larry relented.

"Actually, Larry," she confessed, "I had Martha take me down this afternoon. I start work tomorrow. Please don't be mad."

Larry wanted to be upset. Initially, he felt his position as patriarch of the home had been threatened, but he remained quiet. *How could he be upset?* He thought. She was making this sacrifice to help the family. Olivia had been so good to stand by him and not complain, as he tried so hard to support the family over the years. She truly was his partner in life.

He walked over and took her face in his hands. Tilting her head forward, he kissed her forehead. "I love you, Sweetie," he whispered.

She stood up and hugged him. "Oh, you know I love you, too."

"Well, I guess Robert will be ok with me. I don't think I'll mess up the little guy too bad," Larry said jokingly.

"Little Robert loves his daddy. I think he'll be just fine."

The next evening, Olivia showed up at the *Poultry Palace* for her new position. It was more of a diner than a restaurant, having only ten tables adorned in red checkered tablecloths. The jukebox that sat in the corner was more apt to play Patsy Cline or Hank Williams than the Rolling Stones and the Beatles. Along the back of the room was a counter with stools. The clientele on the evening shift weren't riffraff as Larry had feared. Those shady customers came in on the graveyard shift, though. Police always got free coffee to ensure their protective

91

presence. The sign outside said *Home-Made Chicken and Fixins,* but Olivia thought her own chicken was better, but the burgers and fries were tasty.

On Olivia's shift, there weren't a lot of families. Maybe once or twice a night, the bell of the front door would sound with the opening of a little child with her family in tow. Mostly, though, the customers were single men coming in from the factory with nowhere else to go. They came not only for the food and coffee, but for company and a listening ear.

Olivia—like most of the family—adapted quickly. She learned the new job well and started to get a string of regulars that would come in to sit at her tables. All her regulars were men. They wanted to have her ear in talking about their woes. She, in turn, supplied that ear and was generally rewarded with a generous tip.

At home, little Robert loved having his daddy to himself. The other Rhodes children were off doing their own thing, but Robert spent his evenings around his dad. Even though he was completely exhausted after his hours of toil at the mill, Larry would come home, kiss Olivia goodbye and head straight to the family garden to work until dark. His garden work was somehow cathartic to him. As he moved up and down between the rows, his stress filtered away. While his hands were in the cool red dirt between the plants, he thought clearer, felt more confident, and somehow felt closer to his creator. He felt fulfilled in seeing his work come to fruition in bounteous vegetables for the family table. In his garden, there were no debt collectors or wives of buddies to burden his life as vermin. Larry dealt with the garden's vermin with a quick slam of his shovel. Dad tried to get Robert to help, but his little hands did more harm than good, so Larry didn't prevent the boy from wandering off.

Since summer arrived, Robert and Ricky played together much more often, sometimes every day and sometimes late into the evening. Regularly, though, Robert preferred to be by himself. He often retreated to his own company after Ricky had tricked him or made fun of him. Ricky's ways were unusual for the younger boy. Robert didn't know if this was the way that friends treated each other, but he knew he didn't enjoy it even if it was.

Ricky Goodman's personality revealed itself early through his actions toward his young prey. Though it started slowly, Ricky's teasing got more frequent as time went on. The mistreatment started with little things, such as making fun of the smaller boy's bare feet or telling him a lie about something. One day, he took Robert out into the woods and told him to wait until Ricky retrieved something he left back at the house. After what seemed like hours, Robert made his way back to the house to see Ricky sitting on the porch, taking great delight in the gullibility of his new plaything. Ricky's skills at taunting were very well refined and seldom good natured, as some people's teasing can be. He would be nice to Robert for several days and then unleash his emotional abuse on him unsuspectingly.

On a summer evening after sunset, when the only lights were the glowing porch light and the darting fireflies in the lawn, the Goodman family entertained visiting relatives. Ricky called to Robert to play hide and seek with him and his cousins. The young lad was reluctant because the summer sun had already set and the dark scared him. Wanting to be included in the children's laughter, he climbed through the hole in the fence and walked to the Goodman house to play. Each time the hiders went out into the darkness, Robert got more and more bold and went further and further into the abyss. On the fourth or fifth time they went out, the little boy found a spot behind a bush outside the halo of the porch light. He huddled under the bush, knowing he would certainly be the last one found. He was so excited about his hiding place—but so scared of what lay behind him in the dark woods. He hadn't noticed how quiet it had gotten. He peeked around the bush toward the house. At first, it surprised him to see how open the seeker had left home base. If Robert ran, he was certain he could get home free, but he wanted the victory of not being found while hiding in the best hiding spot in the whole yard. After a few minutes, he was aware of how *completely* quiet it was in the yard. No one was yelling, "home free!" or "One, two, three on Billy!" Looking back into the dark woods, he suddenly got a haunting feeling that made him not want to be there anymore so he started inching his way toward home base. As he entered the edges of the circle of light, he finally became aware that he was alone in the night. He ran but wasn't sure exactly where he was going. He was half running to home base and half running toward his actual home beyond the fence. Even if he wasn't sure what he was running toward, he knew exactly what he was running from—the dark woods! Now he was running as hard as he could across the Goodman's lawn. He glanced toward their house and saw all the hide-and-seek kids looking out the front room window, laughing mockingly. It was obvious to Robert that Ricky had planned this all along and that Robert was again the butt of mean teasing. He ran past home base and sped toward his home, fueled by adrenaline, embarrassment, and fear. Tears streamed down his freckled cheeks and onto his neck. As he neared the hole in the fence, Ricky added the crescendo to his sick symphony—he turned the outside porch light off. With the sudden wall of darkness in front of him, Robert couldn't determine where to direct his inertia. He hit the fence at his full speed, then fell through the opening, which he had intended to find.

Inside the Rhodes home, Mom was taking some time to hem several pairs of pants during one of her few nights off. She heard a piercing scream coming from her baby somewhere in the yard. As a protective, grizzly mother, she leaped up and raced to his rescue. She could see the young boy, lying on the Rhodes' side of the fence, writhing in pain. She carried him in and sat on the brown naugahyde couch. By this time, the commotion had alarmed dad who also came to investigate. Laboring to catch his breath as his crying did not subside, he turned blue from lack of oxygen. Larry noticed what Olivia had not detected while comforting the boy. On the lower part of his shin, was a gaping tear in his flesh caused by the fence's barbed wire as his leg ripped across.

"Oh, my!" Mom gasped as Dad pointed it out.

"Get a towel from the bathroom and wrap it around his little leg to stop the bleeding." She directed her husband.

"I'll get some water and peroxide to clean it out, too," Larry replied calmly. A defining characteristic that the Rhodes parents had developed over the years was the ability to remain calm during crises.

As they cleaned the wound, they could see the tear was about three inches long and very deep.

"Can you see bone?" Olivia asked in a whisper.

"Almost ... maybe ... I dunno," Larry replied.

"Should we take him to the hospital?" Olivia questioned, revealing her maternal instincts.

Larry's mouthed words and gestured with his hands in such a way that the boy didn't know what they were discussing. Yes, it looked as if it needed stitches, probably plenty of them and yes, it would cost a lot of money that they did not have. Even though Larry worked for a good local company, in the sixties, not many employers offered medical benefits to their employees.

"It looks as if the bleeding has stopped. Let's see what how it looks in the morning." Larry concluded.

"All right," Olivia responded, knowing fully that her baby's ripped skin would have to heal on its own.

Robert cried himself to sleep that night, lying next to Mom. He couldn't determine which hurt more, the open wound in his leg or memories of his humiliation.

Over forty years later, as he drove across the desert, Robert could still feel the humiliation and fear that Ricky had caused him that night. Going eighty miles per hour down I-40, he pulled his pants leg up and could tell that neither scar—emotional nor physical—had healed from that night.

Chapter 12

In the fall, Robert started first grade at Mountain Springs Elementary School, about two miles from his house. As his mom got him ready for his first day at school, she tried to read the young boy's emotions.

"Are you excited about your first day of school?" she asked Robert while tying his shoes.

"Yeah, I guess so," the first grader reluctantly replied.

Knowing her son would not share his true feelings willingly, Olivia had to work it out of him craftily. "Tell me, young man, what is the most exciting thing about going to school?"

Not knowing he was being psychoanalyzed, he thought for a second and then replied, "I guess riding the bus with my sister."

"Yeah, you will sure be a big boy riding bus number eighteen all the way to the school. What else will be fun?" Mom probed a little deeper.

Again, he thought. "Uh, I don't know. I guess playing at recess … and learning math!"

"You're going to be great at math *and* recess. Now, what do you dread the most?"

Robert drooped his head a little. "Nothing."

"Oh, come on now. There must be something," she persisted.

"Seeing Ricky every day," he finally mumbled. Since the night of the hide 'n' seek incident almost three weeks before, Robert had been able to avoid the neighbor boy. Now, the two boys' meeting could not be avoided since they were just three grades apart.

"Oh Robert, he was just teasing as kids will do. Your leg is about healed. He's probably forgotten all about it and so should you," Mom said unsympathetically.

Robert didn't tell her any more since his first answer had not yielded any sympathy. She finished tying his shoe. He hugged his mom, then ran to where the bus would pick them up in front of their house.

His school was a leftover relic of Arkansas school systems fifty years earlier. While all the elementary schools in the city of Russellville were modern buildings, this outlying community was not yet afforded the capital budget to build such an edifice. Mountain Springs was a two-room school on a big curve in a dirt road. One classroom housed grades one through three and the other room had grades four through six. Robert didn't know any difference and the school fit his needs just fine. He enjoyed being around all the kids. His teacher, Mrs. Pearson, was a perfect mix of discipline and motherly concern.

Because of the small number of students, Robert could not avoid seeing Ricky at recess or on the bus. Surprisingly, Ricky avoided Robert for the most part—almost as if he did have a conscience and it was eating at him for the way he had treated his young friend. Then, after several weeks into the school year, Ricky made his simple move toward offering an olive branch to little Robert. During lunch recess, while Robert was trying to tie his shoe—a skill his boney hands had not mastered—Ricky walked up behind him.

"Do you want me to do that for you?" Ricky asked in a surprisingly kind voice.

Robert was certainly astonished to see him standing there. "Sure, I guess."

After Ricky tied the shoe, he said, "Do you want to play?" as if nothing had ever happened.

"Sure," Robert said without hesitation.

Later in life, it still amazed Robert how children could forgive so easily and move past any differences they had.

The two boys continued to play together almost every recess and before and after school. They played at each other's house every school night. They became almost inseparable, as if they had known each other their whole lives. Robert was happy with Ricky and was glad he finally knew how it felt to have a buddy and best friend.

The two kids were mostly unsupervised. Larry didn't start thinking about Robert and where he might be until the sun went down. He was just glad his son had a playmate. Undoubtedly, Olivia would have paid better attention, but since she worked most nights, Robert roamed freely. Ricky's mom and stepdad simply didn't care where he was, so the two boys had plenty of time to play, explore, and get into mischief. The two were quite adept at climbing trees and scaled the canopy of the neighboring woods as if they were spider monkeys in the Amazon.

Necessitated by the lack of toys growing up, Robert had developed a keen imagination and soon taught his neighbor how to make fun out of seemingly nothing: An overturned car in the field behind the Goodman's became a pirate ship. A row of trees on the edge of the property became the walls of a pioneer fort where the boys retreated from the attacking Indians. The propane tank behind the house became a bucking bronco in the rodeo. They seemed to never run out of objects that could entertain them.

Randy Judd

If just one object could entertain them, then the field behind Ricky's house offered a plethora of possibilities. Over the years, when the neighbors had a car that had given up the ghost, they hauled it to the back field and left it. This resulted in a large cluster of relic vehicles from the forties, fifties, and early sixties. This automobile graveyard included station wagons, coupes, sedans, pickup trucks and even convertibles that had outlived their usefulness and now whose highest calling was to be used for parts. The two youngsters spent hours moving from car to car. No one cared what they did to the cars, as long as they did not purposely break anything that could possibly be sold. Robert loved to pretend to drive and sometimes would make his way out to the field by himself and turn one of the cars into his own private racing car. When the children were in the cars, they felt isolated from the world. Since the field sat beyond a small crest in the landscape, hid it from the houses even though it was less than a hundred yards away.

For the most part, there was very little friction between the boys; however, once in a while—almost out of nowhere—Ricky would change face. One day, while the boys were play wrestling, the older friend became more and more agitated, until Robert realized his friend was no longer playing. Ricky started punching Robert, then sat on his face until he couldn't breathe. As he got off, the younger boy started to cry and Ricky taunted him.

"What's the matter? Is the baby crying?" Ricky asked mockingly. Then cupping his hands in front of Robert's face, "come on, cry my hands full. Cry little baby, cry my hands full." He then strutted back to his own house as a gladiator who had just felt victory in the coliseum.

Robert lay in the dirt, crying. After he composed himself, he wondered what he could have possibly done to make his friend so mad. One minute they were playing and the next minute he was being pummeled. He didn't tell his parents.

100

He felt as though he was growing up enough not to run and tattle on everything that happened to him.

The next day, while waiting to catch the bus, Ricky was back to his normal friendly self as if nothing had happened. This confused Robert even more.

Olivia was now working five nights per week at the *Poultry Palace*. Though she complained about her feet and back after a night of waiting tables, she actually enjoyed her job and secretly relished the attention she received from the men who visited the diner. Many regulars would make sure they sat at her tables.

This hillbilly beauty may not have had the looks of a Hollywood movie star, but the girl from the hills was definitely more pleasant to look at than most. Her honey blond hair was shoulder length and her jade-green eyes accented those locks. Her build was petite, just over five feet tall. Though small, her buxom appearance caused men to twist their necks to catch a glimpse as she passed. Olivia wasn't oblivious to their stares. In fact, she delighted in them. Being married to a man many years her elder, it enchanted her to know she was still desirable to other younger men. Her need for their attention certainly wasn't based on any lack of attention from Larry. Her husband still found her desirable and was proud to be seen in public with his bride of twenty years. Her needs were based on some deeper insecurity and caused her to be flirtatious to a level that was inappropriate for a married woman.

Larry was trusting by nature, but if given a reason to doubt, could become irately jealous. Olivia knew this and was careful about how much she shared with him about her nights at work.

One evening, as Olivia returned home from work, it surprised her to see Larry sitting in the corner armchair in the living room. Because he had to get up at five, he was seldom awake when she ended her shift at midnight or one o'clock.

She greeted him in a tired, dragging voice, "Hey Hun, what're you doing up? Can't sleep?" As she finished the question, she noticed he had a beer in one hand and a lit cigarette in the other. His cigarette had burned almost to his fingertips and had left behind a long stem of ashes hanging precariously. Larry didn't drink much, and it was even more unusual for him to drink this late on a work night. Even though he had only finished a couple of beers, the alcohol had taken some of his inhibitions away.

Larry avoided her question. "Today at work, one of the fellers came up to me and said, *I hear that girl Olivia down at the diner is your wife.* When I said yes, he said *the boys around say she is one fine filly and you are one lucky man.*"

"Well, that was nice of him. What did you say?" Olivia asked in a quaint antebellum accent.

"What do you mean, *what did I say?*" He asked, raising his voice a little more than he should have. "I told him you was my wife and to stop talking about you that way. What kind of ideas you givin' those men down there, shaking your behind for all to see? Don't they know you're married?"

"Oh, settle down. They don't mean no harm. It's just part of the job," she said calmly, trying to keep him settled down.

At this, Larry stood up and threw his hands up in the air in disbelief. "Part of the job? Parading around for the men is part of your job?"

Trying to calm him down, Olivia said, "Larry, you know you're the only man for me. If I had wanted to stray, I would've done it years ago, but I don't want to."

"I want you to quit!"

"You know that's just the beer talking," she continued. "I'm not doing anything wrong and you certainly don't complain about the tips I bring home, do you?"

"I don't want the tips if you get them that way." He snapped.

Olivia knew it was useless trying to reason with him when he was drinking. Although Larry was generally a gentle man, he could be a jealous man, and he didn't hold his alcohol well. "I'm not staying around here while you're this way. I'm going next door to Martha's to sleep. Don't look for me until you've sobered up."

Olivia headed back toward the same door she had just entered. She heard rustling behind her, which she assumed was Larry coming to stop her. As she turned to see him, she saw him release a four-legged coffee table he had lifted over his head. As he threw it toward her, she darted out of the way to avoid being hit. The table hit the wall opposite the kids' bedroom. The force of his throw caused the cheap piece of furniture to shatter into splinters against the wall.

"That's it! You'll regret that, Larry Rhodes!" Olivia said as she exited, slamming the door behind her.

Larry swirled back around with a growl. He sat back down in his armchair, breathing angrily.

In their room, the children were lying in their beds with their eyes wide open with fear. Lou snuggled up next to her terrified little brother and rubbed his side. "Don't worry little brother, everything's ok. Mom will be back in the morning," she said, although not feeling sure of her claim.

Mom and Dad had fought before, but it didn't happen often and seldom involved violence. Most of the time, it was little more than a loud argument, which was settled with a kiss and make-up session. This was the first time any of the kids were aware of either of them throwing something. The event was disturbing for all the kids. Sleep came slowly and lightly that night.

In the morning, Lou helped Robert get ready for school. Dad was still asleep and was apparently calling in sick from work. The kids were very quiet while getting ready. As they stood in front to catch the bus, the first grader watched over the fence at the neighbor's, hoping to catch a glimpse of mom to know she was ok.

To Robert, the second hand on the clock moved slowly, as if it were drops of water from a faucet needing a washer. With only a month until summer recess, Robert wanted it to arrive sooner. Mrs. Pearson noticed that Robert was daydreaming and reprimanded the boy for not paying attention. He hated the confusion and sadness he was feeling and wanted to know how to make it go away. On his way home, he was tentative about what he would find at home.

It was unusual to get off the bus and see both his parents' cars parked in the dirt driveway. Usually, Dad did not get home till after six o'clock and sometimes Mom had already left for her job. Robert didn't know what to think about both cars being parked haphazardly in the dirt.

As Robert hesitantly opened the door, he saw his mom and dad sitting in the same corner chair. Mom was sitting on Dad's lap. They both greeted the boy with a cheerful welcome. Robert rushed across the room to hug his parents. As he laid his head into his mom's bosom, he smiled and felt loved. All was right.

The next day at school, the class made construction paper pinwheels that were attached to a pencil's eraser with a straight pin. They walked along the road to make their pinwheels spin. The late spring air felt great to Robert. Once again, it was a good day.

Chapter 13

Many storms blew through Russellville that late spring and early summer. On one of the last days of school, the teachers herded the students into a smaller room of the school because of the threat of a funnel cloud which was sighted coming up the Arkansas River. Robert—having heard that the best place to be in a tornado was in a ditch—slipped out of the front door of the school unnoticed. He ran across the road and climbed down into the culvert until the storm passed. Although it rained and the wind blew, no tornado hit the area. As the skies cleared, the boy climbed out muddy and slightly embarrassed that he had taken such a drastic measure. He walked home from school without telling anyone, taking shortcuts through the woods. The teachers searched the school for the missing boy but with no success. Finally, one of his friends told the teachers that he thought he saw Robert walking home. When Robert got home, his teacher had just arrived and was talking to his mom. It embarrassed Olivia that the teacher had visited, but grateful that her baby was ok. Larry just laughed about it when he came home.

There were other disturbances in the atmosphere that summer. Will, the oldest Rhodes sibling, decided it was time to become a man. He was coming up on two years working at the furniture plant and spent most of his money on his cars and now on his small trailer on the opposite side of Russellville. Will was no longer able to help the family. Lou was still working a part-time job and helping however she could financially. No one except the Rhodes parents knew how tight their finances were. One day, a truck plodded down Skyline Drive—dust billowing behind. The large white box truck pulled in at the Rhodes home, occupying most of the small yard. In a scene reminiscent of being back on the mountain, the men began carrying furniture out of the house. The couches, chairs, lamps, and tables that mom and dad had bought on their shopping spree a year earlier were being taken back for slow payment. Olivia stood in the kitchen crying, unable to watch.

When Larry came home, Olivia explained what had happened, and the two talked once again about finances.

"It humiliated me, Larry. I'm tired of being humiliated. This seems as though it's our lot in life and I don't like it one bit! We keep swimming but we can't get anywhere. Are we ever going to have our own house, or after today, even our own furniture? With your pay getting garnished and Will moving out, we don't have much money at all to live on. We can barely pay our rent and utilities." Olivia said with frustration.

To Larry, the situation reflected much more than just finances. Not providing for his family threatened his manhood. He felt emasculated … neutered. He also could see reality. The fifty hours a week he was working at the mill was taxing to the man of his age, especially given his background of broken bones and injuries from working in the timber of the Ozarks. He couldn't do much more than he was already doing.

"What do we do?" he asked sheepishly. "I've got to get a full-time job that pays more. I don't want to be away from home more, but what are we going to do otherwise?"

Larry didn't have an answer.

But Olivia did. "Martha, next door got a new job at the shirt factory and she says they are hiring some new hands later this week. I think I should go check it out."

"Well, I have to say, it would sure be nice to have you around at night," Larry said.

"Actually, I was thinking if I can get the job, I might keep the waitress job for a while too, until we can get caught up," Olivia revealed.

"Why, you can't work that much, Olivia! You'll kill yourself."

"I'm younger than you and I think I can do it. Just for a while. After we've caught up a little, I'll quit the café."

Larry relished the idea of her quitting the café and getting away from the men's leering eyes, but he didn't bring that up. "What about the boy?"

Olivia sighed. "Lou is around here most of the time. He's pretty responsible and in a few months, he'll go back to school during the day and I will get to be with him at night."

Reluctantly, Larry conceded. Two days later, they hired Olivia at the shirt factory. She started the following Monday for the minimum wage of one dollar and forty cents per hour.

Randy Judd

Chapter 14

On Mom's first day of her new job, Lou was supposed to be taking care of Robert. She was sleeping late, and Robert was climbing a tree out by the chicken house in the backyard. As he stretched to reach a limb, the young boy lost his balance and fell over backwards. In a blur of limbs, leaves, and bark, Robert fell headfirst to the ground. He landed facing the tree. Upon impact, the rest of his body folded over and he lay flat on his back, unconscious. He wasn't sure how long he had been out, probably only for a few seconds. When he regained consciousness, he needed a little time to orient himself. While lying on his back, the boy could see the tree above him and realized what had just happened. He tried to breathe, but the air wouldn't enter his lungs. The landing had knocked the breath out of him. His efforts to suck in oxygen were soon rewarded so his breathing eventually his normal breathing returned. Robert took a quick inventory of his body. Although he was aching, nothing seemed bad enough to be broken. He was aware that his head was on a board—probably one off the chicken coop that he had previously played with. As he turned to look at the board, to his horror, he saw a large nail within inches of his head. He began to cry, knowing that he could have been dead if the nail had been a couple of inches closer. He wanted his mom, but at that moment, his mom was slicing the cloth on the assembly line. He missed her and wanted to be held and comforted by her. That would not happen today and maybe not even in the near future. After laying there for several minutes, he stumbled inside the house to rest, careful not to wake up Lou.

In that summer, when Robert turned seven, his innocent childhood began to leave him. Lou felt no overwhelming responsibility to watch over him, so the boy often found himself without supervision. At first, this was very scary, but eventually, it became routine. He knew how to scramble an egg or warm a TV dinner, so he knew he wouldn't starve. He didn't let his parents know she left him alone so often for two reasons: Robert didn't want his sister to get in trouble, but mostly, he didn't want to lose his newfound freedom.

Robert and Ricky spent a lot of time wandering the woods of Norristown Mountain. It was hardly a mountain at all, but a long hill that rose five hundred feet from the floor of the valley where Russellville lay. As the two boys increased their boldness every day, they got further and further from home. Some days, they would end up several miles from home. It was at least a mile through the woods to Chapel's grocery store, the nearest place to buy anything. The store sat on the edge of Marina Road—a paved two-lane road tracing along the western edge of Lake Dardanelle. On the side of the road, they collected bottles which drivers had launched at these times before littering laws. The bottles brought two cents each and the boys could collect a dollar's worth on the trek to the store. At the store, they bought sodas and candy, then meandered their way back home—along trails and through brush and trees.

On one of these expeditions early in July, Ricky revealed another side of his personality to his little friend. After they had walked ten or fifteen minutes toward home, Ricky stopped on the side of the trail and reached deep into his pocket.

"Want to see what I just found?" Ricky asked slyly. The boy then pulled from his pockets a handful of small fireworks.

"Where did you find those?" Robert asked naively.

"Oh, back there on the trail by some rocks." Ricky lied.

"Wow," the younger boy said in awe. "Wait a minute, Ricky. These are just like the ones back at Chapels."

"Are they?" Ricky responded. There was something in his voice that made Robert uneasy. A feeling similar to *If you accuse me, I'll pound your face.*

Robert knew what stealing was, and that it was wrong. His parents had cemented this concept in his mind at Christmastime the previous year. As the family was shopping in town for gifts, Robert saw some tootsie rolls that tempted him so much that he took two in his little hand and shoved them into his pocket, unaware he was being watched. As his family was leaving, the manager stopped them and told Olivia what he had seen. Olivia made Robert give the candy back and apologize to the manager. When they got home, though, Mom went into a rage with him. As she whipped him with one of Dad's belts, she talked about embarrassing her and making people think she was a terrible mom. Oh yeah, and that stealing was wrong.

Out here in the middle of the woods, where no one could hear his screams and cries, he didn't want to accuse the older boy. "They're really cool," was all he said.

On the remainder of the way home, Robert tried to mask his fear of the older boy. Robert was happy to get home and even happier to see Will's car in front of the house. This was not the last time Robert—nor the community— knew of Ricky's kleptomaniac ways.

Ricky was also responsible for introducing Robert to more worldly vices. In a barn behind the Goodman house, Ricky initiated Robert to his first cigarette.

There were three smokers in the Rhodes' home—Dad, Will, and Lou. On a hot summer day, when all the family was home, a cloud of smoke hung at shoulder height in their living room. As the boy walked through the front room, he would sometimes hold his hand up and cut the smoke. They scattered several ash trays about the house. The new wallpaper yellowed within a few months after they had moved in. Even though there were three smokers in the Rhodes home, Robert had not dared try to smoke on his own before. In the hayloft of the sun-bleached gray barn, Robert hacked and choked and eventually threw up all to the amusement of Ricky.

Behind the locked door of the Goodman bathroom, the two boys opened a stolen six-pack of beer. To Robert, the liquid was unpalatable and tasted as he imagined pee would. He ended up pouring more down the drain than he actually drank.

The summer of 1967 also brought some fond memories for little Robert.

Later that month, as Dad arrived home from work, he wore an elfish grin when he said hello to his youngest son. "Do you want to see what I've got outside in the truck?"

"I guess. What is it?" Robert asked.

"You'll have to come see." Dad teased.

After opening the passenger side of the truck, out jumped a furry little bundle of canine joy. The little yellow pup ran around the boy's legs who was giggling uncontrollably. "A puppy, a puppy, a puppy! Do we get to keep him?"

"You bet. He's yours, son!" Dad said with a huge grin and moist eyes.

"I love him. He's great, dad! Thanks!" Robert exclaimed as he picked up the little fur ball. "What's his name?"

"That's up to you, son. I just took him away from his mother. She was a stray that had puppies at the mill. He was the biggest boy dog of the litter and looks as though he knows where he's going."

"Then I'll call him Ranger!" Robert declared, and the name stuck.

The rest of the summer, the seven-year-old spent more time with his new canine friend than he did his neighbor. Whenever he went outside, Ranger was waiting. The dog's young owner decided Ranger was a golden retriever from a picture of puppies in a magazine. His dad never argued the point, although he knew the dog was a mutt. The rest of the summer passed too quickly, as it does for most kids his age. Soon the shoes would have to be put back on and the pencils would have to be sharpened.

Mostly, the summer had been a good one, but there was a noticeable void in Robert's life. He rarely saw his mom. Olivia left before he got up and returned after he had gone to bed. On weekends, he hardly left her side, and she tried to make up time by being especially attentive to him. The lack of time at home was creating more strain on Larry and Olivia's marriage. They tried not to argue, and when they did, they made certain it was out of the range of the children.

Lou had used this summer to celebrate her rocket launch into puberty. There was not a shortage of young men hanging around the Tastee-Freeze to give her attention. As her mom did, she enjoyed the interest. She was learning to get what she wanted with a sly grin and a tight pair of shorts. She was much too developed for her age, so even the older men paid attention to her—assuming she was probably at least eighteen and not jailbait.

Will had finally found a group of friends to hang out with. A couple of his new friends were ones he had met at the factory, but they had older brothers who were slightly more interesting to Will. The older boys had a rock band which attracted Will. He tried his hand at playing drums and found it so thrilling that he couldn't get enough. William had found a way to overcome his hillbilly reputation. When he played the drums, he was cool. It was also in the barn where the band practiced that they introduced him to marijuana. In 1967, the herb was just taking hold and winning its way with the subculture of America. He enjoyed the way it relaxed him and how good it made him feel.

Unfortunately, two darker events defined Robert's summer.

At the back of the Rhodes property, lurked the lone storm cellar. If it had ever been used, those uses were ancient history. The cement structure sat half buried and fully forgotten. They had built the shelter to provide a refuge from tornadoes that occasionally haunted the area. The structure was roughly eight feet square and five feet high and made completely of cement, with no windows. Only half of the structure jutted out of the ground. A heavy wooden door—covered with tin—rested at a 45-degree angle against the dungeon. After accessing the entrance, four steps led to the bottom of the pit.

When the original owners built it, there's no doubt they maintained the cellar with pride and kept it clean. As time went on and they rarely used it for storms, it became a place for storage. It was perfect for storage of quart mason jars full of home canned fruit. Eventually, it became forgotten and became a haven for spiders, rats, and imaginary creatures of the dark.

The boys played around the cellar and occasionally (on a dare) heaved open the door to peer into the web-covered abyss.

During a lull on a summer day, Robert noticed Ricky standing with the cellar door open, staring in.

The younger boy walked over and looked—first at Ricky—then at the moist, web laden darkness.

"What's you lookin' at, Ricky?"

"Just thinkin' how horrible it would be to be trapped down there with all those spiders and snakes and who knows what else. I wonder if someone died down there and that's how come no one ever goes down there, because his bones are still down there, with a snake crawling out his eye sockets. It's like something from Edgar Allan Poe!"

"Stop it, Ricky! That's scary!"

"Oh, the little baby Robbie is scared, is he?"

Robert was familiar with the taunting tone of Ricky's voice. Before he could react, Ricky grabbed the shirt of his young victim and thrust him past the open door. Seven-year-old Robert missed the top step altogether and rolled down the remaining ones. The last sound Ricky heard was the thud of Robert's head hitting the cement floor. Fearing he had killed Robert, Ricky shut the heavy door, looked around to make sure no one had seen him, and ran.

After a few minutes, Robert stirred. He opened his eyes. Or had he? Everything was still dark. He blinked his eyes several times. His eyes were definitely open, but where was he? He had no memory of being thrown down into the dungeon. His head was pounding, but he had no recollection of why. Aware of the mustiness that enveloped him, he frantically forced his fingers to crawl around, trying to determine where he was. As he swung his arms, he struck some long forgotten jars of home-canned peaches. The jars fell to the floor, crashing and releasing the fermented, putrid odor. His memory of standing at the top of the cellar came back and along with it, the horrible realization of where he sat. In panic, the boy started screaming and flailing his arms wildly. Spider webs wrapped around his forearms. He darted around in the darkness, terrified of what else was in the cellar with him. As his eyes adjusted, he could see a hint of light at the edge of what he supposed to be the door. He crawled quickly toward it. His first efforts to open the solid slab of wood were futile. He

115

was no longer screaming, but he was now crying deliriously in fear. Remembering how his dad always turned around and used his legs to push a car which wouldn't start, the boy turned—facing all that terrified him—and pushed upward on the door with his back. It elated him when the door actually moved a little. His little success caused the adrenalin to pump even harder. His next push opened the door enough for him to slip through. Once out, his imagination let him believe the dead body in the dark was coming after him. Robert ran toward his house.

As he ran, he could see the windows on the side of the Goodman home. Ricky stood in the center window, watching. As far as Robert could tell, he showed no emotion. He sat there, observing his victim. Robert wondered if it disappointed the bully that he hadn't died after all.

Chapter 15

Now fifteen hundred miles and forty years removed from the event, Robert questioned why he had kept letting Ricky back into his life. He speculated he must have been much like an abused wife. His self-esteem was shattered so badly that he would do anything with the hope of things being different in time. But they never were.

A few days before the start of second grade, Robert was chasing Ranger around the front yard. The two-month-old pup had almost doubled in size and loved his owner as much as his owner loved him.

As he played in the yard, he saw Ricky running toward him. "Good, you're here. Come with me," he said, grabbing Robert's hand and pulling him along.

"Where are we going?" Robert questioned.

"You'll see."

Ricky was not holding Robert's hand anymore, but was running just ahead of his young friend toward the pasture of cars. Ranger eventually retreated to the yard. The boys ran over the crest, out of the sight of the houses. There—near the back of the field—was a brown 1957 Nomad station wagon. As they got within fifty yards of the car, Robert could see Ricky's older brothers and some other older boys standing in a circle, cheering.

Having been completely unsupervised most of the summer, a game had evolved amongst them that often turned violent. While the rest of the boys formed a circle, they would place a single boy in the center who then tried to break out. Earlier, it had been as innocent as Red Rover, but eventually it had progressed as the boys pushed the center person harder and harder. During today's game, there had already been a bloody nose, but the boys' machismo would not allow anyone to back out.

"Isn't this cool?" Ricky asked Robert. "We call it the *Sissy Circle!*"

Robert couldn't see what was so cool about it but dared not contradict him.

When Ricky took his turn in the circle, he began swinging his fists until he struck one of the older boys—Jerry McCain—in the side of the head. When this happened, all the other boys had to hold Jerry back from retaliating. For a moment, it threatened to be an outright brawl.

The entire event scared young Robert, and he quietly tried to slip back to his home for safety. After he had gotten only about thirty feet away, he heard Ricky Goodman's voice.

"And where do you think you're going?"

"Home," Robert whimpered.

"I don't think so—don't you want a turn in the circle?"

"Stop it Ricky," One of his brothers said. "He's way too young."

Robert kept walking. He was trying to hide his fearful tears. Resembling a predator on the Serengeti, Ricky lunged at his young friend and pushed him to the ground. The younger boy lay face down in the dirt with the older boy sitting on his back. Still fueled by the anger displayed in the sissy circle, Ricky began hitting Robert. Although he gave him a few blows to the back of the head, he concentrated most of the hits around the kidneys, a move he had seen on television wrestling.

The sight was pathetic and after a flurry of punches, Jerry McCain came to the aid of the youngster. He charged Ricky and pushed him off onto the ground beside Robert. Immediately, Ricky stood up, reached into his front pocket, and pulled out a knife. With the knife outstretched, the younger Ricky held all the older boys at bay. Everybody remained where they were for several seconds. Robert was on the ground, face down. Ricky was standing beside him with the knife held in his right hand. The rest of the boys were ten feet from him. Stalemate!

Then, in a Jekyll and Hyde moment, Ricky folded his knife, put it back in his pocket and said, "Wow, that was fun."

Relieved, all the boys started milling around Robert. "Why don't you head on home, little guy," one of Ricky's brothers said. "Make sure you don't tell anyone about our fun out here today."

Robert returned home to his empty house.

There was no way a boy his age could fully assimilate in what he had just been involved.

That summer day's events were pivotal in little Robert's life. They were memories he could never erase. Things he should have been protected from were thrust upon him at the back of a Nomad and in the dark confines of a storm cellar. Ricky had cheated the boy out of the remainder of his security.

Randy Judd

Chapter 16

Fifteen-year-old Lou had never been involved in current events. Her rearing as the only daughter of poor Arkansas dirt farmers kept her busy enough to avoid the foibles of the world. That innocence of the outside world changed in April 1968.

On the fourth of April 1968, standing on a hotel balcony in Memphis, an assassin gunned down Martin Luther King Junior. Whether it was the fact that this occurred a few hours away from Russellville or because she had become mature enough to fully understand such events, Lou nevertheless was affected. She had been only ten years old when President Kennedy died, so her child-like innocence had protected her from fully processing the gravity of that occasion. Now, five years later, her compassion and understanding had grown.

The Rhodes children—especially the older two—had grown up fully aware of how different the races were treated in 1960s Arkansas. Although great strides were being made in race relations in the south, leftovers such as *white's only* water fountains and all black or all white churches were still visible remnants of antebellum days gone by.

In Russellville, the Negroes generally lived in their own area around Independence Avenue and they sat at their own lunch tables at school. The races did neither action out of compulsion, but out of a sense of comfort and tradition.

Lou—as most kids her age—didn't carry much of the prejudices of her forefathers and mixed well with her classmates, regardless of race.

Larry, having always been sensitive to his children's feelings, noticed his only daughter had become increasingly morose during the days immediately following the shooting. He couldn't remember a time like this when she sat in front of their black and white television watching Walter Cronkite.

The assassination had occurred on a Thursday. Early Friday evening, Larry Rhodes found his daughter relaxing quietly in the living room. Sitting down beside her on the brown naugahyde couch, Larry put his arm around his girl.

Over the years, Larry had made a tradition of greeting his kids after school with the question, "So, did you get educated today?"

Today deserved a different greeting.

"What's wrong Lou?" Larry asked. "I couldn't help but notice you've been a little down in the dumps."

Lou replied quickly, as if she had hoped someone would ask. She had never had problems relating her feelings to others. She especially trusted her dad. "It's about Martin Luther King. I've been watching all the news and reading the newspapers. It just makes me sad that someone would want to kill a man who was so good. All he seemed to want for his people was for them to be treated fairly.

"Why would someone hate him so bad to want him dead, Daddy?"

"Yeah, there's a lot of hate in this world. Some people hated him because they thought he was trying to stir up trouble. Others hated him because they think the races are different and they shouldn't have the same rights."

Lou, who had been laying her head on her father's shoulder, pulled away and looked at him.

"How do you feel, Daddy?"

"Well, to tell you the truth, Honey, because of my lot in life, how I can never seem to get an even break, well, I guess I feel I'm pretty much in the same boat as them. I guess I see life a lot as they do.

"Just the other day, I was eating lunch with some of the niggers down at the …"

At this statement, Lou jumped away from her dad. "Daddy, you can't use that word! It's horrible! It's so … degrading!"

"That's just what I call them," her dad said, with only a hint of defensiveness. "That's the only word I've ever thought about calling them. I never thought it was bad. It's just what I call them, even when I'm with them."

Lou was becoming agitated with her dad, even slightly disgusted. "You're so prejudiced, Daddy! You might as well be part of the KKK!"

"Look here, young lady!" Larry replied, offended. "I'm not even sure what being prejudiced means, but how dare you say I should be in the Klan! I don't treat those niggers down at work any different than I treat the Whites."

"Stop saying that word, Daddy! I told you it's horrible! You're just a bad white man!" She screamed, running out of the house in tears.

Larry wondered if he should've run after her. He wondered if he should have punished her for raising her voice to him and being disrespectful, but he knew that she was upset and hurt, so decided to let her work it out within herself.

Later that night, at the Tastee-Freeze, Lou heard of a rally being planned in Little Rock on Monday. The assembly was to be a peaceful march around the State Capitol and was open to all who wanted to participate. They had chartered a bus and scheduled it to leave the TG&Y department store parking lot Monday morning at nine. As soon as Lou heard about it, she called her best friend, Margene, and they decided immediately that they had to go.

Lou decided not to tell her parents, fearing that her father's prejudice would be a source for him to prevent her from going. The two girls would have to skip school, but they easily convinced themselves to do so.

Sunday night, Margene slept over at Lou's so they could carry out their flawless plan. On Monday morning, the two ninth graders boarded the school bus as usual to head off to Gardner Junior High. Conveniently, the school bus had to stop daily to pick up kids just a few blocks from TG&Y. As the doors opened near the rendezvous point, the two girls pushed their way through to get off the bus.

"Hey girls, what are you doing?" the bus driver yelled. "You can't get off here! You'll have to wait till we get to the school! I'll tell your parents!"

The girls ran away from the bus, giggling that they had pulled off such an amazing feat. In their minds, it had been planned as well as the getaway in the movie *The Great Escape*. They didn't worry about Chuck, the bus driver, telling their parents. He would either forget it or hold it over their heads for the rest of the school year, threatening to tell if they did not do what he said.

As the adolescent girls neared the chartered bus on the edge of the parking lot, they had an unusual feeling for which they had not prepared. For the first time in their life, *they* knew what it was to be a minority. They could only see five other white people in the entire congregation of Negroes.

Even though they knew their purpose was pure, they were reluctant and slightly scared to approach the silver Greyhound bus.

"You girls goin' to Little Rock for the rally?" a man who had usurped some authority asked, "if so, y'all better get on now 'cause we're leavin' soon."

124

The crowd funneling onto the bus was as diverse as the population at large. There were a few militant looking men, each holding up one fist in a menacing *black power* symbol as they boarded. The action scared the girls and—for the first time—they doubted their judgment. In contrast, though, they also saw several elderly ladies in their proper dress and hair done up in a bun with bobby pins. The girls could not have known it, but these grandmothers were the granddaughters of freed slaves. The elderly women looked peaceful and safe. There were old men as well, some in white shirts and bow ties, some in their cleanest overalls. There were also a few black students the two girls recognized from school.

As Lou and Margene boarded the bus, people stared at them, silently questioning their motivation. The two girlfriends found an empty seat in the middle of the bus and confined themselves there.

Soon the bus was in route to the state capitol—an hour and a half away. As soon as the bus entered the freeway, Reverend Washington—the organizer of the event—stood up and spoke. He was a tall, thin Negro man in his sixties who—as revealed by his tales—had seen his share of injustices in life. He wore a nicely pressed brown wool suit and a thin striped tie. The only hairs that remained on his head were little tight curls of salt and pepper. James Washington had found his calling to preach when he was in his fifties and was the minister at the First Assembly of God Church on the corner of Independence and Eleventh Street in Russellville.

The Reverend began speaking in the rhythmic tones typical of a southern black preacher. He preached about the injustices his people had suffered from the time slavery ripped them from Africa until the killing of their spiritual leader this past week. His sermon was well rehearsed with many rhyming catch phrases. As he spoke, the itinerant congregation periodically rewarded him with shouts of *Amen* and *Halleluiah*! A few of the lines of his declaration were pointed directly at the White race. This certainly made Lou and Margene uncomfortable, and they felt as if they personally were to blame. The wise Reverend, though, pointed out and thanked their White friends who had joined them on this ride and the Colored folks on the bus applauded them.

After thirty minutes of preaching, the Reverend patted the sweat from his head, said amen, and sat down. The remaining time, the congregation on wheels sang hymns and old Negro spirituals, including *Swing Low, Sweet Chariot* and *We Shall Overcome*.

The ride to Little Rock was a treat for Lou. She sat by the window, watching the scenery fly by. Even though the event that motivated her trip was a sorrowful one, she was enjoying the beautiful spring day and the ideal temperature of the air blowing through the open windows at sixty miles per hour. The trees were emerald, and the flowers were in bloom. It would be months before the grasses alongside the freeway would turn brown in the summer heat. Now everything was a luxurious carpet of green.

As they neared Little Rock, Lou began getting excited about the city itself. The Rhodes family had been to the city just once before, when Lou was only eight years old. She didn't remember much about that trip, but now she was definitely enjoying the hubbub of the city ten times as large as Russellville.

Pulling into a parking lot near the Capitol, the bus stopped, and the driver held tight to the stainless handle and pushed open its door. They invited the riders—who were escaping one by one down the steps as ants from an anthill—to pick up signs to carry for the rally. Lou picked up one on which was printed, *We love you Reverend King* and Margene's read *We Have a Dream*.

As they approached the Capitol itself, the scene in front of Lou astounded her. Even though she was young, she realized this was a monumental even that she would carry with her for the rest of her life. Tens of thousands of people were milling about the capitol grounds. When she saw the Arkansas State Police and National Guard in full uniform, Lou worried about the potential for violence. In a parking lot near the Capitol, some Klan members gathered dressed in full attire—white robes and hoods under which they shamefully hid. She was aware of the dark feelings she got when she looked at them. She was also ashamed that she had accused her daddy of being as bad as they were. She knew he wasn't.

Soon after their arrival, the pilgrims from Russellville joined a line of marchers circling the domed Capitol. They quickly joined in the chants and singing. Arkansas built its Capitol as a smaller version of the United States Capitol in Washington. With an abundance of stopping and starting, the march that circumvented the grounds moved slowly toward its cause. The girls had begun their march in the back of the building and as they neared the front, they saw thousands were gathering on the Capitol steps where they had set up a podium. Speakers—ones that Lou had never heard of—spoke eloquently of Doctor King and his mission while marchers continued to march. Lou and Margene looked awestruck as they witnessed history.

Nearing the parking lot where troops confined the Klansmen, it surprised the girls to hear the hooded bigots slinging hateful speech toward them—two young White girls marching with the Colored folks. All the taunts were offensive, but some of the jeering was downright obscene. The teenagers singularly looked ahead and tried to ignore the insults.

A shrill "watch out!" behind them did not give the girls enough time to see the baseball sized rock hurled their way. The rock skipped off the pavement and hit Margene in the back, just above her belt. She immediately crumbled to the ground, holding her back at the point of impact.

The police seized on the group of Klansmen and quickly had one of them in handcuffs and the rest under control.

The marchers who had witnessed the attack gathered around Margene to comfort her while the speeches proceeded at the podium. It was quickly determined that the wound was superficial and would probably only give the teenager a bruise to explain.

The two White girls cried together, not understanding the level of hate that the Klansmen inflicted on them. Once again, Lou recollected calling her dad a Klansman. She again regretted the accusation. He was a much better man than this.

Not wanting to continue the march, Lou and Margene spent the next two hours sitting with their new friends and listening to the profound pronouncements from the podium.

After all speakers had concluded and the crowd began to disseminate, the two girls used a portable restroom and then ran toward the bus, fearing they would be late. They were the last passengers to board. After receiving a chastising glare from the bus driver, the girls found that there were no empty seats left that were together; therefore, they took the first open seats they came across. The word of the rock attack had already made them accepted and welcomed amongst their new comrades, and some of them applauded as they boarded the bus. Margene sat next to a grandmotherly lady who had already fallen into her afternoon nap. A tall man who appeared to be in his fifties—although Lou was not skilled at making such determinations—welcomed her.

The bus driver closed the door and maneuvered the large greyhound out of the lot and found his way through the labyrinth of side streets and onto the freeway.

"I'm Leroy Watson," Lou's bench partner said as an introduction, holding out his hand. Leroy was a man of six and a half feet tall. "But they call me Stretch." Stretch wore overalls and a flannel shirt. His clothing was clean and pressed for the day's activities. He had a full head of hair, which had only recently started turning gray around the edges. His teeth were unusually white, and he showed them with pride. The wrinkles on his face were such that one could tell immediately he had known years of smiling. He was an attractive older man, generally. Leroy's breath smelled of black licorice, which he was eating.

"I'm Louise Rhodes, but they call me Lou," Lou responded, taking his hand reluctantly. Although she was normally a very animated and outgoing girl, she had become somber with the events of the day.

"Well, it's nice to meet you, Lou," Leroy responded. "Thanks for helping us out today, we sure do 'nough appreciate it. Do you want some licorice?"

Lou responded with a coy smile to the man. "No, thanks," she said, not revealing that she despised the candy.

The bus swayed and lunged until it was finally on the freeway. The return trip to Russellville was less orchestrated than the original ride had been. Some people slept. Some had calm conversations. A couple of men were playing cards in the back. The mood was generally quiet and reflective.

After half an hour of silence, Leroy turned again to his bench mate.

"Did you say your name was Rhodes?"

"Yeah, that's right. Lou Rhodes," she replied.

"You're not kin to Larry Rhodes, are you?"

Lou worried what an affirmative answer would mean, but she answered, "Yes sir. He's my dad."

At this, Stretch put his hand on the shoulder of the man in front of them. Similar to Leroy, the other man was also dressed in nice work clothes, although he was shorter and stockier.

"Hey Karl, you know who this girl's dad is?" Stretch asked the man. The man then turned to look closer at Lou. Lou immediately noticed that Karl was not as pleasant looking as Stretch. Karl had a face that she would've feared on other occasions. A scar ran down his left cheek. He was unshaven and his teeth were yellowed.

With his glasses resting at the end of his nose, Karl answered his friend. "No, I reckon I don't."

"She's Larry Rhodes' girl!" Stretch revealed.

"Is that right? well whadda you know?" Karl said with surprise.

"How do you know my dad?" Lou inquired cautiously.

"Well, I've known your dad for a few years now. I work down at the mill with him."

Lou still didn't know if this was good or bad. She had chastised her dad a few days before about the way he described the Black men at the mill. She wondered what Leroy's opinion of her dad was.

After a split second of Lou's angst, Stretch ended her wonder.

"Yo' daddy is a good man, little girl. One of the best white men I've ever known. He will help our people out when all the other men at the mill won't even acknowledge us. He'll even share your mama's good leftovers with us sometimes."

"Really?" Lou questioned apprehensively.

Detecting her apprehension, Leroy turned to Karl. "Tell the kid what Mr. Rhodes did for you."

Karl started recounting his story. He appeared to be looking off in the distance, but was really just looking back into his memory. "One night, I was on my way home from the grocery store when my ole truck broke down out near Pottsville. It was raining somethin' terrible, you know, and all my groceries were in the back just getting soaked.

"Car after car of white folk passed me, even though I was trying to flag them down for help. Some even swerved to get as far away from me as they could. There I was, wet as a drowned cat, feeling lower than a pig's belly in the mud and it was gettin' dark too.

"I'd about given up so much that the next car I see, I didn't even bother flagging it down, but it began to slow down, anyway.

"Now, you understand, for a Black man to be on the road by himself when it's getting dark is a little scary. It hasn't been that long ago that we had to worry about lynchings and such.

"Well, this car pulled right up behind mine. A short, bald, White man in overalls got out and asked me if I needed help. He looked at my truck for a few minutes. He asked where I lived and said he'd take me home.

"I'm sure you've guessed by now that man was your pa! Not only did he take me home, but we loaded up all the groceries in his car. After we got them all to my house, we got some tools, and he even came back and fixed that truck in the rain by the headlights of his car. It was about ten o'clock by the time we got all finished and went back to my house. My wife fixed him a big bowl of beans and collard greens. He wasn't ashamed at all to be eatin' in a Colored family's house. As a matter of fact, he was so grateful for the food, you would've thought we did *him* a favor."

Karl finished his story. "Lil girl, yo daddy's one of the finest men around. They don't make many good as him, that's for sho!"

131

"Yeah, he's got quite a reputation. Why, I bet he could run for the mayor of Independence Avenue ... and *win*!" Stretch said with a chuckle.

Lou sat quietly for a few seconds. She was feeling an odd mixture of pride and humiliation; pride in being Larry's daughter and humiliation for having treated him as if he didn't have any compassion—when, in fact, he had shown more compassion than she ever had.

The girl still had trouble reconciling something in her young mind. "I know he's good and all, but he talks about you folks and uses the ... well, the 'n' word."

Stretch asked a question, suspecting he already knew the answer. "When he talks about us, is it good?"

"Well," Lou thought, "yes, I guess it always is."

Karl smiled and spoke up. "I would rather have a man treat me with respect, no matter what he calls me. Words ain't gonna kill me! I hate that word more than a young white girl will ever appreciate. It's a dark word, but I don't hold it against yo' daddy for saying it. I know he was just raised with it. Funny, when he says it, I don't feel put down at all, because I see into his heart and it ain't dark at all in there."

Stretch chimed in. "I would rather no man use that word at all, but even more important than that, I wish everyone treated us like your daddy does. This whole day today—celebrating Dr. King—it's all about how we treat each other. That's all Reverend King wanted, is for us to treat each other as equals. The Good Book says *faith without works is dead* and I say *fancy words without works is dead, too.* All the good words in the world don't mean nothin' without the works to go along. Little girl, *your daddy* has those good works!

"And you being here with us today must mean you got the works, too. I bet Mr. Rhodes is awfully proud of you!"

During the last thirty minutes of the trip, Lou became more reflective on life than she had ever been before in her tender years. She started thinking about what was really important, words or actions. She knew the answer and hoped that in some fashion her life could be full of meaningful actions and not just empty rhetoric. Her day had taken a completely unexpected turn. She grew up a lot that day. The trip had been her renaissance.

The bus pulled into the TG&Y parking lot a little after three o'clock. Her school bus would pass in a few minutes and she would be able to return home without anyone knowing of her adventure. Lou shook the hands of the friends she had created, and the girls made their way back home.

A little after six o'clock while relaxing in her room, Lou heard her daddy come in the door. She met him in the living room and gave him an unexpected hug.

"Well, what's this all about?" Larry asked.

"I'm so sorry for the mean things I said the other night. You're a good man, Daddy. I know you treat all people right."

"Thanks, honey. I know you didn't mean those things you said. I have been thinking, though. I am going to try harder to not say that word that bothers you. I may slip now and then—I've said it all my life—but I'm gonna try. Is promising to try, ok?"

"I love you Daddy, so, so much."

"Right back at ya, little girl, right back at ya!" Then he proceeded to ask his usual question. "So, did you get educated today?"

He had no idea the education she had gotten.

Chapter 17

A few days after the episode in the pasture, Robert began second grade. As he sat at his little wooden desk on the first day of class, he wondered how many other second graders had ever been treated that way. He decided that most others had never known this brutality because Ricky Goodman wasn't their neighbor.

He was excited to have Mrs. Pearson again as his teacher. She taught first through third grade, so he would get two more years with her. He treasured this reality. Mrs. Pearson was a petite lady in her forties. Her hair was curly and short. She wore dark horn-rimmed glasses which she looked over the top of when she was speaking directly to you. She was nice to the class if they behaved, but was capable of being stern if needed. If pushed too far, she was not afraid to bring out the wooden paddle she kept in her top drawer and take a student outside. Mostly, though, she loved to teach. She was delighted to see her pupils learn new skills and pick up new techniques. Mrs. Pearson had a way of letting every student think that they were her favorite. Robert looked forward to her passing by his desk. She had a homey smell of freshly baked bread that made him feel safe. Much as the beginning of first grade, Ricky and Robert didn't interact much. Robert was glad to meet up with some of his first-grade buddies, which he hadn't seen in the summer.

Each of his school friends provided a safe friendship that had already proved itself unfettered with mood swings or ulterior motives.

One morning, Mrs. Pearson announced an upcoming school talent show. It was going to be held as part of the school Halloween party. She said that anyone could participate and there were money prizes for the winners. The teacher told them to think about it and if they wanted to be in it, they should come see her during recess.

Although he was apprehensive, it sounded fun to be part of something new. During the afternoon recess, he left his buddies on the swings and went back in the building to speak to his teacher.

"Mrs. Pearson, can I sign up for the talent show?" the boy asked timidly.

"Ok Robert. What is your talent?" she asked, while getting the appropriate pad and pencil.

"Uh, I don't really know," the boy stammered. "What kind of stuff do people do?"

"Well," his teacher tried to explain, "some kids do magic tricks, some kids play the piano or other instrument, some kids sing, some kids read poems they have written. Do you do any of those things?"

The boy searched for an answer. "No, not really. I sing a little, when I'm walking around the yard or sometimes in the car when I'm with my parents."

"Good," she said with hesitation, but still a little encouragement. "What song do you want to sing?"

"I guess my favorite is *I've Been Working on the Railroad*. Do you know that one?" he asked innocently.

"Well, sure I do. I'll put you down right here. *Robert Rhodes is going to perform I've Been Working on the Railroad.*" She penciled him in. "Now there will be a practice with everyone on the day before the show. So, you need to practice on your own and in front of your family so you can get really good. Ok?"

"Alright," he replied as he ran back outside to finish recess.

In the days leading up to the talent show, Robert sang his song every time he was by himself. He wanted to sing it for his family, but since they were never together at the same time, he attempted to get them one at a time. Lou heard part of it, and then her friend drove up and honked his car horn.

"Gotta run, little brother. It sounded great," she said as she flew out the door, grabbing her purse on the way.

He sang it to his dad while he worked under the hood of the truck. Part of the way through the song, Dad rapped his knuckles with a wrench and swore at the truck. Robert decided another time might be better.

His mom listened to him on a Saturday before she went grocery shopping. She listened all the way through and had him repeat it.

"That was wonderful, son. When did you say the talent show is?" Mom asked with sincere interest.

"It's the day before Halloween at the school." He reported with pride.

"Well, I'm supposed to work, but I'll see if I can get off," she promised. "But if I can't, you'll know I'll be thinking about you. We'll at least make sure Daddy and the kids go to hear you."

"Cool," the boy replied, looking forward to his day in the sun.

On the day of the event, Robert asked Lou, as she was getting ready for school, if Mom had mentioned getting off work to attend his show.

"Oh, she didn't say anything about the show, but I know she has to work tonight. I can't come either, little buddy. I've got a date with a guy in high school." His sister informed him.

A disappointed "Oh," was all he could reply.

Throughout the day, the kids talked with anticipation about the upcoming Halloween party. Aside from the talent show, there would be games and food. The party was an annual event welcoming all residents within the boundaries of the school. The event was an important social gathering for the small community on Norristown Mountain.

On the evening of the event—as the time approached for the boy to return to school—Larry had still not come home from work. It was not unusual for Dad to work late to get the overtime hours to help the family. With just thirty minutes until the party started and with Dad still not home, Robert whimpered a little, not knowing what to do. While watching out the window for the lights of his dad's truck, he noticed the Goodmans loading up in their family car. He ran out.

"Are you guys going to the school?" Robert yelled across their yards.

"Yeah, do you need a ride?" Ma Goodman asked.

"Yes ma'am, my dad's not home yet," the boy confirmed.

"Well, we can take you. Jump on in. I'll write your dad a note to let him know where you are," she offered.

As Robert got closer, it became obvious to Martha that he had not had help getting ready for the activity. His dirty blue jeans were the same ones he had worn to school, and probably the day before. The left knee was worn through with threads hanging. One of his white tennis shoes had a hole in the toe. She was embarrassed for him, but since he was not her boy, did not say anything. Hopefully, he would get lost in the crowd and no one would notice.

The ride to the school only took ten minutes, but it seemed much longer since Robert had to sit between Ricky and his brothers. This was the first time he had any interaction with them all since *That Day*.

When he got to the school, he quickly lost the Goodman clan and found his friends. The PTA had set up a typical elementary school carnival. The activities included a cake walk, pop the balloon and a fishing game where the children threw a string over a wall and a prize was put on the clothespin.

The anticipated highlight of the evening was the talent show. Robert didn't understand any of the rules which were being outlined by the emcee. He announced something about a senior and junior division, prizes, and the judging, but Robert didn't hear much of it as he talked to his buddies. After several people had performed, the boy heard the announcer say, "Next up, from Mrs. Pearson's second grade class, ROBERT RHODES!"

"That's you, Robert, go on up!" His friends urged.

As Robert walked toward the stage, he noticed the boy who was the previous act coming off the stage. The first grader had a nicely pressed shirt and even a church tie. It was only then that Robert was aware of his own clothing. He quickly surveyed the situation, and it immediately embarrassed him. *Why hadn't his parents been there to prepare him and support him at this moment? Why had they let him come dressed like an urchin without any supervision?* Walking up the steps to the stage, he heard some children giggling and a comment from an adult about how he dressed.

As the second grader perceived it, he had two choices—run away or sing. So, he sang.

Holding the microphone too close to his mouth, his words rang loudly throughout the room. *"I've been working on the railroad, all the live-long day ..."*

Robert sang the song a capella and sang it with so much gusto that the crowd could not help but love him. He sang clear and loud and right on key. After it was over, he was delighted with the unexpected applause and even a few cheers. He then returned to his seat as his buddies patted him on the back.

After all the contestants performed, there was a break while the judges conferred. The principal, Mrs. Warner, stood and raised her hand to hush the crowd.

"Tonight," she began, "there will be two sets of winners—one set for the three younger grades and one for the older grades. Each set of awards will have a first, second and third place."

Principal Warner, a stern-looking spinster in her fifties, began with the younger grades. First, she awarded third place to Francis McVey who had performed a piece that Robert had never heard of on the black, upright, slightly out-of-tune, school piano. Second place went to a boy who did tricks with his dog. Robert thought the tricks were pretty good, but Ranger was a much more handsome dog.

"Now, for the first-place award," Mrs. Warner announced. "The winner gets a blue ribbon and two dollars and fifty cents. The first-place prize goes to Robert Rhodes for singing *I've Been Working on the Railroad*!"

As the audience erupted in applause, Robert proudly walked to the front of the room and upon the stage. For a moment, he forgot his Dickens appearance, and a smile enveloped his face. He accepted the awards and walked back down into the crowd, proudly showing the ribbon to his friends. He walked toward the next room as the older grades' announcements faded behind him.

Suddenly, in the quiet vestibule between rooms, Robert felt very alone. With all the school giving him accolades, his family was nowhere in the audience. He wondered if his dad had forgotten his performance or they forced him to work late. The seven-year-old watched all the supportive moms and wondered where his own mom was at that moment. He had no way of knowing she was serving a second cup of coffee and a wink to a wavy-haired truck driver.

The irritating sound of Ricky's voice interrupted his solitude.

"Well, aren't you special, little neighbor?" Ricky said. His brothers and sundry friends accompanied him. "You weren't *that* good. I think they probably just felt sorry for the poor little boy with holes in his britches." They all laughed.

Ricky's cutting sarcasm had unfortunately become familiar to Robert.

Ricky's older brother, Ernie, butted in. "Hey Robert! Let me borrow some money to get a hot dog!" His voice was more demanding than requesting.

The smaller boy hesitantly handed his winnings over to Ernie—looking first at the money, then into the threatening eyes of the older boy.

"Let's go," Ernie said to his brothers and friends. They turned and disappeared into the crowd. "I can't believe he gave me all his money, like he's ever going to see it again."

Despondent, the boy walked outside into the night. He sat on the cold stone steps of the schoolhouse. Hidden there, he could hear the jubilation just inside the school behind him. Somewhere in front of him, he heard a truck door slam. He looked up to see a man's silhouette coming toward him—emerging from the glow of a streetlight. As the gentleman got closer, Robert could see it was his dad. Larry couldn't tell if his son was crying or mad, as his head hung low.

"Sorry, little fellow," Larry said while rustling the boy's hair. "They kept me overtime at the mill. Do you want to go back to the carnival?"

"No. I'm ready to go home, I guess," he replied hesitantly.

"I'm sorry I missed your singing. How'd it go?"

"Ok, I guess. Let's go home," Robert said, pushing the blue ribbon into his right pants pocket so his father wouldn't ask about it.

Randy Judd

Chapter 18

Robert spent the second night of his trip in Flagstaff, Arizona. The high-altitude city was only about four hours from Las Vegas, but his late arrival was caused by spending the morning taking a tour of Hoover Dam. He decided not to push the day any further than five o'clock. The trip was originally to be just a quick jaunt to retrieve his new car. Now he was enjoying the solitude and reflection he was experiencing.

After eating a sandwich at the Subway restaurant near the hotel—but wishing they had Firehouse Subs in Flagstaff—he changed into shorts and a t-shirt to call his wife. His heart raced, as it always did, when he heard her voice. They talked about the events of each of their days. Robert explained the unexpected relaxation he was finding in the seclusion of his car. Although he could think of nothing better at that moment than to be nestled in her arms, he asked her if she would mind if he took a little more time getting home.

At first, she thought he just wanted to spend more time with his new roadster—which he could do at home just as easily—but she thought she could hear something deeper, more of a need than a want.

"Well, Honey, I always want you here by me," she responded. "But I know you enjoy your private time, too. It wouldn't hurt you to take the rest of the week off work."

"Thanks, Babe," he said in a quiet, loving voice.

They spoke for an hour and then said their goodnights among many *I love you's*.

After hanging up the phone, Robert lay back on his pillow with his hands under the back of his head. How much effect had his young life had on who he was today? How much different could he have been? He wished he could drift off to sleep thinking of his wife, but instead, he was thinking of his childhood on Norristown Mountain.

Chapter 19

The night of the Halloween party was not a restful night for the Rhodes children. After having slept for a few hours, the children woke to a swelling of voices reverberating through the walls. Although it took a few seconds to identify the sound, it soon became clear that the disturbance was the upset voices of their parents arguing. Regretfully, this sound was becoming more familiar and seemed to always occur about this time of night, just after mom came home from work.

The commotion generally didn't last long, as one of them would go to bed or walk outside for some air. Robert didn't get accustomed to the uproar and there was no way to accept it, but he learned to go to sleep afterward.

The next day at school, Robert enjoyed the attention and the congratulatory accolades of his fellow students. Mrs. Pearson asked all the winners to stand up and get another round of applause. It did not embarrass Robert in the least to receive the attention being heaped on him.

Soon after the morning recess, Mrs. Pearson came to Robert and told him his dad was outside and wanted to speak to him. Larry had never visited his son at school before because he was usually at work. Robert thought his appearance was odd.

"Hello son," his dad said, again rustling Robert's hair.

"What are you doing here, Daddy?"

Larry took a deep breath and released the words he'd been practicing in the truck. "Well, son. There's no easy way to put it, so I will tell you straight up. Mom and I are splitting up. I'm moving out right now. I'm sorry, son."

Dad didn't know what reaction to expect from his young son. He had pictured in his mind his son breaking down in tears and howling cries, but in an unexpected reaction, his son just sat looking at the ground.

Not expecting this non-reaction, Larry continued. "I'm moving up to Morrilton to live with some other fellows. It's only thirty or so miles, so I'll still get to see you a lot."

Finally, Robert spoke. "Can I come with you? I won't be much trouble."

"No, son. It wouldn't be a place for a boy to grow up," his father responded.

Larry put his arm around his son as they sat on the cement steps of the school. Larry was not a man of many words and didn't know exactly the right thing to say to his boy. On the outside, Robert was handling the news well, but on the inside, his world and heart had just shattered. He knew his family wasn't typical. They had always been poor and his family didn't come to Halloween parties to support him, but at least he had a mom and dad at home that loved him. Until now.

Robert broke the painful silence. "I'd better get back to class. They're getting ready to do spelling."

"Ok, son." Larry let his son get up, then pulled him back and wrapped his arms around his baby boy, pulling his face into the bib of his overalls. "I love you so much, Robert. You're my little man."

"I love you too, Daddy." Robert released his father and went through the door.

The boy stood in the foyer before returning to his classroom. He could hear his father's pickup driving off—the tires spitting gravel up, hitting the fenders—and yearned to be sitting beside him. He appeared fragile as he stood in the quietness, wiping his few tears with the sleeve of his plaid flannel shirt.

After returning to his seat, Mrs. Pearson found a moment to stand beside the boy and put her hand on his shoulder.

"It'll be ok Robert. Sometimes parents just can't get along," she whispered down at the boy.

Olivia was home when Robert got off the bus. He ran to his mom and hugged her without saying a word.

"I need to talk to you, son," Olivia said. "It's about your dad."

"I know about it, Mommy," the boy replied. "Dad came to school and told me."

"He what!?" She stopped short of saying exactly what she felt. How could a father break such news to his son at school—then leave him?

"What's going to happen to us, Mom?" Robert asked.

"We'll be ok," Olivia responded. "We'll probably even be better off without him."

"Well, I won't!" Robert said, breaking away from his mother's clutch and running toward the house.

"Oh, son! I didn't mean …" Olivia immediately regretted her words, but now they ingrained permanently in his memory.

Finally, in the privacy of his room, he lay face down on his pillow … and cried.

Getting out of bed the next day was tough for Robert when he realized the previous day's events had *not* been a dream. His heart ached. Permeating sadness filled the boy's soul for the next few days.

After two weeks away, Larry showed up one night at *The Poultry Palace*. Olivia placed her apron aside and told her manager she would be back in a few minutes.

Larry was sitting on the fender of his truck. "Hi Sweetheart," he said. "I've missed you."

"Don't *sweetheart* me just yet. We've got some talking to do!"

"I know. I want to come back home. I miss the kids and I mostly miss you," he said sincerely.

"What has happened to us? We used to never fight, at least not this way. We've been through all kind of things and we never got into more than a spat."

"I don't know. I guess it's all the stress. That, and it seems we never get to see each other."

"Of course, I want you to come back home, but it can't be the same. Not for my sake. Not for the kids' sake."

"I'll change, honey," he said.

"Oh, Larry, it's not just you. I am so tired all the time, I can't even think."

"Then you've got to give up one of the jobs. Make this your last week here."

She wanted to protest, but knew he was right.

Larry continued, "We've got to make this work, Sweetie. We've been in this for over twenty years. No one else will have us."

Olivia smiled. These were the words of the husband she loved. They said little else. She approached him and fell into his body. His embrace wrapped around her as it always had for over two decades.

All of Robert's seven and a half years had been full of change and unpredictability. Most of the time, the changes were frustrating, but two and a half weeks after dad had appeared at his school, Robert was treated to a welcome change.

He woke up expecting it to be the same as most Saturday mornings: he would go into the front room, light the only source of heat in the house and watch cartoons until the rest of the world woke up. This Saturday, though, he woke up to hear some low mumblings in the front room. As he walked out through the bedroom door, he first saw his mom with a big smile on her face. He then saw his sister standing beside her. As he came around the corner of the door frame, his daddy came into view.

Robert ran to his dad and jumped on his lap.

"Son," Larry spoke, "we were just telling the other kids, your mom and I are going to make another go of it. I've brought my stuff back home."

This overjoyed the Rhodes children, but none more so than the youngest.

Olivia continued the announcement where Larry had left off. "You'll like this next news, son. I'm going to quit my job at the café, so I'll be home with you every night!"

At this news, the boy's eyes lit up. His smile showed that this news was better than any present at Christmas.

He never knew what had happened between his parents. He was just glad to have them together again.

This wasn't the end of hard times for the Rhodes parents. But it was a healing time and a time to move on.

Randy Judd

Chapter 20

Robert's relationship with Ricky was still inconsistent at best. Sometimes Ricky could be nice to the boy for weeks, then suddenly turn on him and beat him. The beatings were never just play wrestling, but intended to cause pain to the younger boy. Even though Robert didn't trust his neighbor, when Ricky was nice to him, it at least gave him someone to play with.

For the next couple of years, life in the Rhodes home became at least predictable—and sometimes, predictable is good. Mom and Dad both worked their daytime jobs while the kids were at school. The parents were both home in the evening. They remained busy working in the house or out in the garden.

William continued living in the trailer park on the other side of town and continued to spend his money on his cars. In 1969, he became the owner of the first new car in the history of the Rhodes family: A blue, two-door Olds Cutlass with a white, vinyl top. The car was his identity, and it made him feel significant, as if he had escaped the weight of the Rhodes' poverty.

Will's involvement with his band increased. In parallel with his music, he also became more and more involved with marijuana. Although his parents were oblivious to his newfound love, the other Rhodes family members knew. Even Robert had come across some of Will's hidden herbs one day when visiting his brother's house. He gave Robert strict orders—threats—not to tell, ever. William became less dependable at work. This was very frustrating to his parents, who spent every waking hour working in some capacity. Their son began following the beat of a different drummer, literally. In August 1969, Will announced to the family that he and the band were going to Max Yasgur's farm in New York to attend a huge concert. They loaded up his friend's VW Microbus and headed to join Jimi Hendrix, Joe Cocker and four-hundred-thousand other people in being part of history. William and his friends were gone for several months and missed Christmas with the family that year. He subsequently lost his secure job.

Lou flew past puberty and into full-fledged womanhood. In the summer between her sophomore and junior years, she showed significant changes, her skirts got shorter, and her blouses more revealing. Her personality became less fun-loving. The teenager's temper revealed itself quickly, and the family noticed they wanted to be around her less. That wasn't a tremendous problem, since she was unavailable to them most of the time. Lou spent most of her time away from home even during the week. Her older brother was aware of the rumors in town surrounding Lou and didn't doubt them. All Robert knew was that he just missed his big sister.

The Rhodes parent's relationship continued to experience more changes. The two were adequate partners in managing the household, but their friendship waned. Their arguments were common, but not violent, and they tried to hide the conflict from the children—especially little Robert—as much as possible. They tried a few times to heal their marriage and family by attending local churches of various denominations, but the older kids had no interests and the parents soon lost theirs.

Robert's life became very predictable. He adopted Norristown Mountain as his home. He knew the area well and most of his childhood memories were there.

As the summer of 1970 approached, Robert assumed it would be much as the others had been on the mountain, but the summer he turned ten was very different than the others had been.

On the first day of summer recess, Robert went to Ricky's house to get his neighbor to play.

"He ain't here and he ain't gonna be here all summer!" Mrs. Goodman proclaimed joyfully.

"How come?" The boy inquired.

"Well, he was gettin' to be a handful around here, so I sent him to live with his dad in Missouri for the summer," she responded.

Robert knew Ricky had a real dad but had never met him. They had named Ricky after his real dad. Big Ricky was a stock car driver and had made a name for himself on the quarter mile dirt tracks of the Show-Me State. To hear Ricky tell it, Big Ricky was a superstar. The way Ricky had talked to Robert about his real dad, he felt assured that Ricky was surely happy to be with him for the summer vacation.

Ricky's stepdad was a cranky old man who scared his step kids. Robert had never spoken to the man and went out of his way to avoid him.

With his neighbor gone, Robert realized he was to be all by himself during the summer. As this thought sunk in, he instantly felt lonely, but slowly the idea became very palatable to him.

The summer of 1970 became the summer of autonomy for the youngster. Although he sometimes called on his other buddies, Robert became comfortable with his own company. He spent the days wandering the woods and roads of the small mountain, his beloved dog in tow. There was no one to give him mischievous ideas, on the other hand, there was no one to talk him out of them. Larry and Olivia never knew the trouble he got into during those months that he stayed by himself.

When Robert got bored, he got creative. One hot Tuesday afternoon, when all that was on television were soap operas, the ten-year-old took his toy soldiers out and set them on the freshly plowed dirt road. He set six soldiers in the middle of the road and returned to the house and retrieved his dad's twenty-two caliber rifle. Guns were not foreign to Robert. He had gone squirrel hunting with Daddy many times. It took almost a box of shells, but the young marksman was finally able to kill all the soldiers. The mis-aimed bullets sailed into the woods and into the resting town below. Near the end of the massacre, the first car made its way up the road. Hiding behind a large bush in front of his house, the boy tried to hone his skills on the white sedan, kicking up dust at fifty miles per hour. As he aimed at the taillight, he squeezed the trigger. He felt instant regret. Relief followed the regret when he realized he didn't hit his target. The thought of harassing the car gave him a new idea, though. Robert grabbed a two-gallon metal gas can—which was almost full. With some matches that his father used to light his cigarettes, he marched a quarter mile up the road in order not to be too close to his house.

He waited by the side of the road with a gas can hanging from one arm and a book of matches in the other, listening for an oncoming car. When he heard a car approaching the small crest in the road, he poured the gas across the road—emptying the entire two gallons. Before the driver could see him, he jumped into the roadside bushes. As the blue pickup approached the sweet spot, Robert lit a match and threw it into the river of gasoline on the road. In his excitement, he started the process a little too early.

Seventy-three-year-old Bosco Watkins had a hard time explaining to his family that afternoon how—as he was driving down the road—the road flashed on fire in front of him. The old man slammed on his brakes and slid to a stop just before the curtain of fire. He got out and started stomping on the fire, which was quickly fading from lack of fuel. Mr. Watkins sat there scratching his head, wondering what he had just witnessed. As all quieted down, the man could've sworn he heard the animals in the woods snickering at his puzzlement.

But being unattended also put the boy in danger.

The Goodman family next door had found a source of extra money by allowing people to use the field of cars as a grazing pasture for horses. Although Robert was fearful of the half dozen quarter horses that roamed the field, he wasn't so reluctant of the little Shetland pony that shared the space.

One day, while he explored amongst the cars, he found the Shetland standing next to a 1961 Dodge carcass. Robert climbed on the car, all the time talking softly to the horse. As the boy got near enough to touch the pony, he slid one leg over and then the other till he was mounted on the little brown and white horse. All was well until the horse realized the boy was on and suddenly took off running at a sprint. With the boy on its back, the horse quickly ran toward the herd of full-sized horses. In the midst of the larger horses, the Shetland stopped and spun around, sending the lad flailing. Robert landed face down on the hard pasture dirt, in the center of the larger horses. This action startled the quarter horses and as they took off, the ten-year-old laid low to avoid the thunderous herd of horses as they retreated. He was relieved to see them running away, but was in horror as they circled back toward him at a full gallop. Before he could devise a plan, the horses were back again. The horrific stampede shook the ground around the boy and soon reached a crescendo. Burying his head and instinctively putting his hands behind his neck, he felt the weight of a horse's hoof on his tender back. The thunder of the horse's hooves subsided as they kept running to a distant end of the pasture. Writhing in pain, he opened his mouth to scream, but nothing came out. The weight of the horse had forced the air from his lungs. He thought at that moment that he would die. As the air returned to his lungs, his first sounds were screams of pain. As soon as he could get his strength, Robert made his way to a car and crawled into the backseat. With the steel of the car door protecting him from the stallions, he took inventory of his condition. His pain was intense. Looking in the Chevy's rearview mirror, he surveyed his injury. Although his back was already starting to bruise, he could tell the hoof had barely torn the skin. *Maybe I won't die*, he thought. With the devil-horses at the other end of the field, he made his way across the fences and back to his house.

For the rest of the day, he lay on the brown nagahyde couch and watched reruns of *Gilligan's Island* and *The Andy Griffith Show*. Robert felt he couldn't let his parents know of his stupidity, so he tried to avoid them that evening and the following days. He discovered a new talent that he was pretty good at—hiding his pain.

Although the horse incident could have led to an untimely death for the boy, another incident that summer had the potential to lead to something even worse.

Having just cashed in some pop bottles for candy money, Robert walked down the side of the road toward home. After a half mile or so, he could hear a car slowing down behind him, dropping the right two tires off the side of the blacktop as it pulled up next to him. He turned to see a beautiful red Chevy Corvette. To the poor lad, a Corvette was something his brother talked about, but nothing in which any of the Rhodes ever dreamed of riding.

Inside were two men in their twenties. The one on the passenger side had blonde hair with long bangs swept to one side. He sported a blonde mustache which dropped over the corners of his mouth.

"Hey little man, do you want a lift?" the passenger asked.

Robert's eyes brightened with delight and, without hesitation, said, "YOU BET!" His brother would be so jealous that he had gotten to ride in such a car.

"Well, climb on in," the driver said.

With only two seats in the sports car, the boy straddled the console as they sped off. The driver checked his side mirrors to make certain no one had seen them.

"What's your name, little man?" the blonde stranger inquired.

"Robert, sir. Robert Rhodes." the boy said unwisely.

"Well, Robert. Does anyone know where you are?"

"Nope. My parents are at work. I was just cashing in some bottles for candy."

The two men glanced devilishly at each other. "We've got lots of candy where we're going."

The blonde man with the mustache patted his leg. "Why don't you sit on my lap, Robert? It would be a lot more comfortable than that console."

As Robert moved toward the man, a car sped past them. Suddenly, the driver of the Corvette slowed, then pulled to the side of the road and, for no apparent reason, stopped.

"This is as far as we can take you today, Robert." The driver said. The passenger looked at his partner with confusion.

"Thanks guys," the boy said innocently.

"And by the way, don't tell anyone we picked you up and gave you a ride," the driver continued. "If word got out, every kid would want a ride from us and we just can't do that."

"Oh, you bet, mister. It's our secret," Robert said just before the pretty car sped off.

Robert never told anyone until the day he told his wife thirty years later. As he reflected on this incident as an adult, he wondered what would have happened that day in 1970 and what the men had planned. Could that have been the last day of his life? If he had stayed with the two men, what evil things might he have experienced? An even more intriguing thought to Robert was why the men had suddenly let him go? Did they get scared by the passing car? Did they have a sudden pang of guilt and conscience? Or did some unseen force take control of the situation to protect the young boy for greater things in life?

The incidents with the horses and the men reminded Robert of what the doctor told his parents after his snake bite: *This is one fortunate little boy; the good Lord must have something in store for him.*

Decades later, Robert was grateful life had spared him, though he couldn't say exactly for what.

The boy and his dog spent a lot of time together that summer. Robert discovered a route through the woods which would take him to downtown Russellville in a little over an hour. A few times that summer, he set out toward town with Ranger at his side. Robert took the money he had saved and then bought lunch for himself and his dog. At the Piggly Wiggly grocery store in town, he could get a three-wing chicken dinner for ninety-nine cents. Ranger waited by the automatic door of the store while his master went inside to get the meal. After returning, Robert sat on the curb in front of the store and shared his meal with his canine friend. Ranger waited patiently as Robert took a bite and shared the bones and part of the meat with his friend. The streets of Russellville were certainly busier than the dirt road in front of the Rhodes house. Ranger protected his boy by stepping in front of him to prevent his master from crossing in front of cars and only then move out of the way when it was safe.

During the days alone, his parents gave Robert chores. It was his job to clean the house, wash the dishes and generally, have things tidy for his parents when they came home. Although rare for a boy his age, Robert used this house cleaning time to play house. When he cooked his lunch—scrambled eggs, pot pie, or something else very simple—he sometimes pretended he was making it for his wife and kids. A ten-year-old pretending to have a family was certainly a sign of an unmet need in Robert's life.

For doing this, they gave him twenty-five cents per day, payable on Friday. The young housekeeper was great with his money and bought his first watch and many of his toys with his own money.

Chapter 21

The beginning of the fourth grade brought a bittersweet change for the students at Mountain Springs Elementary. The small two-room school was retired. Sequoyah Elementary was the newest school to grace the Russellville School District. It was a thoroughly modern school, named after the inventor of the Cherokee Alphabet. All the students in Mountain Spring's boundaries moved to the new school. Unlike the former school, this new school had two classrooms for each grade and two teachers for each classroom. Robert felt thrust into an enormous world. He took solace that Mrs. Pearson was at the new school also and he could wander down to the first grade rooms and see her almost anytime.

Ricky returned to Russellville shortly before the start of school. The two boys reunited for the first time on bus eighteen as they headed for the first day of school. The conversation was awkward, so they rode most of the way to school in silence. Ricky seemed older to Robert. He wondered if something had happened to his friend that summer to change him. He would never know. Ricky was in seventh grade that year, which meant he was no longer in the same school as his young friend. They would only see each other after school and on the bus. During that moment—while the ride to school seemed painfully quiet—silence was ok with Robert.

That school year, Robert and Ricky did less together than they had the previous years. Robert continued to notice the change that Ricky had gone through and the two friends seemed to have less and less interaction. As the end of the school year approached and summer was nigh, Robert looked forward to spending another summer by himself. He was dismayed and slightly worried when he heard that Ricky would not be going to his father's house again that year.

Events in the summer of his eleventh birthday caused Robert to find out his older friend was not just mischievous, but actually *bad*, maybe even *evil*.

Several weeks into the summer, the Goodman boy knocked on Robert's house.

"Hey Robert, I got something to show you!" he said, walking off the porch.

Although Robert was reluctant to go, he was also afraid *not* to go.

They didn't speak much as they made their way down deep into the woods and around the backside of an enormous boulder forming a cliff out of the mountain.

As they turned the corner of the precipice, Robert could see a stash of sundry items. At first survey, he saw there were two bicycles, and a pile of various toys piled up against the rock. There was some electronic equipment and even clothes piled up near the edge.

"Where did all this stuff come from?" Robert quizzed in awe.

"I stole it!" Ricky announced proudly. "There is a trailer park down the hill and people who live there are too stupid to lock their doors, so I just walk in and take what I want."

Dumbfounded, Robert just stared at the loot. Finally, he started realizing how ludicrous some of the items were. "But Ricky, you have a toaster and women's clothing. What are you going to do with stuff like that?"

"It's not about what I get," Ricky revealed. "It's about the high I get from doing it. Come with me right now and see what I mean."

The younger boy couldn't quite understand what he meant by getting a high, but soon found himself going down the mountainside behind the older boy.

As they neared the edge of the woods and could see the trailer park, Robert hesitated. He knew stealing was wrong, but also found a certain thrill in being involved.

"I don't think I can do it. Can I stay here and watch you the first time?" Robert asked.

"Man, you are such a sissy, aren't you? OK, stay here and you'll see how easy it is!"

As Ricky exited the woods, he stayed close to the boundary for an easy retreat. Circling as a wolf around a campfire, he closed in on an unsuspecting trailer house. With no cars in the driveway, he checked for signs of life. When a mutt emerged from under the porch barking, a lady opened the door to the trailer and yelled to quiet the pooch. She was dressed in a pink housecoat and slippers and had foam curlers in her hair. She closed the door again, apparently not noticing the lurking stranger.

With one target eliminated, Ricky moved on down the street to another residence. Again, there were no cars in the driveway. He tossed a small rock toward the trailer, which glanced off the front door. Nothing. He walked confidently closer, looking around as he approached. Nearing the back door of the house, he reached for the doorknob to see if it was open. It was. *Stupid people deserve to have their stuff stolen,* Ricky had said. He slipped inside.

He was only inside for a few minutes, but to Robert, it seemed forever. Periodically, Ricky opened the door a little, looked towards the woods where Robert lay, and tossed his booty on the ground below the door.

When the amateur thief had tossed enough to fill his arms, he slithered back out of the trailer.

Robert watched with fear, afraid the older boy would get caught. He also feared for himself, being associated which such activity. As he watched Ricky collect his things, Robert noticed peripheral movement. The lady who yelled at the dog had apparently seen Ricky after all and was watching his activity.

From the edge of the woods, Robert could tell that the woman was still dressed in her nightgown and slippers. She leaned down to unhitch the mutt. When she did this, Robert could see she was also holding a rifle at her side. Robert wanted to run, but froze where he was. As the dog took off toward Ricky, the woman raised the gun to her shoulder and squeezed the trigger. The bullet arrived a split second before the sound and caused a pop on the metal side of the trailer. Immediately after, the sound of the gunshot reached Ricky's ears. He looked to see the dog approaching quickly, with the lady running behind it.

The young criminal dropped his goods and ran immediately towards the woods. *No, don't come this way!* Robert thought. The lady's next shot caused Ricky to change direction and head toward the highway. The dog got distracted by a cat and—since the woman couldn't keep up with the intruder—he got away. As she went back in her house to call the sheriff, she hesitated and looked toward the woods where Robert lay. He was sure he hid well enough, but he stayed right where he was, anyway.

As the sheriff's car pulled into the trailer park, Robert knew it was time to move. He army crawled deep into the woods, then stood up, still slightly crouching, and ran further into the woods.

That evening, one of the county deputies made his way along the mountain road, door to door, in similitude of the prince looking for Cinderella. The deputy had no glass slipper, just a description.

"We're looking for a boy about thirteen or so who has been stealing a bunch of stuff down at the trailer park," the deputy explained.

As the deputy stood at the door speaking to Larry Rhodes, Robert stayed in his bedroom, praying to the god of crime to save him.

"Have you got any boys about that age?" the deputy asked.

"I've got one that'll turn eleven this year." Larry turned his head toward the inside of the house and yelled, "Hey Robert, come on out here!" As Robert shyly approached his dad, his father turned to the officer. "This here is my youngest boy, Robert."

The Deputy looked the boy over for a few seconds, and then said, "Naw, doesn't match the description. The boy we are looking for is thin, with longer blond hair. Your boy's hair is too short."

Robert couldn't remember a time when he was so glad to have a flattop haircut. Just as the deputy was leaving, Larry interrupted. "That does fit the description of the boy next door. His name is Ricky. He's quite the hellion."

"Thanks, Mister Rhodes. I'll check it out," the deputy said as he headed to the house next door.

Watching from his bedroom window, Robert could see the deputy lead Ricky to the patrol car. In a few days, he heard that Ricky had to spend thirty days in the Pope County Juvenile Detention Center. Afraid that Ricky would blame him for being caught, Robert dreaded the next time he would see him—and for good reason.

Randy Judd

Chapter 22

The summer was almost over when Robert heard of Ricky's release from juvenile detention. Lou told him in passing. Robert stayed inside for the next few days. Peering through the curtains, he had not seen much activity next door, and certainly no sign of Ricky.

On the third day after Lou's announcement, Robert went to the mailbox on the road to retrieve the family's mail. As he got back to the house, it startled him to see Ricky's older brother, Ernie, standing on the porch.

"Hey Robert. Guess What?" Ernie said, not really caring if the young boy guessed or not. "Ricky's home and he wants to show you something cool he learned about in lockup."

"I can't go right now. Let me by," Robert mumbled, shaking in fear.

Ernie grabbed the boy and maneuvered him to the Goodman house. He pushed, pulled, dragged, and did whatever it took to get the boy to the house. Robert was trying not to cry—knowing it would only exasperate the situation. There was no need to scream or yell, since there was no one to hear him.

Ernie dragged the boy through the front door, past the front room and into the second bedroom. As he came into the room, Robert could see the other two Goodman boys—Joel and Ricky—waiting. Ernie pushed him toward the other two boys and Robert stumbled, not quite falling. When he straightened up, he was face to face with Ricky.

"I sure had fun in Juvy." Ricky started out. "Yeah, three meals a day. Not much to do. Not a bad gig. I had a lot of time to think, though."

Ricky started moving to his left, circling the boy. Robert didn't move, but remained as he had been, looking at the floor.

"I thought about why you would turn me in to the cops. Wondered why you would do that to your best friend in the whole world." By now, Ricky had circled behind him.

Robert wanted to say so much. He wanted to say that he didn't turn him in. That he didn't want him to go to jail. He also wanted to tell Ricky he wasn't his best friend. He said nothing.

Ricky continued, "I thought a lot. I thought about how I could possibly repay you. Robert, I learned a lot in detention. I learned how people in jail pass their time. Do you want to know, little buddy?"

Robert stared at the floor, speechless.

Suddenly, Robert felt an abrupt push on his back, which propelled him to the bed on one side of the room. He fell face down on to the bed. Immediately he felt weight on both arms. Joel and Ernie were pinning him down. Since they were full-grown men, eleven-year-old Robert didn't stand a chance of moving from their grasps.

Joel removed the Marlboro from his mouth and handed it to the youngest Goodman. Ricky sucked on the cigarette, causing ashes at the other end to flare up into a miniature inferno. With pinched fingers, he removed it from his lips. With his other hand, he pulled up Robert's shirt. Seeking his target, Ricky's hand circled momentarily. He then pushed the red embers of the cigarette into the center of the young boy's back.

A shrilled scream escaped the room and the house, then traveled into the woods as he felt the intense heat scorch his pure pale skin. With a devilish grin, Ricky repeated the torture twice more, causing Robert to squirm in pain under the weight of the older boys. The torturer then passed the cigarette to Ernie.

After all the brothers had taken their turn, they released their grip. Robert fell off the bed and landed on the floor. Writhing in pain, the tears gave way to shock. He was aware of a smell he had never known before—the smell of burning flesh. The pains of the ten burns on his back started to subside somewhat.

For the first time, Robert looked somewhere aside from the floor. Strangely, he noticed that the three brothers appeared rather embarrassed by what they had inflicted on him. They were avoiding each other's glances.

Ricky glared straight into the eyes of young Robert and said, "If you tell anyone what happened over here today, we'll kill you! Do you believe that?"

Robert nodded in response and he *did* believe it. If they were capable of doing what they had just done, they were capable of doing anything.

Then, as a finale, Ricky kicked Robert in the side as hard with all his might.

The defeated boy shuffled home. Walking into the empty house, he felt so alone. He wanted to be held by his mom and protected by his dad, but they wouldn't be home for several hours and even then, he couldn't tell them. Robert locked all the doors and pushed one of the chairs up against the front entrance. He sobbed most of the afternoon and resolved that he would never let that happen again. He would rather die.

Randy Judd

Chapter 23

He kept his dark secret from the rest of the world. For the remaining weeks of summer, the boy didn't talk much to anyone. His family really didn't notice because they were so busy with their own lives. As he began fifth grade, he put on a cheerful face to hide his shredded soul. His friends didn't notice a difference and being at Sequoyah during the day helped him forget for a while.

Robert rarely saw the Goodman boys, and that was the way he wanted it. Joel no longer lived at home and Ernie was out of school, nowhere to be found. Robert didn't know where Ricky was. He didn't ride the bus anymore. Robert had heard rumors that his mom had kicked him out after his bout with the law and he was living with some cousins. That wouldn't surprise Robert, since Ricky and his mom had never gotten along. It was only natural that the young Rhodes boy was nervous about being home alone. He often went to his friends' houses after school and played.

Time began healing the lad, albeit in small degrees. Life returned to normal, at least as normal as it could be in the Rhodes' home.

Will had found a girlfriend, and they planned to be married the following spring. Robert liked Mary. She had long brown hair and looked soft and innocent. When her thick lips parted, they revealed a brilliant smile that made

Robert feel happy. As odd as it was for an eleven-year-old boy, he already longed for the day he could have someone special as his constant companion.

Will and Mary moved to a house in town. It was a white wooden house with two bedrooms and a big yard on Glenwood Street in Russellville. The young couple didn't have much furniture but were gradually building a home. His hippy ways started to mend and marriage led him back to responsibility. He now worked at Butler's Auto Parts in the neighboring town of Dardanelle. His love for hot rods had led him to Tony Butler, the owner. The two men became fast friends, and Tony hired him to learn more about the business.

Will worried about the draft. The family had friends serving in Vietnam and knew there was always a chance their son's time could come. Starting in 1969, the draft board drew numbers randomly and assigned numbers based on birthdays. The lower the number, the better chance a young man had of being drafted. Every year, they watched the draft lottery with trepidation.

Lou was now a senior at Russellville High School and if she hung in, would be the first Rhodes ever to graduate from high school. She enjoyed high school for the social aspects, but had become increasingly aloof. Not surprisingly, she ran with a dangerous crowd. Now a heavy smoker and drinker, she was lucky to even be able to concentrate on schoolwork. She still worked at the Tastee-Freeze, but had other part-time jobs as well.

Mom and Dad Rhodes had determined fighting wasn't accomplishing anything, and their marriage seemed to be mending.

By the time winter bowed and spring introduced its daffodils, Robert was feeling much more comfortable with life and much more secure in his safety. On a Sunday afternoon in April 1972, Mom sent Robert over to borrow some eggs from Martha. Without thinking much about it, he ran to the neighbor's house and rapped on the front door. Prepared to ask Mrs. Goodman for some eggs, he was taken back to see the door opened by Ricky. The Goodman boy had watched him come up the steps and was prepared when he got there. As the door opened inward, Ricky reached out and pulled the young boy inside the house. The two boys fought on the floor of the front room, Ricky trying to get control and Robert trying to get away.

"That was a lot of fun last year. Did you come back for some more?" Ricky grunted.

This time, it was just Ricky, without his brothers. Robert knew he had a chance to escape, maybe not a significant chance, but a chance anyway. But Ricky was still stronger and pinned the boy face down on the wooden floor. While struggling, Robert kept waiting for the first blow, but so far, it hadn't come. Robert tried to roll side to side to get Ricky off. It wasn't working, and he was getting tired, but he knew he could not give up. Unlike the first time, he thought, this time there may be someone nearby to hear him. So, he started screaming for help.

In response to the screaming, Ricky wrapped his hands around the younger boy's throat and began choking him.

Hearing the screams, Martha woke up startled from her Sunday afternoon nap. Still somewhat asleep, she stumbled to the front room. There on the floor was her youngest son sitting on the next-door neighbor boy, choking him. Fearful of what he might do, but somehow not surprised, she grabbed a table lamp and swung it at Ricky, striking him in the right temple. The impact knocked the older boy off Robert—who then jumped up immediately. Gasping for air, he ran toward the corner of the room, where he cowered.

"You little inbred!" Martha screamed at her son. "What are you trying to do, kill him?"

"You watch it, woman!" Ricky screamed back. "Or I'll kill *you*!"

"I have a good mind to call the sheriff and have them lock you up, boy."

"You'd better watch your step, you witch! I'll slit your throat in your sleep!" Ricky ranted. Then looking at Robert, he continued, "and you too. You little piece of crap!"

Once again, Robert believed him.

Robert made a mad rush to the front door, but no one tried to stop him. He ran back home and, without shutting the door behind him, went straight into his room. Olivia was still in the kitchen.

"Where's my eggs, Robert?" Olivia yelled.

"She didn't have any." The boy shouted the lie.

"I'll send Lou down to the grocery store to get some then," Mom said, never getting close enough to see Robert's distress.

Before dawn the next day, a shadowy figure fled the Goodman home. A few minutes later, Larry went to his truck to head for his day's work. An uneasiness fell over the man. A flash coming from the neighbor's house caught his attention. As he looked toward their house, he could see the flicker of fire through the window of Martha's bedroom!

Instantly, he ran back inside his own house and yelled at Olivia—who was getting ready for work—to call the fire department. Larry darted back outside and sprinted the short distance across the two properties. Without much forethought, he went through the front door into a blazing living room. With the heat scorching his skin, he immediately retreated out to the porch. While wondering what he should do next, he heard the terrorizing scream of Martha in her bedroom. The haunting screams were like nothing he had heard since the war. The screams were not just fear, but the intense pain of her flesh burning. Larry was subconsciously motivated by the same spirit that had saved his friend,

Howard, in Guadalcanal. Without considering the consequences, the man went back into the inferno and found his way to the room of the burning woman.

Grabbing a blanket lying unburned on the floor, he threw it over Martha, whose bed clothes were on fire. Her eyes locked on him with a panic that showed she knew the end was probably near. He picked her up, wrapped in the blanket, and carried her out to the front yard. By this time, most of the house was ablaze. Larry didn't know if anyone else was home, but with walls falling and the house enveloped, he knew he couldn't get back.

As he got a safe distance from the house, he laid Martha on the grass. The fire was no longer burning her decrepit little body, but she was dead. As he laid her down, the charred skin of her wrist slipped away from her muscles in his grip. He then heard her last gurgle of life, while smoke still rose from her body.

By the time the emergency vehicles arrived at the scene, all that remained to do was investigate. They treated Larry's burns on the scene and let him go. The rescue workers described his actions as heroic and superhuman. Their quick investigation concluded the fire had started in her bedroom. They guessed she had been smoking in bed. They were right about the location, but wrong about the cause.

Little Robert watched from the edge of the yard under a tree. He could sense in the air the awful smell of burning flesh that—unfortunately—he had known firsthand.

Eventually, they accounted for everyone else. Poor Martha was the only casualty. They buried her a few days later at a funeral which was full of lamenting and screaming, but empty of hope. All her sons put on a good face.

For Robert, his daily actions reflected his fear of Ricky. He looked around every corner before proceeding. He turned on the light before entering a room.

Although he was a very private person, for many months, Robert didn't want to be alone.

The weeks crawled into months and soon it had been a year since the fire.

Robert heard that Ricky was staying with his father in Missouri. He didn't really care where the boy was as long as it wasn't near.

Although Robert became more comfortable with shadows and empty rooms and being by himself, he had a hard time forgetting his enemy and feeling completely comfortable within himself.

Chapter 24

Allowing himself to sleep a little later, Robert finally made his way from Flagstaff, heading east on I-40. He stopped briefly in Winslow so he could stand on the corner and take a selfie. There was not a lot to see crossing the desert into New Mexico. After stopping in the Native American town of Gallup, he ventured on to Albuquerque. The previous night, he had searched on his laptop for places off the beaten path to explore on his way home. He chose to go north from Albuquerque to Santa Fe. The city was founded sometime in the seventeenth century and he read that it was the oldest state capital in the United States.

As he drove eastward, he became very aware of the road noise beneath him. The road hum was interrupted about every second with a bump where the concrete had been joined. No matter how fast he was traveling or what lane he was in, the hum and the rhythmic clicks were still there. It resembled the hum of Ricky Goodman that had followed him throughout his life.

His time he spent in Junior High was not a pleasant experience for the boy. Slowly, his friends from Sequoyah drifted to fresh groups of buddies. Unlike his sister before him, Gardner Junior High became a futile exercise in perseverance. Going to class was difficult. He prayed in each class the seating would be assigned, otherwise, his lack of friends would be more painfully obvious as he sat in the back of the room by himself. As hard as it was to be in class, it was twice as hard to be out. During recess, he spent his minutes trying to be unnoticed. On occasion, he pushed himself to go stand in a group of people who had been nice to him, but without anything to add to the group, he found himself shut out of the circle.

The three-fifteen bell was parole from a prison, but sadly just a day-pass as he had to return the next morning.

Lou moved to Memphis during her senior year—as soon as she turned eighteen. She was an inspiration to Robert. She apparently found success in the big city. Whenever she returned home for a visit, she always brought nice presents for her little brother. She always drove newer cars and wore nice jewelry. She had certainly made something important of herself.

As a student, Robert performed adequately: An A grade here and there, but mostly Bs and Cs. He didn't mind the schoolwork, just the social aspects of school.

Although going home at the end of the day was a relief, it was lonely. The teenager's loneliness and pain led him to experiment with alcohol. At first, he just swiped a little of his dad's beer, but eventually he squirreled away enough alcohol to satisfy his need but not to be noticed by his father. Robert also stole a little when he was visiting William's house. Additionally, he knew a boy down the mountain that would sell it to him for twice the price. By whatever means Robert could get it, he would.

Alcohol certainly numbed the pain but didn't cure the cause. It lured him deeper into his depressed state. He removed himself from almost all social situations. His parents dismissed his aloofness. *He's just a teenager.*

Robert had always hated fall. As the leaves died around him, it seemed all hope of life was gone. The air was chilly, and the landscape was gray. On a gloomy day in early November of ninth grade, Robert stayed home from school. The thought had been entering his mind for weeks. Now the solution to his problems had almost become an obsession for the teenager. He got out of bed about eleven and walked into his parents' room, then opened the door to the closet that held his father's guns.

He had grown up around guns and knew that each one served a particular purpose, depending on its caliber or gauge. The shotguns—twelve, sixteen, and twenty gauge—were all meant for hunting birds and game at close range. At longer ranges, the pellets spread too much to be accurate. They used the rifles—twenty- two and thirty-aught-six—for hunting squirrels and deer at longer range. They were also great target guns. But none were appropriate for his purpose today.

The troubled boy did not want to make a statement by creating a mess for his parents. He just wanted to slip suddenly out, so he steered away from the shotguns. The rifles were too long to hold. He settled on a twenty-two caliber pistol his dad used for killing annoying varmints living around the house and in the neighboring woods.

He chose the bathroom as his place to do the deed. It would certainly be an easier place for his mom to clean up. As much as he loved her, he didn't want to create more work.

Robert contemplated a note, but couldn't think of anything he wanted to say. He felt sorry for his family. He knew they would be sad, especially Lou, but they would eventually move on. Their pain would become tolerable. He didn't want to hurt them; he just didn't want to go on in his current mental state.

Closing the lid, he sat on the toilet, raised the pistol, and put it in his mouth. The steel was cold to his tongue and cheeks and he could still taste the gunpowder from its last firing. With his thumb, he pulled the hammer back and locked it. Then he quickly removed the gun from his mouth and uncocked the hammer. He realized at this angle, the bullet would exit the back of his head, splattering blood and cerebral matter onto a picture on the wall. His mom had bought the watercolor painting of purple lilies at a yard sale. She really treasured it!

He swung his legs around ninety degrees so that his back faced the bathtub. *Much more sanitary*, he thought. He once again put the gun in his mouth and engaged the hammer.

As he prepared to pull the trigger, Robert noticed Ranger's warm head resting on his master's leg. Through the entirety of his pain, the faithful dog had never been far away. For ten years now, the dog had been close by to lick Robert's wounds, both physical and emotional. Ranger would miss him, that was for sure.

Suddenly, the image of the horses in Goodman's field came vividly to his mind. Couldn't he have just died then, avoiding all that came after? And what about the men in the Corvette? If he were meant to die, that would have been a great time. What about the snakebite on the farm? What was it the doctor had said? Something about the Lord having a grand purpose for this little boy. If he were meant to be dead, wouldn't all those situations have been better?

Maybe he shouldn't act so hastily. If there is a God, maybe He is not ready for me to die. Maybe there is a purpose. Although he couldn't see a purpose now, these thoughts gave him a sliver of hope. That little hope was all he needed to lower the gun and disengage the hammer a second time.

Ranger seemed to be panting his approval and moved in closer to be petted.

Robert returned the twenty-two back in his dad's closet and reached instead for a bottle of Jack Daniel's he had hidden under his bed.

A few months later, on his way out the door to school, Robert rustled the fur on his dog's head. As the bus pulled away from his house, he saw Ranger sitting contently on the porch. Robert knew his dog would be waiting faithfully for his return, as he had for a decade.

Sadly, that was the last time Robert saw Ranger alive. For several days following, he scoured the woods, yelling desperately for his dog, but there was no answer. He talked to neighbors, hoping to get some clues, but there was no sign of his dog or its potential demise. Then, as if by inspiration, Robert saw in his mind a large oak tree in the woods where he and Ranger had played often when they both were much younger. He went deep into the woods to their secret spot. There, near the base of the tree, lay Ranger—his body was curled up as if he had laid down to sleep, then simply slipped into death. The dog's master returned with a shovel and buried his companion beneath the oak. Robert mourned for weeks. Ranger had been his only true childhood friend and now both were alone. He would never know what happened to his dear friend that day, but wished he could have been there when he passed.

Randy Judd

Chapter 25

He finished Junior High that year and yearned with everything in his soul for tenth grade to be better.

By the start of his sophomore year at Russellville High School, Robert had grown quite a bit. He had always been a tall kid, but his summer job in the lumber yard with his dad had filled him out with muscle. On the first day of school, one of the football coaches approached the fifteen-year-old. "You play football?" the coach asked, putting his hand on the boy's shoulder.

"No, sir," he replied, looking at the floor.

"What's your name, boy?"

"Robert, sir. Robert Rhodes."

"So, you don't play football, huh?"

"No, but I like watching it, though."

"Who's your favorite team?"

"Oh, I root for the Cowboys! Especially a couple of years back when Staubach and Morton both quarterbacked."

"Yeah, that was a good team, probably the best ever. Even better than those undefeated Dolphins." The coach changed gears. "Listen, if you want to try out for the team, I think you're big and stout enough that you might stand a chance.

We're having tryouts all week. We already started two-a-day practice a couple of weeks ago, but you're welcome to try."

"I'll think about it," Robert replied as the coach released his shoulder and scanned the commons for another undiscovered all-star.

Robert went to the tryouts and ended up making the Russellville High School Cyclone football team. After a couple weeks of staying after school, he missed his bottle and quit the team.

The only extracurricular activity he enjoyed—besides the booze—was working. He had been working since he was twelve when he started mowing neighbors' yards. At fourteen he was working washing dishes at a diner near the marina and at sixteen a convenience store on Main Street. Just recently he secured a job at the newly built Motel 6. He worked there from nine at night until two in the morning, checking in guests for an inflated rate of eight dollars per night and seventy-five cents extra if they wanted a key to turn on the black and white television. The new job gave him abundant time to think and be by himself—which he savored.

The years of watching his parents struggle with finances shaped Robert's relationship with money. He spent little and saved much. He was soon able to buy a 1974 Pontiac GTO. It was a blue two-door coupe with a white vinyl top and a racing strip down each side. His auto gave him newfound freedom. Robert was a responsible worker who never let his drinking get in the way of his duties. Dropping out of school—like his siblings—tempted him. He could find more instant rewards from cashing a paycheck than dissecting a frog.

At school, he was torn between his comfort level of staying in his social cocoon and his desire to be someone different from what he was. He watched silently—from his private table at lunch—other kids in their groups of five or six. He longed to be in one of those groups. It was a new school and a new chance to start.

In actuality, he wasn't a total recluse. In class, if they assigned him to a group, he would participate—even taking a leadership role—but if there were no such assignment, he didn't know what to do, so stayed in his protective social foxhole.

Slowly, throughout the tenth grade, he tried sitting with different groups at different tables. Soon, he was able to sense which groups were amiable to his unassuming nature. He landed in a group of misfits which welcomed him. He felt comfortable and a genuine part of this group of half a dozen boys and girls.

By the end of his sophomore year, he had developed enough friendships to make coming to school tolerable if he could slip back home at the end of the day to the comfort of his liquid friend. His group had learned their new member was quiet, but had some noble qualities. They found him to be very gentle and intelligent. In fact, one of the girls in the group had given him the Native American name *Deep Waters*.

His junior year was uneventful, but he gained more confidence in his social abilities. His grades were decent, and he started to wonder if he would be like his siblings and drop out of school or if he should try to persevere. He leaned toward the latter.

As Ricky Goodman was becoming just a haunting memory, Robert was again reminded of the evil that was the Goodmans.

The first week out of the eleventh grade, Lou was home from Memphis visiting the family. As usual, Robert's hero was driving a nice car and dressed in fashionable clothing. He didn't want to do anything except be in her presence and feel the loving spirit of his big sister.

After a couple of days, it came time for her to leave. Robert's sadness was obvious to Lou.

"What's wrong, little brother?" Lou asked.

"I hate to see you go, Lou. You're the best thing in my life." Robert responded sincerely.

"Oh, come on. I'm hardly that good," she said modestly.

"Yes, you are, Lou. You're nice. You're also successful and important in Memphis," Robert continued. "You drive impressive cars, have cool stereos, talk about going to the best discos. I want to be like you."

Lou hugged her brother for a short time and then released him. She was looking down as if embarrassed at the scene. Robert noticed the tracks of a tear on her cheek.

"Let me come with you Lou," the boy asked his sister. "If not permanently, just for the summer."

"No, little bro, I can't do that," she replied. She called him little brother, but this was purely about birth order. He wasn't little anymore. As she lifted her head to look up at him, she realized—at almost seventeen—he was a grown man. He knew more about the world than she wished for him. It was time for her charade to end. She had to tell him the truth. "Sit down with me, Robert."

They sat on the edge of the concrete front porch. Things had changed a lot since he first sat on this porch twelve years earlier. The dirt road that he had once set on fire was now paved. New houses peaked out from the woods where he ran and played as a child with Ranger. Sitting there with Lou, he could hear the saws and hammers of construction work from amongst those hardwoods.

"I need to tell you some things, Robert. Some things that might be hard for you to hear, but you need to hear them."

186

Robert looked at her—his eyes dilating with interest. Like a pup, he tilted his head slightly and listened intently.

"Do you have any idea what kind of work I do in Memphis?" she asked.

"No, not really. Mom said you were in some kind of business with a man over there, but I really don't know what kind of business it is."

Lou took another sigh and forced the words out. "It's time that you know, Robert. It's hard to say. I am not some successful businesswoman. Robert." She hesitated. "I'm a call girl in Memphis. Just a high-priced hooker."

Robert took a punch in the stomach. He couldn't breathe well and he looked at his sister with desperation. He stood up and walked away a little to gather his thoughts. His hero had fallen.

Lou remained quiet, allowing him to sort through his thoughts. After a few minutes, he turned back and faced her. "I can't believe I never knew, but as I look back on it. There were clues, huh? How did this happen, Lou?"

"You act as if it's a disease, Robert. Look at me, I have nice things and live in a nice apartment. It's not that bad." Her words didn't hide the shame in her eyes.

"But, how? Why?"

"You were too young, Robert," she started, "to know all that was going on around here when we first moved in. With Mom and Dad gone all the time, I got into some trouble. I met some men at the Tastee-Freeze. They weren't very good, but by the time I found out, I was in deep. Drugs, drinking, overall partying.

"I wanted to finish school, I really did, but so many times I would wake up hung over or high. I couldn't keep up with school.

"I fought to get rid of my demons, little brother. I really did. In the eleventh grade, I started doing better. I even started thinking about college, believe it or not.

"Then one day, when I came home from school, Joel Goodman met me getting off the bus and asked me if I wanted to come over to their house and smoke some weed. I knew I shouldn't go, but I went anyway.

"When I got there, the three brothers were all there, with a buzz on." Lou paused for a breath. The hardest part was yet to come.

"Ernie sat beside me and after I had a few tokes, he started getting fresh with me. I pushed him away, but he came back more aggressively.

"They raped me, Robert. First Ernie, then Joel, then their little brother, Ricky. Then they took turns again."

The brother and sister sat quietly on the cement front porch, only fifty feet from where both their abuses had taken place. Only a charred foundation remained of the house, which had never been rebuilt. Lou quietly sniffled. Robert put his arm around her and pulled her close.

"I know this is hard for you to hear, Robert. Especially since you were such good friends with Ricky, but it really happened."

For the first time in a while, Robert spoke. "I believe every word of it, Lou. Those Goodman boys are bad people."

Robert wrestled with himself about whether to tell her of his own ordeal. He carried so much shame with him that he had not told anyone. Part of him wanted to, but he couldn't. Listening to her tell the story reminded him of all the feelings he had felt immediately after the attacks—the shame, the confusion. He wasn't ready to tell, not even his favorite person in the world.

"Not long after that," Lou continued, "their house burned and it killed Martha. I never quite believed it was an accident, but I don't know why. The boys all went their way, and I've only seen them once or twice since.

"The attack caused me to start having doubts about myself. I constantly felt ashamed and felt as if everyone around me could see into my soul and know it happened. I stopped going to school and put my dreams on hold.

"In the middle of my senior year, I ran into a man and a woman I had met while at the Tastee-Freeze. They lived in Memphis and invited me to come over and visit him. More than anything, I wanted to get out of Russellville, so I went with them. I wasn't there long before he introduced me to some wealthy friends who would pay me to be with them. As they say, the rest is history."

"Do Mom and Dad know?" Robert asked.

"Yeah, everyone knows. Mom had the hardest time with it. She wouldn't let me come home for a while—called me a whore. But, hey, all of us have had problems in this family except you, Robert! You're the Rhodes' only hope for a legacy."

If she only knew, Robert thought, *if she only knew about the drinking, the anti-social behavior, and the suicidal thoughts.*

"I'm sorry Robert. I'm sorry for who I am," she said despondently.

Robert took his big sister's face in his two hands, forcing her to look at him. "Lou, I love you! You're my big sister, no matter what. You've always been good to me. I guess … I just want better for you."

"I must really disappoint you."

Her little brother responded with wisdom beyond his years. "I am not disappointed *in* you, Lou. I'm disappointed *for* you!"

"Thanks Robert! I love you! I want better for me too. I've been thinking about getting my GED. This doesn't have to be my life."

As Robert walked Lou to her car, the convertible didn't seem as nice as before. Her clothes had an old stench about them. But his sister was still his sister and now they had a new bond, even if she didn't know about it.

As he watched her pull out of the driveway, he felt a twinge of hope for himself and his sister. He didn't understand what could possibly cause him to feel hope in such pitiful circumstances, but he cherished the hope.

Chapter 26

Suddenly one day, someone turned on a light.

Two weeks into his senior year, they introduced a new student in Robert's first period psychology class. Her name was Carla Morton, and she had just moved to Russellville from Utah. Robert didn't know anything about Utah, but the young lady who had just entered his class enthralled him. She was short; a little over five feet tall. She styled her blonde hair in a Dorothy Hamill cut—which was common for that year's trend. She dressed fashionably in white painter pants and a blue cowl neck sweater. As she walked toward him—taking the only open seat directly in front of him—she glanced at him and smiled. Her glance was not flirtatious, but genuine. She emitted a certain goodness that Robert could not remember ever feeling before. Her blue eyes were piercing and beautiful. As she sat down, the smell of her perfume drifted back and engulfed him. First period elapsed much too quickly. Soon she was gone again—lost in the sea of students. Robert anticipated the next day.

When Tuesday's opening bell rang, Robert made sure he was one of the first students in psychology. He deliberately wanted to be in class before Carla—hoping she would smile at him again. As the class started to fill, what Robert saw amazed him. The new girl walked into class with no fewer than four girls around her, laughing and talking. In one day, the new girl from Utah had made as many friends as he had made in his whole high school experience. As he sat in the middle of the class, he watched her and listened to her interaction with the other students. It was easy to understand why they instantly accepted her. Her conversation was unpretentious. She laughed easily and sincerely. Her countenance was a warm fireplace in the corner of a cold room. Everyone was instantly attracted to her and wanted to be her.

Her easy entrance into popularity was not a positive thing for Robert. He had hoped she would have a difficult time meeting people, thus giving him a chance to become friends with her. Now there was no chance of her getting to know him or even noticing him.

As the teacher entered the class and the students settled into their seats, Carla walked toward her same seat in front of him. As she approached her seat, to his surprise, she looked directly at him.

"Hello, Robert, how are you today?" she said as she sat.

He wasn't prepared to be greeted. He muttered some response and was instantly embarrassed that he did not possess her social savvy.

When the teacher had to excuse himself for a minute, the girl turned to Robert.

"So, Robert, I haven't really had much of a chance to say hi to you. I'm Carla Morton," she said, holding out her hand to shake his.

He shook her hand and was immediately aware of how soft and gentle it was. He responded awkwardly, "It's nice to meet you. How did you know my name?"

"Oh, it wasn't magic. It is written on the top of your notebook. I saw it when I sat down yesterday," she proudly replied before continuing. "Hey, I was wondering if you could help me get caught up in here. I know we're only a few days into the year, so it shouldn't be hard. Could you take some time at lunch and show me what I've missed?"

Robert's heart pounded so loudly—he was sure she could hear it. Girls generally didn't want to even talk to him, let alone be seen with him. Just then, the teacher returned to class and called everyone to order.

Robert couldn't let the moment pass. "Sure," was all he said.

"Ok then, I'll look for you at lunch," she whispered, then turned around to face the front.

The rest of the classes before lunch were a blur for Robert. He was so focused on his lunch meeting that he couldn't think about anything else. His insecurity led him to have a self-defeating dialogue within himself. *I'm probably going to say something stupid. She'll probably find someone else to do it. Someone will tell her I'm a loser and she won't even show!*

As the lunch bell rang, he swam upstream through the river of students to make sure he was one of the first ones in the lunchroom. After a few minutes, he saw her. She entered the commons area with three girls flanking her. They were laughing and gesturing as they got in the pizza line. He observed as she sat across the room from him with a half dozen socialites.

As Robert's table started to fill with the usual classmates, he remained quiet. Robert was deep in thought—reflecting about how abnormal and socially inept he was. He couldn't help but think of the Neil Diamond song, *The Story of My Life* and how this was truly the story of *his* life.

The surrounding table cleared and as it did, Robert looked across the commons area again and saw she was gone. *Why did he let himself feel normal?* He felt one of his lunch mates slide over beside him. As he looked to see which one it was, he saw Carla.

"Here you are. I've been looking for you all over," her smiling voice uttered. "I know lunch is about over, but can you help?"

For the last twelve minutes and forty-three seconds of lunch, Robert had a highlight of his life. Carla was so unassuming, so natural. She looked at him as if she really cared about what he had to say. He was so enthralled by her that all else around them melted away. When the second bell rang, Robert wanted to freeze time. He wanted this moment to last forever. The boy had honestly never felt anything resembling what he was feeling at this instant. But reality set in. He knew it couldn't last. He closed his psychology book and picked up the papers.

Carla wrote something on a small piece of paper and handed it to the clumsy boy. "I want to be all caught up by tomorrow. Can you call me tonight and go over the rest?" she asked, handing him the paper with her number on it.

"Sure, I can do that. Talk to you tonight," he replied with a teaspoon of confidence and a cup of anticipation.

As she walked away from him, her stride took him. She bounced as she walked, as if there was life and energy pulsing throughout her body, just waiting to get out. As she disappeared, he could've sworn the lunchroom dimmed slightly.

Calling any girl can be a traumatic event for a teenage boy, but for someone who was such a social dinosaur as Robert, it was almost impossible. He practiced all his opening lines. He even practiced dialing the numbers on his home's rotary phone, stopping at the last one. He decided he would call at six o'clock. No, her family was probably having dinner. He would call at seven. As seven approached, he talked himself out of it again. At seven-thirty, he put his finger in the hole beside the three and dialed the last number.

A pleasant-sounding woman answered properly. "Morton residence."

"Is Carla there?" the boy asked awkwardly.

"Why, yes, she is. Whom shall I say is calling?"

Robert thought this was a great time to hang up. He had never even known anyone who used the word *whom*. "Uh ... Robert ... Robert Rhodes."

As the woman went to retrieve Carla, Robert wanted to hang up, but he knew he couldn't now because she would know who ... or *whom* it was.

Soon, he heard the angelic voice. "Hey Robert, thanks for calling. How are you?"

"Good." *Crap! I should've said FINE.* "Is this a good time?"

"Yes, it's a great time! We just finished dinner about half an hour ago."

Robert relished his wise decision and wondered how it would be to eat dinner with his own family.

As she retrieved her psychology book, Robert took a deep breath. *So far, so good*, he thought.

When she returned, he started going over the pages and assignments to bring her up to speed. He took his time, hoping to keep her on the phone longer. Eventually, though, he ran out of material with which to bring her up to speed.

An interesting thing happened at that point. She didn't say goodbye and hang up, instead she asked Robert about himself. He embellished most facts, but was careful to make it believable. Then, after she had gotten all the information from him, she continued talking about herself.

She had just moved from Utah because her dad had taken a job with the nuclear power plant just outside of town. She had three older brothers. Her mom was a stay-at-home parent, and her family lived in Western Hills—a newer development with neatly organized brick houses. Carla had many interests, but her strongest passion was running. She told him how running made her feel liberated. She didn't run competitively but ran for the freedom. She didn't care what she would become in life, as long as she could run!

Robert delighted in hearing her talk. Her voice was smooth, yet full of life. He marveled that she wanted to talk to him. He certainly wasn't a skilled conversationalist, but with Carla, it came to him more naturally. Looking at the clock, he couldn't believe that they had been on the phone for an hour. This was by far the longest he had talked to anyone on the phone in his whole life.

As they said their goodbyes, Robert hung up and fell back on the couch. He was glad for the silence in his house because it allowed her voice to reverberate in his ears for several minutes more. *What was happening here? Was it possible she was interested in him? Doubtful, but why did she spend so much time?* With as much pain as Robert had experienced already in his life, he wouldn't allow himself to be off-guard. He decided he would proceed with caution and not with haste.

But he sure enjoyed how he felt at that moment.

As Carla hung up the princess phone on her end. She, too, was slightly confused. What had started out as just a way of catching up in psychology had left her with some feelings for which she was not ready. She had enjoyed the time on the phone with this boy. He was nothing like the boys she had dated in Utah, where the socialite mingled with boys who were of an acceptable social class and college bound. She couldn't allow herself to have feelings for this boy. She had guessed from their conversation that his family was poor and uneducated.

She also had to worry that she was just feeling lonely. She missed all her friends from her old school. Her parents had lovingly warned her to choose her new friends carefully. Carla didn't know what kinds of friends Robert ran with and what kind of influence they would have on him. At this moment, she lay down on her bed, enjoying the silence of her room, alone with her thoughts. She decided to proceed cautiously and without haste.

But she sure enjoyed how she felt at that moment.

Randy Judd

Chapter 27

The next day at school, she said hello to him as she sat down in class. The greeting was neither aloof nor overzealous, but it *was* friendly. After class, she met up with some friends and left the room without having further interaction with him. This left him wondering where things stood. Was she being evasive with him, or was he hoping for too much? He wouldn't make a judgment yet.

His feelings were so strong for her companionship that he had made up his mind the previous night that he would ask her out on a date. The only problem was, he had never asked anybody out and didn't know exactly what to do.

Between the first and second after-lunch bells, when students were gathering their belongings and dumping the healthier parts of their lunch into the trash, he approached her.

In all his teenaged awkwardness, he spoke. "I sure enjoyed talking to you last night!"

"Aw, thanks. I did too," she replied.

"I was kinda curious if you needed someone to show you around Russellville?" Robert blurted out before the moment passed. "I was wondering if I could. Maybe Friday night?"

She tempered her grin at his struggle to ask her. She could tell he hadn't done it often. This somewhat endeared Carla. "Well, actually, I've already got some plans for Friday."

Dang it! He thought. *Why did I put myself out there like that? I'm so embarrassed.*

She ended his pain. "But I bet we could do it on Saturday. If that works for you!"

They worked out the details, and Robert walked away, trying to conceal his smile.

When he got home from school, he wanted to tell someone, but his relationship with his parents wasn't such that he could. He went for a walk to release some of his energy.

That night at work, he couldn't help but think of her. One thing about working a late-night shift at a hotel, it gave him plenty of time to think. He thought of how her cute, round face illuminated him. He thought of how her soft and confident voice comforted him. He thought of how her presence warmed him.

He pulled into his house just after 2 a.m. Turning off the ignition prematurely, he let the GTO roll quietly for the final twenty-five feet to not wake the family. Since the family never locked the front door, he quietly entered the house and slid into his bedroom, where he laid down to get five hours of sleep before waking himself up for school.

That night, he dreamed.

In the dream, he was running through deep, dark woods. It was nighttime and something was stalking him. Robert couldn't see the something, but without a doubt, something lurked behind him. As he ran, he flung his arms violently to fight off the weeds and limbs that were slowing him down. Things got worse in the dream as the unknown follower started throwing golf ball sized rocks at Robert. The stones never hit him, but he could hear them whiz past his head. As hard as he tried, he couldn't run fast enough to lose the unseen enemy.

In the morning, Robert remembered the dream but dismissed it immediately.

Saturday arrived slowly for the boy. As he pulled up to her Western Hills home in his freshly cleaned GTO—he felt out of place. Soon after picking her up, though, he felt comfortable.

He took her to all the usual places on his tour. They stopped at Whatta Burger—the spelling differentiated it from the national chain. They ate on the tables under the awning since there was no indoor seating. It was a warm windless night where the crickets and passing cars competed in making the loudest sound. Cold beads of condensation clung to the strawberry milkshakes in paper cups between them. Although it was early, the night was going flawlessly. Robert thought he could even learn to endure the fall if he could stay around Carla all the time.

As the darkness chased away the remaining light, they made their way to Old Post Road Park outside of town. The park, built beside the Arkansas River a few years earlier, was a hangout for teenagers providing tennis and basketball into the early hours.

They walked around the park full of people. The six tennis courts were full of players, as were the four basketball courts. Many other high schoolers sat on rocks and benches with no particular purpose. Robert felt slightly uncomfortable because he didn't have any friends to introduce. In fact, she talked to more people from school than he did.

As they walked back to the car, he began to get anxious. He didn't know much about this boy-girl dating business. The fact is, the seventeen-year-old did not know how to properly interact with a girl. Most of his models of relationships came from Lou's sexually charged existence or movies and television. With his lack of experience, it wasn't surprising that when they were back in the car, he leaned over to kiss her.

Immediately, Carla pushed him back. "What do you think you're doing, mister?" She snapped. "I don't know you well enough to kiss you, and it looked as though you were going for even more." She huffed and if there had been enough light in the car, he could've seen her face was flushed and red.

Robert didn't know what to say. Seeing how angry she was, the girl slightly scared him.

"I'm sorry, Carla," was all he could muster. "I didn't mean to make you upset."

They sat there for a few minutes in awkward silence. She looked at him in the moonlight and saw a clumsy teenage boy who was unsure of himself.

"Look, Robert. I'm not sure what is happening here. Maybe I gave you some wrong signals, I don't know. Maybe that's how you do things around here, but that's not how I work."

He still cowered and appeared embarrassed, so she explained further. "I have standards that may seem a little weird to some people. I don't kiss until I know someone well enough and feel the connection that I *want* to kiss them. Don't get me wrong, I like to kiss—*really like it*—but there must be a connection. I don't just do it for recreation.

"This may surprise you even more, Robert. I don't plan on having sex before I am married."

That did surprise the boy. In the world he had been raised in and in the movies, it was unheard of.

He finally gathered his courage to speak. "Really, why not?"

"It's because of my religion. Do you know anything about Mormons?" she asked.

"No, not really," He replied. "I mean, I've read about 'em in history. Aren't they the ones with lots of wives? Does your dad have lots of wives, Carla?"

Unseen by him, she rolled her eyes. "No, and that was like a hundred years ago!"

She continued to tell him about her beliefs. Aside from no premarital sex, she didn't believe in drinking or smoking or lots of things teenagers in his town did.

There was no way that he was going to reveal some of his activities to her. They would probably disgust her. He started to wonder if the good feelings he had when he was around her had something to do with her faith.

"Carla, did I mess up tonight? Did I mess up the chance of us being friends?" Robert asked meekly.

His humility touched Carla. "No, Robert. I think you're kind of cool, but why don't you take me home now?"

By the time they got to her house, the conversation had returned to its comfortable place. They sat in the car and talked for another hour. They talked about their backgrounds and likes and dislikes. Robert was very protective not to reveal too much.

At 12:13 a.m., there was a knock on the car window, which startled them both. Carla's dad had come to retrieve her—pointing at his wristwatch. He scowled at Robert, then returned to the house.

"Robert. I really had fun tonight. Thanks for being my new friend."

"Me too. See you later," he responded awkwardly.

He watched her walk to the door. Just before she went in the white brick rambler, she turned and waved. His heart leaped. This was possibly the best day of his life.

Chapter 28

Over the next several months, their friendship grew. They spoke several times a week and periodically did homework together at lunch. As friends, they had fun. They enjoyed watching movies together and eating out. Sometimes they took rides in the Arkansas countryside. She enjoyed exploring new places, but mostly they enjoyed talking.

Carla did most of the talking, but Robert knew the right questions to ask and how to respond to her. She quickly determined his sense of humor was sharp and she appreciated that quality. She concluded early that—although he was rough in his social graces—deep down, he was a good person with a good heart.

She had not become as popular in high school as Robert had originally suspected she would. As the socialites found out she wouldn't party with them because she was Mormon, they didn't pursue her as much. She was still very much liked, though. Students saw her as someone who was genuine and easy to talk to. She joined the yearbook staff and track team and loved meeting as many people as she could. Carla wasn't preachy about her standards, but she wasn't ashamed of them either.

Carla introduced Robert to some people who attended church with her. There were only four other Mormons in the school, three boys—two of which were brothers—and a girl. Billy Ray and Steve Simpson were brothers. The other boy's name was Kelly Bell. Kelly was the junior class president for Russellville High School. Molly Milsap was the girl. The group of six started sitting together at lunch and Robert really took pleasure in their company. He felt welcomed, accepted.

Periodically, the group would invite him to activities at their church. Although he felt honored that they wanted him to attend, Robert couldn't bring himself to go. He trusted them, but wondered if the only reason they hung around with him was to get him to church. If he resisted enough, the legitimacy of their friendship would surely shine through. The teenager had been hurt many times in his life by trusting. He was reluctant to concede.

On some level, he also worried that somehow the people at church could see into his soul—see the weak character he had. See his dependence on the bottle. See the shame of his abuse.

Each morning before school, the gymnasium at the high school was open for pickup games of basketball. A painting of a large red cyclone—the school mascot—graced the center of the court, where Larry Bird and Magic Johnson wannabees displayed their prowess.

Billy Ray and Steve were talented basketball players. The two brothers were only a year and a half apart in age. They were equals on the court. Both brothers had—at one time—been on school teams. Robert loved to play basketball also, but his love for the game had not transferred into tremendous talent. He wasn't awful and even possessed basic hand-eye coordination, but they would never choose him for a varsity team.

As the school bell neared, and boys collected their possessions, Billy Ray approached Robert. "Hey, if you enjoy playing ball, our church has a team that practices every Wednesday," he said, patting the sweat on his brow with a towel.

"We play teams from other churches around the state on Saturdays. It's pretty low-key. You ought to come play with us."

Something sparked in Robert. "Maybe I will. What time?"

"Usually around seven," Steve said as he approached Billy Ray and Robert, "you ought to come."

"We'll see," was all Robert could muster.

Wednesday evening, Robert pushed himself out the door and drove to the gym where the Simpson boys said they were playing. He saw them immediately, and they trotted over to welcome him. The brothers introduced him to the group. They played basketball for a couple of hours in the old, rented gymnasium. Before he left, Robert agreed to join them for a game in a neighboring town on Saturday.

It was a cold, frosty morning in January and the teenagers loaded up in two twelve passenger vans. There was plenty of room to spread out, but Robert made sure he made room for Carla—who was there to play on the girls' team—and she was glad he did.

They talked, which was what they did best. They talked about music, cars, relationships, and anything else they found interesting. Even after these four months, they never tired of being together. The two youths from completely different backgrounds had quickly formed a tight bond.

They had become as inseparable as two kindergarten friends.

Robert enjoyed spending time at Carla's house. At first, her family found him to be socially inept and slightly uncouth, but over time, had discovered in him a good heart and a steady soul. Robert enjoyed the atmosphere at her house. Even though her father was slightly unapproachable, Robert could see the love that Carla and her siblings had for him and thus surmised he must have some good qualities underneath all his gravitas. Mrs. Morton gave an *Ozzie and Harriet* feel to the household. She worked hard at being a homemaker and was very good at it. Their house was complete. He felt great essence in the Morton home.

The day was good. Robert enjoyed the basketball game, but days later, he could not even remember the score. The highlight of the day had been cheering for Carla as she drove her five-foot figure down the court to score a layup. He was so proud of her. He enjoyed the day mostly because of how at home he felt with the people he was around. They welcomed him with open arms. He did not feel judged because of his background or appearance.

When they returned to the church where they had left their cars, Carla asked for a ride home from Robert.

They climbed into the Pontiac and Robert immediately chose an eight-track tape to listen to. He chose the *Masque* album of *Kansas,* which he had just discovered and wanted to share with Carla. They stopped by the Sonic drive-in on Fourth Street—enjoyed a couple of coney dogs—and talked while the engine ran to keep warm. The full moon was peeking periodically between the flowing clouds.

It was eleven o'clock when they arrived at her house. The house was dark except for the light in her parents' room—her mother always waited up for her.

Robert hadn't parked his car in the Morton driveway since her dad had seen the oil leaks his Pontiac had left. After he pulled his car up next to the curb and parked, he got out to say goodnight to her. He leaned back against the fender of the car to watch her walk to the door as he had done dozens of times before.

"I hope you had fun today, Robert," she said as she gave him a goodnight hug.

"I really did," he responded as they released. "I really, really did."

She said goodnight and then walked toward the house. Halfway between the house and car, she stopped. She stood there on the lawn for a few seconds and then turned around and walked back. She was walking with a little apprehension, biting one of her fingernails.

"What's up, buddy?" he asked. She smiled when he called her that. It so defined their relationship.

She paused a little more, then spoke. "I need to say something to you, Robert."

Robert discerned some seriousness in her tone. "Ok, what's going on?"

"You know I'm great at saying what's on my mind. It's usually not a problem." She was right. Carla generally said whatever was on her mind. "But tonight, I'm having to force myself.

"I have gotten so close to you so fast," she continued. "I feel I could tell you anything, as if you'll understand everything I'm feeling."

"As we always say, our relationship is a big, yummy bean bag chair, so easy and so comfortable." Robert added.

"Now I'm starting to feel some confusing feelings."

"Like what?" Robert asked, worried bad news was coming.

"I am having a hard time pushing back feelings that have been building for some time now. Robert, I think I want to be more than friends. I think I am falling for you."

Her words pleasantly shocked Robert, but he didn't interrupt because it was going in a great direction.

"When I moved here, I had no intention of getting involved with anyone. After all, I'm going to be leaving in the fall to go to college, so Russellville was just somewhere to be for a year.

"Then I met you! You slipped into my life out of nowhere and became someone very important to me.

"Now I feel like ... " she paused. "I'll go ahead and say it. Like I'm falling in love."

There it was, out on the table.

Robert had romantic feelings for a long time, but had squelched them for fear of messing up a good thing. Now his waiting was apparently paying off. If teenaged boys can be described as being giddy, that's what he was.

"Please say something, Robert," she pleaded.

Robert thoughtfully started. "Carla, I've lived a hard life. I've lived a lonely life. When you came along, I couldn't believe that I could be so lucky to even know you.

"For a while now, I've felt stronger about you than I have let on. I didn't want to lose you, so I just decided to keep those feelings to myself and enjoy what was.

"You're the best! I say I love you a lot because it comes so easy to me, but I really do love you." Robert finished up.

They hugged, but this hug was different. It was a new hug, a first hug.

After they held each other for several minutes, Carla spoke. "I might as well see this thing through, Robert. Would you think I was too forward if I kissed you?"

She initiated the kiss, leaning into him and slightly opening her lips. It was a passionate first kiss that left everything they had pent up flowing between them. After the kiss, they hugged again and held onto each other. Although they didn't want to let this momentous occasion end, they also didn't want her dad to come out. So, they said goodnight, and she walked to the door and inside.

As she entered the house, Robert noticed the curtain in her parents' window was moving. He wondered what discussion was going on inside.

Robert drove home that night wanting to celebrate. He had never had a girlfriend—it had been his first kiss. As he drove, he childishly kissed the back of his hand, trying to relive the moment.

After driving into his yard, he saw a light was still on. His mom was up sitting in the front room, finishing up a movie on the *Late, Late Show*.

"Hello son, how was your day?" she asked sincerely.

"It was really good, Mom." He replied.

"I'm glad. Well, I'm tired and going to head to bed."

"Mom," he paused until she stopped and turned around, "Carla and I are dating now." He wasn't sure why it was so hard to say the words or why it embarrassed him to tell her. Robert had not established a relationship with his mom that allowed for revealing feelings.

"Oh, my little boy has a girlfriend!" She said, making him feel as if he was ten. She hugged him—although he wasn't sure quite why. "Carla is a nice girl, although you don't bring her around much."

Olivia proceeded to bed, leaving her son in the living room alone. He continued to sit in the chair, reliving the events of the day. This had been a good day. A really good day! As he thought back to the best days of his life—and it didn't feel as if there were many—it didn't surprise him to realize most of them had occurred in the last few months and included Carla.

Under his mattress in his room, lay a bottle of *Jim Beam*. He had ignored it for many days now, and tonight it wasn't needed either. Maybe it wouldn't be needed at all this winter and then the daffodils would appear in spring.

Randy Judd

Chapter 29

Arkansas winters are unpredictable.

Sometimes a winter will generate an icy chill from the time the foliage starts falling until the first daffodil blooms around the foundation of a long-abandoned homestead. In those years there will be snow, rain, and freezing rain—sometimes all on the same day. Ice storms, with their crystal coverage of all things horizontal, are the worst. They can cripple a town as traffic ceases, tree limbs snap and downed power lines refuse to yield their electric life.

The very next year, the winter could just as easily be pleasant. There are years when the mercury seldom falls below freezing. In these winters, new coats remain on the racks at Wal-Mart untouched for the season. They are quickly marked down for clearance. It's not unheard of to watch temperatures rise to the eighties for a day or two in February.

Most winters, though, are somewhere in between. A cold spell for a while yielding to an Indian summer, then back to cold again.

In late February—as Robert's car meandered down a country back road—it pleased him to see hundreds of daffodils populating a small field. Daffodils were Robert's favorite. To him, their bright yellow petals emanating from the tall center stigma resembled the sun itself. They were a sign. He picked them every year for his mom. Now an additional woman would be the recipient.

Robert and Carla's bond continued to build until their souls seemed to be woven together. Their love—which began as a friendship—had grown into something that most teenagers never experience. It was not simply puppy love infatuation, rooted in a purely hormonal foundation. They couldn't have realized it, but the two of them had stumbled into a love that was extraordinary—deeper than many adults ever experience.

Robert could easily imagine himself being married to Carla so he could enjoy her laughter forever. Carla admired his heart and his integrity.

As the weather warmed and basketball season wound down, Robert missed his association with the other youth at church. So, when Carla invited him to come to Sunday services with her, it was a simple choice. He found things at church that he had been yearning for all his life. Some things he could define—acceptance, friends, fun, and structure. Some things, though, he had trouble defining—the good feelings he felt, the new determination to live a better life, the envelopment of love he felt from an unseen source. All these things—defined and undefined—made the church a place he wanted to be.

The more time he spent developing these feelings, the less time he needed his bottle. After dropping Carla off after church one particular Sunday, he returned home and poured out the remaining half of his bottle. For the time being, he no longer needed his liquid support.

After school, one day in March, the two picked up some sandwiches and drove to the lake for a picnic. As they finished eating, Robert laid his head down on Carla's lap.

A few minutes of small talk passed when Robert realized how unusually hot it was for March. He sat up and, without thinking, took off his shirt to cool.

Carla had never seen him from the back without his shirt and immediately gasped at the sight of all the burn scars on Robert's back.

"Oh Robert, what are those scars from?"

Having forgotten for a moment about his mutilated back, he quickly pulled his shirt back over his head and pulled it down to cover the view.

"I'd rather not talk about it, Carla. At least not yet."

From his statement, she could tell that her boyfriend had secrets he was not ready to disclose and at this point, she would not push it. She felt, though—in time—she would learn his mysteries.

He laid his head back on her lap, watching the new leaves dance above them.

"Guess what?" she asked, then continued with the answer without much pause. "I got accepted into BYU. I got my letter today!" She tried to sound excited, but knowing how Robert felt, she also said it gingerly.

"That's great, Carla! I'm so proud of you." he said, forcing the words. "I know that's what you wanted. I'm sure glad it's six months away, though."

Neither Robert nor Carla was naïve enough to think things would always remain as they were. They had often talked about the future, but it was always somewhere … *in the future*. Neither one wanted to think about it actually happening. The thought hurt too much. Having lived most of her life in Utah, she had dreamed of going back to attend college with her friends. She was smart—a four-point grade point average—so they knew all along getting accepted would not be a problem. He loved her so much; he couldn't hold her back. He had thought about moving to Utah with her. Everything right now was so muddled in Robert's mind. Carla's future was quite defined. Her boyfriend's wasn't.

"I'm glad too," Carla responded. "Let's make the best of our last months as kids!"

They sat for a little while in silence. The spring birds were chirping quite loudly and a bass boat buzzed with the sound of a mosquito across the lake.

"Robert, we've talked off and on about letting the missionaries teach you about our church. I really want you to let them teach you. I want to share with you completely some of the things that make me who I am."

"I don't know Carla." Robert hesitated. "Going to church is something so foreign to me. I didn't do it much growing up. I enjoy going with you, but I'm not sure I'm ready to commit to anything."

"Robert, you feel good when you're there, don't you?"

Robert couldn't disagree with that.

"Wouldn't you want to feel that way all the time?" She asked.

"You mean even when I'm not with you at church? Well, sure!"

"My faith is soooo important to me," she continued. "It's who I am. It defines me. I want you to know that same happiness."

"Carla, even though we talk all the time, you know there are things about my past that I am not willing to share." Robert confided as he had before. "I'm not sure a God would want me to be a part of His church."

"Robert, stop that!" She chastised. "I know you pretty darn well. You're kind, loving, and gentle. You've got a great soul. You're better than most of the people over there at church."

He thought a little more. "Maybe there *is* something to what y'all have over there. I guess it wouldn't hurt anything if I just talked to those missionary guys."

The following night, Robert met with the Mormon missionaries at the Morton house. Carla's whole family sat around the living room while the young men—barely older than Robert—sold him their wares.

By this time, Robert already had a basic understanding of what his friends believed. Robert found the missionaries to be intriguing. The two young men—

one from Utah and the other from California—had left their families at the age of nineteen of their own free will to do this. He knew they spent most of their time knocking on doors, trying to share their faith. He also knew that his own friends—Steve and Billy Ray—planned on serving missions when they got to the magical age of nineteen. It certainly intrigued Robert how they could interrupt their lives to do this. He actually admired it.

Over the next several weeks, Robert met with the missionaries. He developed a kinship with the two men, although he had come from a completely different world than they had.

Randy Judd

Chapter 30

A boy knows that he is becoming a man when decisions become life altering. The spring of 1978 was revealing itself to be one of those times for Robert. Soon he would graduate, the first in the Rhodes line. He felt proud to have endured so much. He knew he would need to make life decisions soon. Should he consider college? The idea certainly intrigued him. His grades were sufficient, and he had taken the ACT and SAT just in case.

Another decision before him was one of much more eternal consequences. Several weeks into the missionary lessons, the missionaries challenged him to think about joining their church. Baptism was the gateway to membership. It was a commitment not to be taken lightly. The two explained to him that getting baptized and joining the church required some sacrifices and commitments. He would be expected to pay tithing to the church, attend meetings, be sexually abstinent, and abstain from coffee, tea, and tobacco. Even though he loved his mom's sweet tea, these all seemed doable. They also told him they would expect him to refrain from alcohol. This was a hard decision for Robert. He had never revealed to anyone his struggle with the bottle. He had no doubt he could continue to hide it and they would not know. Since he had emptied the bottle down the drain, he drank only occasionally, but for the first time in his life,

Robert felt he was answering to a higher power. Could he hide his habit from God? No, he finally realized.

When one's actions come into conflict with one's beliefs, either changing the behavior or denying the beliefs are the only ways to soften the internal struggle. Robert was weak and diminishing his beliefs was the easier way out. The liquor would win again. He didn't feel he was capable of giving up his current master for a new one.

After church the next Sunday, Robert walked his sweetheart to the door. The newly mowed grass left a refreshing aroma in the Morton front yard. Robert had been practicing how he would tell her. No way was going to be easy. *How would she respond?* He knew she had high hopes of him becoming a member of her faith and living a life resembling hers. He knew he couldn't tell her about his downfall. It would be much too embarrassing, and he feared he would lose her—although he underestimated her compassion.

They stopped and sat on her porch swing. With his arm around her, the chain creaked as they swayed rhythmically back and forth. Her head was resting on his chest.

"Carla," He began. "I need to tell you something."

"OK, what's up?"

"I've been thinking about things lately, about your church," he continued.

"It could be your church too," she teased. "Just say the word!"

"Well, that's the thing. I don't think I can say the word. I don't think I can do it—At least not now."

The swing stopped. Carla lifted her head and looked at him. "Well, when do you think you can, then?"

"That's just it. I don't know if I ever can. I believe it, at least I think I do, but I'm not sure it's right for me."

Carla was uncharacteristically quiet.

"Carla, I love you. I would do anything for you. If you tell me to join the Mormon Church, I will do it! I'm just not sure that's the right reason."

Even though he didn't want to look at Carla, her breathing let him know she was crying. "I'm sorry, Babe. I hope you'll understand"

Wiping her nose with her sleeve, Carla said, "Robert, it must be your decision. You can't do it just because I want you to. I just hoped … "

Carla stood up, kissed him on the forehead, and said, "I need to go think for a while."

As she walked into the house, Robert found himself confused at the reaction. He assumed she would be disappointed, but he had expected they would talk about it. Talking was what they did best.

Robert walked defeated to his GTO, wondering what the future held for them.

Inside the house, Carla's mom passed her as she came in the door. Seeing her daughter's tears, she stopped to find the root of Carla's consternation.

Carla explained to her mother the conversation that had taken place on the porch.

As Mrs. Morton grabbed her daughter's shoulders, Carla assumed it was to pull her close for comfort, as she had done so many times before. Instead, Mom held her at arm's length, one hand on each shoulder. Carla looked up at her mother, confused.

Mom began with a stern reprimand. "Young Lady, I don't think we raised you that way!"

"Wh … What?" was all Carla could summon.

"Carla, you don't just turn away from someone who has just made such a heart wrenching decision," Mom explained. "Robert has made one of the most difficult decisions of his young life and you have punished him for sharing with you!"

"Punished him?"

"Yes, punished him. You let him know by your actions that his decision was wrong, or at least his decision to tell you was wrong." Mrs. Morton paused, then continued, "I've watched you over the last several months. You really care for Robert, don't you?"

"Yes, of course I do."

"Would you want him to join the church even though he didn't feel it in his heart?"

"Of course not, Mom," Carla replied. "I just want so bad for him to know the happiness in his life we know. He had an unhappy childhood. This is a significant chance for him to see a change."

"It is a significant change, you're right. But it's got to be his decision and no one else's. Otherwise, he will resent you for pushing him into it. Maybe not immediately, but he will carry it deep inside and one day it will reveal itself and he won't like you very much.

"Let me ask you a deeper question. Do you love him?"

Without hesitation, she replied, "I do, mom, more than I've loved anyone. Robert is my love, yes, but he is more than that. He is my buddy, my friend."

"Well, Carla, right now your *buddy* is driving home very confused." Mom dispensed her wisdom. "He is wondering if he made the right decision, even if it did come from his heart. He is wondering how mad you are at him. But most of all, he's wondering if you were his friend just to get him to join the church."

"Oh, no." Carla whispered. "I don't want him to think that of me."

"Then go to him now!" Mrs. Morton implored. "Take the car and go!"

Carla took the Ford Station Wagon and headed toward Robert's home on Norristown Mountain—hopeful he *had* gone home.

When Robert arrived home, he didn't go into the house. He sat on the cement porch as he had done hundreds of times in the last decade. The first time he sat here as a five-year-old, his legs dangled, but now they easily pushed on the grass below.

As the car coming down the road slowed, the pitch of the tires on pavement lowered. Robert looked up to see the familiar green station wagon with faux wood paneling pull in.

He had enjoyed this sight so many times before and his heart still jumped a little in memory, hoping it wouldn't be the last.

Carla had not changed out of her church clothes. The silky teal dress with ruffles around the hem fit her so well. It was one of his favorites—which, of course—was the major reason she wore it.

After exiting her car, she walked gingerly toward him. He stood, and she ran to him, throwing her arms around his neck. Laying her head on him, her tears moistened his shoulder.

Carla was repeating the words, "I'm sorry," between her gentle sobs.

Robert sat her down on the porch in the same area Lou had confided in him last summer. He snuggled up beside her, holding both her hands in between his.

As her crying diminished, she began to speak to him. "Robert, I was so selfish a while ago. I was only thinking about what I wanted, not about you. I was wrong. If this is something you don't feel you should do—don't do it!"

She continued, "I want you to be happy. I pray there will come a day when you will be ready, but when that day comes, make sure you aren't doing it for anyone but yourself.

"My parents raised me to judge people by their character, not by what religion they were. Even if someone has no religion, they can still be good.

"I know you're good deep down inside, Robert. You're a good man, Robert Rhodes, and I love you!"

Robert pulled her closer, and she laid her head on his chest.

In the coming days, Robert continued to attend church but ceased to meet with the missionaries. Church was still where he felt most at home. He loved the relationships he shared there. Robert Rhodes started to respect the person he was evolving into. He started to feel feelings of hope for his life. Success seemed to be a possibility for the Rhodes boy.

The summer after high school, which can be both magnificent and imposing, is a defining time in life. All that is small has been conquered and all that lies before seems daunting—but achievable.

Robert and Carla used the summer to refine their relationship. They rarely spent a waking moment apart, knowing that before them was an event rarely spoken of between them. In late August, Carla would be leaving for school. As the time approached, they accepted that time would not stand still; therefore, the approaching day was inevitable.

They discussed the future, their plans for writing daily or at least weekly. Promises were made and touches remembered. As the dreaded day approached, Robert felt a pain so real and so deep, he thought he might not survive. Carla too felt the longing, but having a more pollyannaish view, thought if their love was meant to continue, it would survive the separation.

They talked about their relationship, how it meant more to them than they could've imagined. Although their relationship was also very physical, it was based on emotion and love. Carla loved to kiss her man, and she felt safe in his arms. They had been careful not to cross the ultimate physical line—mostly out of respect for Carla, but Robert longed to someday be able to make love with her.

The night before she left, they lay on the grass in her backyard looking at the stars—neither one seeing them. At that moment, Robert thought Carla was possibly the most perfect person ever. He thought of his childhood growing up in the Ozarks. He recollected his fragile time as a pre-teen. He struggled through the memories of his teenage years full of loneliness and depression. He had wondered what he had done to deserve this wonderful young lady lying beside him. He didn't know why; he just knew he regarded her as a miracle.

The twenty-first day of August was a scorching day in the Arkansas River Valley. Robert helped Carla load her suitcases into the back of another freshman's car. As the thermometer's mercury soared to the century mark, Robert watched the most amazing person he had ever known disappear around a curve on her way to her future; a future in which he yearned to be included.

Randy Judd

Chapter 31

Robert found Santa Fe intriguing. Thirteen years before the pilgrims landed at Plymouth Rock, settlers established Santa Fe. As the oldest capital in the United States, there were still buildings in use that were hundreds of years old. With the coral-colored adobe as the canvas, it was no wonder the area has one of the highest concentrations of artists in the country.

Although he found it interesting, the dry, high desert landscape was not pleasing to Robert's palate. He yearned for the humid air of Arkansas, which caused the foliage to grow so deep green. He had chances to move elsewhere, but always remained close to his roots, along with his brother and sister.

By this time, William and Mary had their third child, giving Robert two nieces and a nephew to love—and he did. Playing with them caused him to want to have a family someday. That was his dream—to marry Carla and build a family. Will still played his drums periodically with local bands, but only for fun. He had survived his journey into adulthood safely.

Lou returned to Russellville not long after serving six months for solicitation and drug possession. Luckily, the prosecutor reduced the charges to misdemeanors. She was a waitress at the *Old South Restaurant,* living mostly off tips.

Although Robert wanted to just curl up in a ball and ache for Carla, he knew he had to get on with life. He only worked part time at *Motel 6* and he knew he should be more accountable for his time. A friend helped him get a full-time job at the frozen food factory in town where he worked. Robert's new job was to mix large batches of dough—six hundred pounds at a time. This dough was used to make tortillas which wrapped frozen burritos.

The young man enjoyed work. He volunteered for overtime hours whenever he could. Staying busy prevented him from thinking about Carla too much. He still thought of her constantly, but the thoughts of her weren't debilitating when he was being productive.

At work, he enjoyed the relationships he was establishing. The factory workers were similar to the blue-collar folks he had grown up around. He fit in well with this element. In the break room of the plant, he ate lunch with a diverse group of people. They enjoyed teasing the young boy about his puppy love girlfriend away at college. One night, he passed her senior picture around the table. Her blonde hair, blue eyes and delicious smile were sure to wow them.

Robert found himself hurt when one of the women in the group said, "She's cute alright, but nothing special."

NOTHING SPECIAL?! The statement shocked him. *How* could you consider someone so magnificent as nothing special? As Robert sat cupping the picture in his hands, he looked at his love. Though to the group of workers, she wasn't Cheryl Tiegs—to him, she was even better. To recognize Carla's beauty, one had to know Carla. A person couldn't stand in front of her and be enveloped in her divine smile and not think she was gorgeous. When one was with her in a group and watched her delicately make everyone feel important, one could see her magnificence. With a touch of the soft skin of her cheek, her goodness and splendor immediately enveloped them. To truly know of Carla's exquisiteness, one had to know Carla. No picture could capture her animated perfection.

Because of the cost of long-distance calls, the two young lovers only talked once per week. They spoke on Saturday morning when the rates were lowest. They also wrote at least weekly. She scented her letters with *Babe*—his favorite perfume. He always opened her letters slowly and savored the words on the paper.

From her calls and letters, Robert could tell that Carla was finding her niche. Not only had she met up with old friends from Utah, but as a freshman coed, the dorms were full of excitement. Although Robert was happy for her, he was also slightly jealous that she didn't need him to have fun.

Before she left, the two of them came to an agreement—with hesitation from Robert—that they were free to date other people while they were apart. As Carla had so craftily explained, *it would help them realize the great relationship they had with each other.* Robert didn't feel he needed to date others to prove to himself, but he wouldn't dare hold her back.

He wondered sometimes if he was worthy of someone so great as the girl in Utah. With a little introspection, he also wondered why he didn't feel worthy. He wondered if his feeling of low self-worth was rooted in his childhood and especially in his horrible experiences with Ricky Goodman. Robert had seen an interview on television with a lady who had written a book about abusers. She said most abusers had been abused as a child. Although she hadn't said it was a root cause, Robert worried that somewhere inside he was a monster capable of Ricky-like actions.

Robert's friendship with Steve and Billy Ray became even stronger, and he was glad he finally had good, strong friends who wanted to be with him as well. The three were together constantly after school and on weekends. They played a lot of basketball and tennis. Robert and Steve were both out of school now, and Billy Ray was a senior. Steve was in his freshman year at Arkansas Tech University in Russellville. He was planning to attend until he went on his church mission when he turned nineteen.

Even though Robert had not joined the boys' faith, he still attended events with them and went to church with them on Sunday. His friends did not pressure him into being baptized into the church, but other members of the congregation asked when he would take the plunge. For the most part, he felt he was living the precepts taught by their church. They jokingly called him a *Dry Mormon*, because the only thing he lacked was getting into the waters of baptism.

Even though the three boys had individual standards and morals, they were often tempted as teenage boys. The two Simpson boys were tall, handsome, and athletic and because of this, there were always girls willing to be with them. An interesting dynamic developed between the friends. Whenever one of them was weak, whether it was because of sex, drinking, partying, or even experimenting with drugs, the other two were in a sane enough place to strengthen their fragile friend. They unconsciously took turns being the weak one and the strong two. With this supportive pattern, they were generally able to escape the snares of youthful indiscretions.

Robert started feeling cautiously optimistic about his drinking problem. His need to trust the bottle came with less frequency and less intensity. As 1978 neared its end, the eighteen-year-old made a brave decision. He took the bottle of *Jim Beam* that lay hidden under his mattress and threw it in the garbage to be picked up that day. Even though there was less than a fourth of a bottle of the golden liquid, he didn't want it to be accessible. Although he had vowed to quit several times before, he felt surprisingly optimistic about his decision this time.

On their weekly call on the first week of December, Carla told Robert she would not be returning to Arkansas for Christmas.

"What do you mean, you won't be back? You've got to come back." Robert pleaded pathetically.

"Oh Robert, it'll be ok. I'm just going to spend it with Laura. You remember, my best friend from high school?" Carla tried to soothe.

"But I've missed you so much. The only way I've been able to make it is by knowing you'd be back in a few weeks. I can't stop thinking about you, Sweetie. You belong back here with me, your boyfriend. I love you; don't you love me?" Robert's supplication was not appealing to Carla. The appeal seamed possessive and full of insecurity. Being needy was not an attractive trait.

"Look, Robert. Of course, I love you. I've only been gone a few months. We'll be able to see each other when I come back for spring break." Carla assured him.

"I can't wait that long. Maybe I'll come out there and see you." He suggested.

"I don't think that would be good, Robert," Carla said. "It would cost a lot to fly out here and you wouldn't have anywhere to stay. After all, you probably couldn't get the time off at the factory since you just started."

She was right about the factory, he thought. His friend had pulled strings to get him hired. He couldn't just leave. "But I'm desperate to see you, Carla."

"I'd love to see you too, but the time will come soon. You'll see."

Robert couldn't help but think that the nature of her voice was less loving, less passionate. Something felt different.

231

As they hung up the phone, Robert wanted to look for a bottle like he had thrown away weeks before, but he didn't. Maybe he had overcome his vice after all. As he lay on his back, watching the shadows on the ceiling of his bedroom, his heart ached ominously.

After Christmas, thoughts turned to the birth of a new year. Amongst the thoughts of renewal and resolutions, Robert thought seriously about his own future. He had ample time to think, during his time mixing dough, while the roar of the machinery masked all other sounds. He enjoyed the hard work at the factory. Lifting the fifty-pound sacks of flour night after night had given him an upper body workout. Although physically he was being rewarded, he knew he wanted the ability to use his mind as well. Watching the machinery associated with the assembly lines, he became intrigued with the workings of the equipment and wondered who had designed these single-use million-dollar apparatuses.

The young man became acquainted with the plant engineer, who made nightly rounds examining and tweaking the equipment. The man took an interest in Robert and encouraged him to go to college.

Robert Rhodes began to take the steps to get registered for the fall semester at Arkansas Tech University. This action concerned his parents—he had a good job at the plant and should not jeopardize his union standing.

He did enjoy the hard work and had no intention of quitting immediately. If he were to go to school, he would still have to work to pay for school and support himself. His parents had required him to pay rent since he was sixteen and the amount had increased once he graduated. So, he knew that if he were going to enjoy the privilege of college, it would include working full time along the way.

One coworker seemed to take an extra interest in him. Maggie had introduced herself to Robert a few weeks after he began working there. Over the next few weeks, it was obvious that she had some curiosity about him.

Maggie had little in common with Carla. Maggie Morrison was twenty-two years old and, as such, was an older woman to the newly graduated Robert. She was not the pure, religious girl that Carla was, and Maggie reveled in that fact. Her hair was big. Every morning, she took pride in ratting her curls and sprayed them with aerosol until the mane stood up on its own. Robert couldn't be exactly sure of the color. He thought it once had been brunette, but the chemicals and dyes she used had turned it into a somewhat copper color.

Robert thought Maggie had an impressive body. Her womanly curves were ample and well placed. At work, she wore her white work uniform about two sizes too small, which made it hug every contour the girl had to offer. She conveniently left the top two buttons of her shirt open so that, while standing, there was just a hint of cleavage. When she leaned over—even the slightest bit—every man in the room turned for a chance. She leaned forward a lot around Robert.

Robert enjoyed flirting with Maggie because, as far as he was concerned, it was harmless. Carla had revealed just enough for Robert to know she was actively dating at school. Robert hoped in the end, their dating other people would only solidify their own relationship.

Maggie knew he had a girlfriend away at college. She had seen Carla's picture, but that made him that much more desirable. Maggie wasn't especially interested in commitment. Getting him to forget about Carla would be good sport and she could get what she wanted in the meantime.

At first, the two sat in the break room with a large group of workers, but after a few weeks, they spent their lunch time sitting at a corner table, flirting, and talking with innuendo.

A few weeks into their pseudo-relationship, Maggie found out something about Robert which heightened her interest.

"So, did you and this Carla girl get it on much?" Maggie crassly asked. Robert was evasive in his reply. "Hey, you know a gentleman doesn't tell those kinds of things."

"Hah! I've never known a man—gentleman or not—that doesn't delight in sharing the details of the girls he's been with," she replied.

"Well, not me. I'm not that way. I've got class," Robert said defensively.

"Ah, come on," She pressed, "tell me about it. Where did you first do it? In the back of your GTO? At her parents' house? On a picnic table at the lake?"

Suddenly, Robert felt as if he was betraying Carla's integrity. She prided herself in her chastity and if he let Maggie assume anything, he would be betraying her.

"Actually," He paused, "we never had sex. It was against our … her religion."

"Are you serious?" Maggie asked incredulously. "You dated almost a year and you never …?"

With an ironic mixture of embarrassment and pride, he answered, "No, we didn't. We agreed not to."

"Geez, how could you not? I mean, you must've wanted to, at least some time."

Robert knew that a girl with her scruples could not understand concepts such as fidelity, honor, self-control, so he didn't even try to explain. He just smiled innocently at the worldly woman in front of him.

As the blaring horn signaled the end of lunch, they picked up their lunch pails and headed toward the lockers.

With her disbelief fully disclosed, she continued, "Well, we're going to have to get you laid."

"Oh, are you now?" he said flirtingly.

Jezebel contrived.

Chapter 32

O ne of the reasons that Robert enjoyed the flirtatious nature of the relationship was that he had started to get less fulfillment out of the long-distance relationship that existed between Carla and him.

Their Saturday conversations became sporadic. Her roommates knew Robert's voice well and felt reluctant to tell him she was not there—again. When they talked, she tried to avoid the deep conversations that they had loved so much in Arkansas. Instead, she kept the conversation very superficial. Robert, worried that the relationship was slipping and not knowing how to handle the situation, became increasingly possessive of her. This attitude did not endear him to her.

On Tuesday, after the most recent call—one that ended especially poorly—Robert walked toward his car after work.

"Hey Robert, wait up!" Maggie shouted as she hurried toward him.

In her street clothes, she looked even more inviting. Even in early March, she wore fashionable short shorts, which made her shapely legs look even longer. From behind, the men stared because her blue jean shorts revealed so much. She tied her blue polka-dot shirt at the bottom and had cleavage escaping the top. As she trotted toward him, the natural man in him enjoyed the rhythmic bouncing of the polka-dots.

As she caught up with him, not winded at all from the quick jog, she spoke, "Hey, a bunch of us are getting together Saturday night at *PJ's Bar* up in Morrilton, do you wanna come?"

Russellville was in Pope County and the county was dry—no alcohol was sold anywhere. To get alcohol, a person had to travel to Morrilton, about twenty-five miles down the freeway toward Little Rock.

Robert was familiar with *PJ's Bar*. It was a honkey-tonk which sat across the street from one of the liquor stores he used to frequent once he turned eighteen and could partake legally.

He replied without really thinking, "Naw, I'd better not. I got some things I wanted to do Saturday."

"Come on, Robbie. It'll be a blast!" Her plea was persuasive.

"I already promised my brother I'd help him move." He lied.

"I think you're afraid of me," she taunted. "You don't think you'll be able to resist me? Either that or those Mormons really got to you and you can't let yourself have any fun."

"Oh, you think you know everything about me, don't you, Maggie?"

"I know a certain boy who needs to be shown how to have a little fun."

He said goodbye, got in his car, and drove away.

Lying in bed that night, instead of thinking of Carla, he was pondering polka-dots.

The next few days were laced with an odd feeling around Robert. He couldn't determine whether the feeling was foreboding or downright ominous. He avoided his friends and chose instead to be around family as much as possible. In a spontaneous moment, Robert decided to go fishing with his parents as they headed out the door. Larry and Olivia were delighted to have their son along—although he wasn't much company. He sat on a rock with his red and white bobber surfing the small waves of Lake Dardanelle in an area known as the Strip Pits.

Larry leisurely approached his son and struck up a conversation.

The years had been difficult on the father-son relationship. This gulf was due mostly to the typical teenage rebellion against parents rather than any lack of respect on either person's part. Robert loved his dad. He cherished the memories of the things they had done together over the years. At least once per year, they went hunting together among the hardwoods of the Ozarks. They hunted for squirrel and deer. Robert wasn't necessarily a fan of the sport. He was, however, enamored with spending the time with his dad and learning from his hillbilly wisdom.

Because of his immaturity, Robert had not always been kind to his father. The large age difference between the two had been a source of embarrassment to the boy. As a teenager, Robert was gone so much that he often avoided his dad altogether. Even though Robert wouldn't always give his dad the feedback he deserved, secretly, he cherished the advice that Larry dispensed.

Often, he delivered the wisdom with a direct provocation, but other times he gave it amid humor. Still, other times, it was accompanied by a wink and a nod. The son was even taken back sometimes by the candor of his dad's comments. Robert often smiled at his dad's folksy words of wisdom.

Now, sitting on the banks of the lake, Robert had been secretly hoping to get some time with his dad. As Dad approached, his son slid aside on the rock where he was sitting.

"There's not much bitin' today, is there?" Dad broke the ice. "I bet because it's been raining and muddied up the waters."

"Yeah, probably," Robert responded quietly. "I guess I was hoping for some catfish, though. They usually don't care how muddy it is."

Robert reeled in his line to check his worm. Seeing that the worm was untouched, he took his bobber off the line so the bait would go to the bottom where the catfish swam. After recasting and being satisfied with the line's placement, he sat back down on the rock.

"How's things going at the plant, son?"

"Pretty good, Dad," Robert replied. "I like the work. It pushes me. It's pretty fun and I enjoy the people I work with."

"It's important to enjoy your work, and it's a bonus to like the people you work with," Dad said. "I think I've told you before, but if not, shame on me. You're a good worker, son. You always have been."

The dad's words gave his son a warm feeling inside.

Larry continued, "You've never had a problem going to work, even while you were going to high school full-time. Not many kids your age could do that."

"Thanks for noticing, Dad." Robert sheepishly replied.

In an instant, the back-patting was over, but that was ok. The supportive words from his dad would sustain the son for months. Larry changed the subject.

"So, how's that cute Carla doing at school?"

Even though their relationship had been all-encompassing for the boy, he had tried to protect Carla from examining his home life too closely. He was subconsciously worried that some detail would slip out to embarrass him or appall Carla.

"Ok, I guess. She doesn't call as much as I had hoped."

"Yeah, it's hard when they're away. Some say absence makes the heart go fonder, but sometimes it can also make the heart go wander."

"It's hard, Dad. I never thought I would ever feel the way I did … do about Carla. But now I'm not sure what's happening between us."

"Do you think she is dating other guys?"

"Yeah, I'm pretty sure she is."

"Then maybe you should play the field a little too, son. If it's right that you and Carla are together, you'll end up together." Larry felt confident in his advice. "Have you got your eye on anyone?"

Robert had never been comfortable talking to his parents about girls. Maybe it was because he had never felt completely at ease with his parents about anything.

"Well, there's this girl at work. I think she is interested in me."

"Tell me about her."

"Well, she's more like us than Carla was. Her parents are poor farmers. She dropped out of school and went to work at the plant."

"Well, maybe you ought to give her a shot. You never know."

They heard a commotion down the bank. The father-son bonding moment was over. Mom had hooked a fish, and both men moved down the bank to admire her trophy.

The talk had been good for both men. It confirmed their relationship for another few months, at least.

Robert watched his mom and dad interact. His parents had stopped just co-existing and had developed a great relationship now that they were approaching their golden years. Although they passed through years of fighting, their perseverance had led them back into love. Robert hoped he could someday experience what they had.

The day had started out warm, but as it progressed, winds from the south picked up, indicating an approaching low-pressure system. The wind's strength built until fishing was no longer fun. As the winds reversed direction, the temperature started to drop. It was easy to discern from the weather that a change was about to take place.

As the son sat beside his parents on the front bench seat of the Ford Pickup truck, they passed a field of newly bloomed daffodils. He remembered picking some last year for Carla. His heart ached for things to be the way they were then.

Chapter 33

On Saturday morning, Mom roused Robert out of his sleep, telling him Carla was on the phone. He rolled over to get the phone and saw by the clock that it was only nine o'clock, eight in Utah. They usually didn't talk until later in the morning.

Robert cleared his throat, then put the phone to his ear. "Good morning, babe. You're sure calling early this morning."

"Good morning, Robert. Yeah, I've got a pretty busy day today, so I thought I would call you early."

The small talk lasted for less than a minute when Carla dropped the bomb on him. "Robert, I need to talk to you about something serious."

Robert didn't see it coming. "Well, sure. What's up?"

"Robert, you have been great for me. You helped me when I moved back to Arkansas. I needed a friend, and you were a great one. We really had something great there, didn't we?"

Had? Robert thought.

"The only way I can say it, Robert, is getting right to the point, even though it's very hard for me." She paused. "Robert, I've found someone else and we'll be getting married in the summer."

He felt dizzy and short of breath.

"You can't be serious, Carla! I mean, sure, things have been a little offish between us, but we'll get it back when you come back here at spring break, you'll see. Besides, you couldn't have known this guy very long. What if he's not right for you?"

"I won't be coming back to Arkansas, Robert. This is my home now. He's my best friend's older brother and I've known him for years. He is a senior at BYU and we'll be getting married just as soon as he graduates. I'm sorry to have to tell you this way."

"But …?" He couldn't think of anything pertinent to say.

"I'll always cherish the time we spent together. It was really fun." Her words sounded patronizing.

"*Really fun?* They were the most amazing … you were the most amazing thing I could ever have in my life. Now you're just going to say goodbye?"

"I'm afraid so. It's for the best."

Silence

"Robert, there's really not much else to say. Telling you is one of the hardest things I've ever had to do." Then she finished with, "I hope we can still be friends."

He didn't even know how to answer that. He didn't want to be just friends. Just a year ago, she had given him a reason to exist. Now she wanted to disappear from his life.

"Can't we talk about this?" Robert pleaded.

"No, Robert. It's decided. Please don't make this any harder than it must be for me."

That may have been the first selfish thing he had ever heard her utter.

She concluded the call. "Robert, I have to go now. Try to understand that I wish you all the luck in the world. You're a great man. Bye Robert."

He muttered an ending and then hung up the phone. Lying there in his room, he didn't know what he was feeling. The gut punch he had just received was completely unexpected. All his future plans had included Carla. Now he couldn't see a future.

The rest of the Saturday, he languished, unable to see life in anything around him. He felt like swearing at people on the street that he saw smiling. He remembered the day during ninth grade when he had sat in the bathroom with his father's pistol.

He didn't want to talk to any of his family, so he stayed in his room until noon, showered, and then left for an unknown destination. He didn't want to go to Steve and Billy Ray's house. At least for the day, he wanted to be by himself.

The despondent man drove to Mt. Nebo outside of Dardanelle. After driving up many switchbacks, he arrived at the top and drove out to a lookout point. From his parking place on the edge of a cliff, he could see the forest stretch out many miles and beyond them, the Arkansas River and Lake Dardanelle.

Although it was mid-March, the cold front was moving in and the temperature was dropping quickly. No one else braved the elements on the top of the mountain, so he was alone. Robert had not brought a coat, resulting in his staying in the car with the radio on. Thoughts plowed through his head.

How could he have let himself get so wrapped up in his love for Carla? Hadn't he learned from the events of his childhood that he was not worthy of such a relationship? His time with Carla had been similar to winning the second-grade talent show, having the prize money taken from him. What had lulled him into thinking he was capable of having a life of pure happiness and a promising future? He had been so naïve.

245

On the radio, Neil Diamond sang *The Story of My Life* and Robert again felt the song was appropriate.

He felt shackled by who he was and where he came from. He started to wonder if the thoughts of going to college were futile. His inevitable failure would just be a waste of time and money. He should feel very lucky to even have the union job at the factory.

After a couple of hours sitting at the summit, Robert made his way back down the serpentine curves.

Chapter 34

The rest of the day slipped away and soon the overcast day turned dark. Robert wrestled with what he should do. In his depressed state, his yearning turned to his old crutch. He pulled onto I 40 and headed east for the liquor store in Morrilton. The temperature had continued to drop and now the drizzling rain produced a reflection on the black surface of the highway.

Pulling off the blacktop and onto the gravel parking lot of the familiar liquor store, he parked the GTO. As he sat there, all he could hear was the hum of his engine, the rhythmic squeaking of worn-out wipers, and the whiz of a car passing on the wet pavement behind him. He got out before he could question his decision.

As he neared the store, he glanced around, making sure to go unnoticed. Across U.S. 64, he saw the commotion of *PJ's Bar and Grill* and, in an instant, remembered Maggie's invitation. He stood there, deciding. He returned to his car and drove across the highway.

From the parking lot, he made his way toward the thumping of the music emanating from the building. The building itself was made of dark wood. On this night, the building seemed even darker as the wood planks absorbed the rain. There were no windows which would allow light during the day to ruin the ambiance. The only light on the outside was from a fading streetlight and the crackling neon sign gracing the front of the building. Parking was haphazard in the gravel lot.

As he entered the honky-tonk, a wall of cigarette smoke—even thicker than he had grown up with at home—greeted him. Mixed in with the cigarette smoke was a hint of herbs he had also become aware of from being around his siblings.

On a stage in the back of the large room was a band blasting out the county music melodies of Willy, Waylon, and others. The band needed to be loud to cover the noise of the crowd. Either that or the crowd needed to be loud to hear themselves over the band. Chicken or egg? Either way, the band and crowd escalated their way up to a country crescendo.

Looking around the room, Robert didn't recognize anyone. He made his way toward the pool tables, where he finally saw Maggie flirting with a couple of middle-aged men.

She was dressed much as she had been in the parking lot the day of the invitation. Though it was cold outside, she still donned her Daisy Duke shorts and a red-checkered top tied above her navel. Her blouse had one additional button undone for the evening, *her formal look*.

As she looked his way and recognized him through the haze, an impish smile came across her face. She gently pushed the two men aside and strutted toward Robert.

"Well, lookie who's here," she said. "Decided you wanted to come see me tonight, eh Robbie?"

"Where's the rest of the gang, Maggie?" Robert asked while looking around.

"Oh, they're around somewhere, but I'm all you really need to have a good time," she said in a sultry voice. As she spoke, she circled around him, lightly touching him with her index finger. "Do you need something to drink to get you loosened up?"

She went to the bar and returned with a beer for him. It was the first alcohol he had consumed in about a year. He didn't enjoy the taste of beer, though. It took too long to numb the pain. On his second round, he escalated to gin.

Even though he drank since he was in Junior High, it was always alone—in secret. He had never had alcohol socially and wondered how he would react. But now that he had tasted his demon, he wanted more. He wanted to numb the memory and pain associated with Carla.

Maggie pulled him out to the dance floor. He had danced a few times with Carla but had always felt self-conscious of his awkward moves. The band was on break, and jukebox music from recorded singers filled the room. The couple danced to *You've Been Talking in Your Sleep* by Crystal Gayle. Luckily, it was a slow song which didn't require any rhythmic prowess. Maggie pulled him close. In the midst of the cadenced swaying, he started getting excited for the woman he was with.

After the song, they walked to the back of the room where she held on tight to him while they talked flirtatiously. They spent the next hour cuddled up on some wooden chairs away from the light.

Standing up, she took his hand and pulled him around to a shadowed area slightly behind the stage. Putting her hand behind his head and grabbing his thick mane, she attacked his face in a flurry of drunken kisses. He responded appropriately. He noticed she had hiked her leg up on his thigh and was rubbing her hands on his back. Although he was feeling the effects of the gin, he was still acutely aware of what was happening. He also knew whether in the corner by the stage or the backseat of the GTO, there was no doubt where this train was heading. In his excitement, he still thought of Carla. He wanted to pretend that kissing Maggie was as pleasant as kissing Carla—but it wasn't. Maggie's mouth tasted of cigarette smoke and beer. Kissing her was forced and unemotional. Kissing Carla, however, had been natural, unhurried, and sweet.

Robert was still lucid enough to think reasonably. Even with the passion, he was still able to make decisions. Did he want to lose his virginity at this time to this girl? He didn't think so.

"Whoa, Maggie." He interrupted. "Let's slow down a minute."

"I'm too hot to slow down right now, Robbie!" Then she resumed kissing him. "Let's go out to your car."

He pulled away. "I'm serious, Maggie! I don't want to do this!"

She looked incredulously at him. "What are you talking about? Why did you come here tonight if it wasn't to fool around with me?"

"To tell you the truth, I'm not quite sure. I just know I don't want to do this with you, at least not right now," he said as he walked away toward the door.

"Get back here, Robbie! No man walks away from me!"

"Well, one just did!" Robert said as he walked through the door.

Walking to his car, he stumbled a little, noticing the alcohol had more effect on him than he had previously realized. Since he always drank in the privacy of his own home, he had never driven with any more than just a hint of inebriation.

The cold front had apparently arrived, and by now the light rain had turned to sleet. If this kept up, it would be ice by morning.

Robert was aware of his condition and the danger he posed. At first, he thought about calling Will, but since no one knew he drank, it would be too embarrassing to explain. He couldn't call his friends, Steve or Billy Ray, because he felt they would be disappointed. He decided to avoid the freeway and just drive slowly along U.S. 64, which would lead him to his home on Norristown Mountain.

As he drove, he was keenly conscious of his delayed reaction time. He was not drunk enough to get the overconfidence some drunks get. Robert could just tell that he was having trouble keeping a straight line down the road. The lights blurred through the rain on his windshield.

Fortunately, the bad weather had kept most people home for the evening and Robert only periodically met an oncoming car. As cars approached, he gave all the attention he could to keeping his car in line, then as the car passed, he would loosen up and swerve a little.

After several miles, he built confidence in his driving ability and increased his speed from thirty to fifty miles per hour. He hadn't realized, though, that the road was getting slick and even for a sober driver, fifty was too fast.

As the GTO approached a sharp right turn in the road, Robert applied pressure to the brake pedal. He felt the tires break free from the pavement and the car started sliding across the double yellow line. Around the curve, a Mack logging truck was creeping along, coming toward him. Fortunately, the truck driver was wiser than Robert and had slowed the truck to twenty miles per hour.

It all seemed to Robert to be happening in slow motion. He could tell he was going to hit the truck head on, although he had time to hope he would slide past it to the opposite shoulder.

He didn't.

The impact was so loud and so instantaneous that Robert didn't hear the crumpling metal or the shattering glass. In a moment, the car hit the front grill of the slow-moving truck and spun to the shoulder where the GTO landed. This collision created one big thunderous impact and then all was quiet.

The collision knocked Robert unconscious—but only for a few seconds. The first thing he became aware of was very cold rain landing on the side of his head. He was lying on the blue hood of the GTO, having been launched through the windshield.

The truck driver soon arrived at the side of the car.

"Are you alright, son?" The driver asked in a quivering voice. Seeing Robert was conscious, he continued, "man, I thought you were going to be dead."

Chapter 35

Robert slipped out of consciousness again and the next time he awoke, he could tell he was in the back of an ambulance. The rest felt dream-like until he woke up in a hospital bed.

As he looked around, there were a few medical personnel attending to him. Their lack of urgency gave him confidence that the injuries were not too severe—or they thought he was dead.

Seeing he was awake, the doctor walked to his side. "How are you feeling?"

"My head hurts!"

"Well, that's not a big surprise since you flew through the windshield of your car." The doctor said while examining the boy's eyes with a small penlight.

"You were in a head on collision with a semi. You have a cut on your head and a concussion, but I think it is slight. We'll have to do a few tests."

"Where am I?" Robert asked groggily.

"St. Mary's Hospital in Russellville."

The doctor continued to examine Robert and asked other questions about aches, pains, and the use of limbs.

"We'll keep an eye on you for a while, but as far as I can tell. You're one lucky son-of-a-gun."

After a little while, the truck driver, a short, balding man in a flannel shirt and jeans, waddled into the room. A Pope County Deputy Sheriff followed him. Even in his dreamy state, Robert could tell this was trouble.

"Hello Robert, I'm Deputy Peterson. The doctor tells me you're going to be all right." The deputy spoke in a deep southern drawl. "God was watching out for you tonight. You must have a purpose in this here life."

Robert couldn't imagine any God looking out for him after his careless decisions of the night.

"Robert, I need to get an official statement from you. Where were you heading tonight?"

"I was going home from my brother's house in Atkins." He lied, making sure not to mention *PJ's*. "I wanted to get home before the roads got too bad."

"Well, you didn't." Peterson replied sarcastically. How fast do you think you were going?"

"Probably fifty or so."

"Well, the speed limit is fifty-five, but when the roads are slick, you've got to slow down, boy!" The deputy thought for a few seconds then continued, "I've got to make you responsible, son. It's certainly not the truck driver's fault. I'm going to write you a citation for *driving too fast for road conditions*."

Even in his fragile state, Robert couldn't help but want to smile. There was going to be no breathalyzer. No drunk driving arrest. Not even a mention of alcohol. The deputy had blamed the accident on the weather. Robert had certainly dodged a bullet.

"Your car is being towed to a junkyard. It's totaled."

As the driver and the officer left, Robert thought about the irony of the day. He had lost his girl, his car, and could've lost his virginity, yet amazingly retained his life. Lying in the hospital bed, he wasn't sure if he should be rejoicing or mourning.

Robert was glad when daylight came. His night in the hospital was full of distractions. His parents had visited him soon after midnight. They had been told of his accident by the hospital staff and had come as soon as they could. Robert was glad to see them, but also wanted to sleep, so he was also glad when they left.

The next morning, it surprised him to get a visit from Bishop Houston, the leader of the Mormon congregation in town.

Harry Houston was a tall man in his early fifties. He was a family man with four grown kids who had all left the nest. Because the Church of Jesus Christ of Latter-Day Saints functions without a paid ministry, they choose capable men from the congregation and ask them to volunteer their time for five years or so. Bishop Houston was a dry cleaner by profession. He had always been very kind to Robert. As far as Robert could tell, he was nice to most everyone. He was a gentle man. The bed-ridden Robert was glad to see him walk through the door.

"Hello, Robert," Houston said in his best soft hospital voice. "How are you doing?"

"Hello, Bishop. I'm fine, still got a headache."

"From what I heard, you're quite the lucky duck," the bishop said as he stood at the bed beside Robert.

"How did you find out about it?" Robert wondered.

"I guess your parents filled out the paperwork last night and put me down as your minister." Houston responded.

"Oh, I'm sorry about that. We never have had a church, so I guess they put the only thing they knew."

"Robert, I'm honored to be considered your minister." The bishop looked sincerely into his eyes.

Harry Houston asked for the details of the previous night. As Robert related them, the man listened intently. One thing the Mormon leader had been blessed with in his calling was the ability to listen and discern. Listening to Robert, he discerned there was more to the story, but didn't pursue it.

"I heard about Carla," Houston said softly. "Her mom called me yesterday to tell me she was getting married. I'm sorry, Robert. I know you two were close, almost inseparable."

"I didn't see it coming, Bishop," Robert said, again feeling the pain. "I knew things had cooled off a little, but I always assumed we'd be together."

"I know it must hurt. I know it's hard to understand right now, but let me assure you, time will help you heal, son."

"With the pain I feel right now, I don't know how."

"If it helps any, Carla's mom isn't very excited about it, either. But what can she do? Carla's an adult."

Robert replied, "I think Carla's mom kind of liked me. Maybe she'll talk some sense into her."

"I wouldn't count on it," Houston replied, "as I said, Carla's an adult now."

The room quietened. Not an uncomfortable quiet, just silent as each man was spending time with his own thoughts.

After a few minutes, Bishop Houston broke the silence. "Robert, can I ask you some questions?"

"Sure, Bishop. What's on your mind?"

"Robert, how do you assess your life? I don't mean now or even two years from now, but what do you think it will be in ten, twenty, thirty years from now?"

Robert thought for an instant and then responded, "I suppose much as my parent's life has been full of hard work with little reward."

"Well, nothing's wrong with hard work. I hope you will have lots of hard work, but why don't you think you'll have rewards?"

Robert hesitated. "That's just the way it's been with us. I never think about having good things in life. Every time I do, I get disappointed."

"Yes, there is a lot of disappointment in life—but I'm here to tell you it doesn't have to be that way. There can be more good times than bad."

"I sure hope it starts soon."

Houston could tell in those few words that the boy had indeed seen lots of frustration.

"Robert, a few months back, the missionaries were teaching you. Why did you stop them?"

"I dunno, Bishop. I guess it just wasn't for me."

"Do you still believe that, Robert?"

"I don't know. I mean, I really related to what was being taught. I just didn't know if I could live it," he paused for a moment, "or was worthy of it."

"What do you mean, son?" the bishop asked, putting his hand on the boy's shoulder in a fatherly way. Robert enjoyed the comfort he felt from the action.

"There are some things about me you don't know, Bishop. Things you probably wouldn't want to know."

"Would you want me to know?"

"I'd be too embarrassed to tell you."

"In my position in the church," the bishop said, "I hear a lot of things. I'm not here to judge you, Robert, and it's all in strictest confidence."

Not sure what was motivating him—Robert started confessing his weaknesses to Houston. He told him of his unorthodox upbringing, the abuse he had endured from Ricky Goodman, the lies he had told, his suicide attempt, and reluctantly his drinking problem. The confession poured out as if released from a lifelong dam in his soul. He didn't hold back. He had long wanted to tell someone. Now he finally had someone to hear him—yet not judge him.

After telling these things, Robert was teary-eyed and relieved—and ashamed.

The wise bishop listened intently, then smiled a gentle smile and said, "Robert, you must've been carrying that burden around for quite a while. Now it's time you gave it up. Do you believe in God, Robert?"

"I think I do. I think I always have on some level."

The bishop then proceeded to teach the boy about their Christian belief in repentance and forgiveness. He assured him that nothing he had done was beyond the reach of loving forgiveness. The message rested well with Robert. He openly cried, wiping his eyes and nose on the sleeve of his hospital gown.

"You have not given yourself enough credit, boy." The Man taught. "You have such a splendid chance to be optimistic about life. You are smart and a hard worker. You have common sense and a soft heart. There is no reason you can't accomplish anything in life you want to. It is possible for you to be the first in your family to attend college. There is a way to overcome the bottle. You can overcome the trauma of your childhood. You have that power within you."

The words of solace resonated with Robert. On some level, deep down, he believed it. They released him from the hospital on Monday and he called the missionaries to start the lessons again.

Chapter 36

Returning to work was a mixed blessing. He enjoyed getting back to a normal routine but didn't enjoy seeing Maggie. She had told quite a different story of the night at *PJ's*. Robert spent much of that week thinking about his life and the direction it would take over the next few years.

After work on Friday, Robert arrived home and sought out his dad, who was working in the small shop he had built in the former chicken coop behind the house. The father welcomed his son, who was an infrequent visitor to the shop. The two men exchanged small talk about the day's events. Robert noticed his dad was using the claw side of a hammer to remove nails from old boards, long since worn and gray. He then laid the disfigured nails on the workbench and lightly pounded them as he rolled them along in quarter turns with his finger. When a nail was acceptably straight, he tossed it into an old Folger's can. "Why do you spend so much time straightening out those nails? Aren't nails pretty cheap?"

"You have to remember son, I lived during the Great Depression. I don't throw anything away that hasn't had the chance to be used three or four times. Someday, I might not have the money for nails—then, I'll be the richest man on the street because I'll have a whole can full that I can use," Larry said with a slight grin of sarcasm.

Dad held up one of the nails he had just removed. The slightly rusted nail had a ninety-degree bend and its head was slightly bent. Looking at the nail, he began to wax philosophically. "Robert, did you ever realize how these nails are similar to people?

"We all get kind of beat up, old, bent, and rusty. Lord knows I have over the years."

Robert smiled at his father.

Larry continued, "But even when we think we aren't worth using again, sometimes we get straitened up, polished and get to work once more. The big difference between these nails and people is that the nails are never quite as strong the second time. A man, though, can be even stronger after he's been repaired."

Robert wasn't sure of the purpose of the analogy. He suspected his dad knew of the changes occurring within the boy and was somehow trying to give him hope. He didn't respond, but instead watched his dad pull a few more nails out, straiten them, then put them into the coffee can. He contemplated his father's wisdom, and it added to his optimism.

With the motivating talk of Bishop Houston and Larry's allegory as his foundation, Robert started making changes that would lead to a better future for him. He didn't drink again and started attending group meetings for support. He came clean with his parents about the years of drinking. The news surprised them—he had hidden it well.

He continued his registration for college in the fall. He would be entering uncharted territory and hoped he would be able to do all that was required of him.

Robert got a new job as a server and cook at *Catfish Charley's*—a family restaurant in town. The owner, Charley Stanley, was always willing to help the college students by allowing them to work shifts around their school schedule. Robert enjoyed the restaurant business, especially serving people and making them happy.

In late August, Robert Rhodes was joined by about fifty members of the local Mormon congregation as they watched him go into the swift Arkansas River and be baptized.

The night before the baptism, he had dreamed.

In his dream, he was on the floor of the high school gymnasium. The bleachers were full of yelling people. From the center of the court, he could see the seven or eight doors leading out of the gym. He felt that one of them was the right choice, but he wasn't sure which one to choose. As he was drawn toward one of the doors, the crowd started jeering and mocking him not to choose that particular one. When he backed away from the door, they cheered with delight, but he really felt compelled to go through the one that was unpopular with the crowd. As he got closer to the door and even put his hands on the bar to push it open, the crowd got hostile, throwing things at him, and rushing from the stands. He felt one particular being behind him, jeering at him more than the rest. He recognized the evil spirit that he had felt before. This one led the crowd's screaming. They didn't want him to choose that way, yet he felt it was right.

In the morning, he felt substantiated by his choice.

The mighty change he had experienced in the past five months made him feel as though he was a new being.

He finally felt his future was not predetermined. He felt as if he could be in charge of what his life became, but there was some straightening still to be done.

His religious conversion did not solve his problems and—as he would soon see—it did not prevent him from having future challenges. Maybe, though, it was one right choice on which he could build.

Randy Judd

Chapter 37

Remembering the day with his dad in the shop, Robert smiled reminiscently. At the time of his dad's death, Robert walked to the small building and recovered the can of nails. Even today, it held an honored place in his garage and was one of his most prized inheritances of his dad.

Santa Fe had been educational, but he had rather his wife had been with him to share the event. The couple enjoyed taking excursions to new places. Whether it was for a weeklong drive down the Florida Keys or a weekend getaway to a cabin by a lake in the Ozarks, the pair loved exploring together.

Robert's extended trip home was now becoming too long. He was excited to get back home. He would stay tonight in Santa Fe. Tomorrow, he would make it as far as Oklahoma, his birthplace. Then home.

Nineteen-year-old Robert delighted in the new direction his life was taking. By the middle of his first semester at Arkansas Tech University, he settled into the college routine. He didn't have time or desire for the entire college experience of fraternities, dances or football games. He was attending college purely to further his chance in life.

He was enjoying his time at *Catfish Charley's* and Charley had immediately seen some qualities in Robert that he respected. Charley promoted Robert to closing manager, which allowed him to go to school during the day, have a few hours for homework, then work till two in the morning.

Sunday was his only day off, and he was able to get to church and relax the rest of the day.

Robert's life became very routine for the next couple of years. It disciplined him enough that he could handle the fifty hours per week of work and go to school. He didn't have much of a social life, though. He would occasionally do something with friends from work. Steve and Billy Ray had both decided to serve missions for the church—Steve went to Peru and Billy Ray left a year later to Boston.

Robert rarely dated. He had certainly become outgoing and confident enough to ask women out, but wasn't sure with his work and school schedule if he had the time to give a relationship.

He thought of Carla less frequently. For a year or so after the breakup, his most prevalent emotion was betrayal. It hurt him that she could walk away so easily. He buried the pain deep beneath his new life and attitude. Sometimes, though, he let his mind wonder. He couldn't deny how he felt about her and what could've been.

By Robert's junior year at Arkansas Tech, he had decided on a business degree and was looking forward to graduating in a year and a half. He wasn't sure what he would do when he graduated. There would be time to decide that later.

In January 1982, a family moved into the area and attended church with Robert. The Potter family had moved from Alabama and had four kids, including a nineteen-year-old girl named Patricia. Patricia had long red hair and had a fiery spirit to match. She was a second semester freshman at the college. For the first time in a while, Robert found himself attracted to a legitimate candidate for a relationship.

As he got to know her, he found her to be wilder than he was. That was not to say she was as wild as Maggie had been. Patricia did have some standards, after all. But she could be quite a hellion and didn't worry much about responsibilities. They started dating in the spring.

Robert, again, enjoyed feeling the anticipation of being with someone. She always carried most of the conversation, since she was very outgoing in nature. He sometimes considered her to be too loud and slightly obnoxious, but she did have a good heart and other positive qualities. She talked a lot and did not choose her words carefully.

Robert was in love with being in love again. He was aware that his feelings weren't as strong as they had been for his former love, but he was happy to have someone in his life.

Partially for fear of losing her and being in love with the idea of being married to someone, Robert pushed the relationship along and Patricia was amiable. After only eight months of dating, the two were married.

For most of his life, Robert had dreamed of having a family and now he had taken the first steps to fulfill that dream. Although they had a rough start as husband and wife, they soon fell into the comfortable routines of building a life together. He continued to work at the restaurant and she found part-time jobs to keep her busy in between cruising with her girlfriends.

As his college graduation neared, Robert pondered his future. On a momentous occasion like this, he was supposed to be happy. Instead, the weight of the decisions burdened him. He considered going to graduate school and pursuing a graduate degree, but that would mean postponing being able to properly support his family for another two years. He had also interviewed with a couple of companies seeking recent graduates, but the starting pay was less than he was making at *Catfish Charley's*.

His burden of decision got even heavier as the couple announced in October that they were having their first child in June.

With his need to make a decision looming, Charley Stanley called Robert into his office one day before his night shift began.

"Robert," Charley started. "I've seen a lot of college kids come and go through here. You'd think I would get used to being a papa bear and kicking them out and on their way to their future."

Charley was in his early sixties, but his hair premature white hair made him appear older. He always wore a white shirt which was slightly soiled from helping in the kitchen. He wasn't even sure himself how much he weighed and hadn't seen a scale or doctor in years. Add his weight to his six foot two inch frame and he made a very formidable man. Over the years, he had earned the nickname *Mount Charley*, and it stuck.

"Every now and again, I have someone come through here that I hate to see go," Mount Charley said. "This is one of those times. I hate to see you go."

"I know what you mean," Robert replied. "It just won't seem the same, not coming in here every night."

Charley continued, "I'm not sure what decisions you've made and if any of your interviews have tempted you, but I've been thinking about something I want to tempt you with.

"I know I'm almost at retirement age, Robert, but I don't intend on slowing down at all. In fact, with a little help from some good people, I think I'd enjoy making one more surge at greatness."

"You *are* great, Charley," the younger man replied. "Everyone in town loves you. You could run for mayor and win in a landslide."

"Heck, I don't want to be no mayor, but thanks anyway for the thought.

"I still have a dream that I can't let go. Over the years, investors have come to me wanting me to build more restaurants. To tell you the truth, the thought has always scared the pants off me. *Catfish Charley's* is a local institution, that's for sure, but I don't know how one would do in another city."

Charley continued, "Well, I'm not getting any younger, and if I am ever going to do anything, now's the time. I am going to build at least three more restaurants in the next two years. I've got all the financing in place and I've already found one site in Conway."

"That's great Charley! Good for you!" Robert exclaimed.

"I had hoped, Robert, that you might help me."

"What do you mean, Charley?"

"Well, you've done such a great job while you've been with me. I was hoping you might run this restaurant while I go off and start the new ones. You have a great work ethic and you're honest. I couldn't think of anyone better to leave in charge of my business."

Charley continued, "I will pay you more than the other job offers you've had and you already know what to expect. What do you say?"

"I don't know what to say except thanks! Your confidence in me is very important. I will certainly give it some thought. Let me talk it over with Patricia."

"Why, of course you should. Robert, I don't want you to think managing a *Catfish Charley's* will be your lot in life. If these stores take off, I could see you helping run my entire business. With your book smarts and my savvy, we could rule the catfish world!"

Robert smiled at the old man and then got up, shook his hand, and promised to get back to him in a couple of days.

It was important for Robert to involve his wife in all the decisions he made. He wanted their marriage to be a partnership. Patricia was a superb listener, but seldom provided wonderful insight to the conversation. She often seemed preoccupied when he spoke. She would agree with most things he proposed, but sometimes argue just for the sake of arguing. This frustrated the young man because it sometimes made him feel he was alone in the decisions. Alone to succeed and alone to fail.

After many hours of deciding where his life was to take him, looking at all his options and even the lack thereof, he decided to see where the restaurant business would lead.

Chapter 38

Robert and Patricia's life together soon yielded their first child. A beautiful girl whom they named Tabitha—*Tabbie* as they soon called her—came into the world without a hitch and mom and baby convalesced appropriately. Robert took his new financial responsibility seriously and increased his hours at the restaurant.

Two years went by and Robert and Patricia told themselves they were happy together. Were they in love? It was hard to say. Mostly they were in love with being in love and being a couple and a family. The couple functioned well as a partnership. He provided the money and lawn mowing skills and she kept the home fires burning. They were a good *Ozzie and Harriett*. Although his marriage was less fulfilling than he had once wished, it was certainly better than others he had seen, so on some level, he was content.

One emotion Robert was convinced of was his joy at being a parent. He thrived on being with his little Tabbie. Everything she did was perfect for him. From the moment he got home from work, she was in his arms where he took over the nurturing from a baby-weary Patricia.

Years later, Robert heard a quote from the actor, Johnny Depp. The article quoted Depp as saying, "Parenthood didn't change me. It *revealed* me". That's exactly how Robert felt. The feelings he had for being a father were feelings that had been inside him from an early age. Playing house on Norristown Mountain had been very real to the then ten-year-old.

It wasn't long until the Rhodes family was blessed with a second child, a son they named Russell. Life felt complete.

In five years of marriage, Robert and Patricia had what seemed an ideal life—two beautiful children and a small house in Russellville.

By this time, Charley Stanley had opened a total of four *Catfish Charley's* and though the other locations had not been as popular as his first, they still made money and helped feed Charley's megalomania.

Charley promoted Robert to District Manager over the restaurants and shared—although a minuscule percentage—in the profits.

Robert enjoyed his position, although he felt somewhat unfulfilled. He often wondered if he had taken another position out of college if he would've enjoyed more mental challenges in another industry. He also questioned his decision not to continue and obtain a graduate degree.

Even with his doubts about his career moves, he still was the most successful Rhodes child so far. With a gnawing emptiness somewhere in the back of his mind—and heart—he continued building a life with fun-loving Patricia, a life that was the envy of most of his acquaintances.

Chapter 39

Crossing the panhandle of Texas, Robert pulled the Jaguar into a *Love's* truck stop in Amarillo for refueling and refreshment. It was early afternoon and even though he could make it to Russellville by midnight; he decided to drive just a few more hours and stop at Elk City, Oklahoma, for the night.

His phone vibrated in his front pocket. It pleased him to see it was his sister, Lou.

Lou now lived in Little Rock and with thirty years since their discussion on the Rhodes front porch, she was as far away from her days of prostitution as one could imagine.

Soon after Robert graduated from college, Lou began assessing her own life. Though she was managing a thrift store in town, seeing her little brother graduate gave her new motivation to change her own life. She studied for and passed her GED test. The next fall, she started taking classes at Arkansas Tech. A difficult five years later, she graduated Cum Laude with a degree in English and immediately began attending Law School in Little Rock. Now, decades later, she was a successful civil rights attorney. Her experiences after the death of Martin Luther King had never been far from her heart, and now her passion and avocation had become her vocation. She accepted more than her share of pro bono work. Robert was very proud of his big sister. She was once again his hero.

Although southwest Oklahoma was his birthplace, Robert had no memories of the area. The Rhodes family had left while he was still a toddler. Still, Robert wanted to take some time to see the hospital where he was born and try to find the little store where they had lived.

With no decent hotel having vacancies, he settled into *The Grapes of Wrath Motor Inn,* which was probably in existence when he lived there. He parked his Jaguar sports car outside his door and left it with trepidation.

⚜

As the years of married life passed, Robert noticed changes in Patricia. The changes weren't great or sudden, but gentle, much like the changing of seasons.

Even though he couldn't see the day-to-day differences, he could look back and see how different she was from a year previous. She had never been short of friends, but her friends now were all a different caliber than those of a year or two before. As a mom, she was much easier to lose her patience. Her mood swings were already perceptible to her young children.

One evening while his wife was out bowling with a couple of her close girlfriends, Robert was putting away the laundry and noticed something out of place in back of her pajama drawer. Pushing aside the flannel covering, he saw something very familiar to him—something that ached his heart. There, hidden where her husband wasn't supposed to look, Patricia had hidden a bottle.

It disappointed him that she was obviously drinking. Robert would've been less concerned, though, if he had found out that Patricia had an occasional glass of wine. To find the liquor hidden in her drawer, though, led him to believe that she was in the same place as he had been so many years ago. She must be sneaking around to drink. How long? Six months? A year? Two? He had no clue. However long it had been, she had done an excellent job of hiding it.

He picked up the half empty bottle and immediately felt some of the loneliness of his pathetic life some fifteen years earlier. He knew of the embrace the liquid had on him then, and how it had defined his dismal existence. As he rubbed some smudged lipstick off the neck, he knew he had overcome its clutches forever. He didn't need it now, nor would he ever need it again. Although his knowledge of his conquest was a great feeling, the reality that his wife was using sank in. He tried to think of times where she may have been intoxicated and he hadn't put two and two together. There were times she would come in late from being with her friends and she would slide into bed quietly, barely saying goodnight. Several months ago, she had run her car into a ditch on Weir Road. She walked to a gas station and got a ride from her friend, Jill. Was there more to the story? As he heard Russ calling him from the front room, Robert put the bottle back in the drawer to hide its detection. He had some hard decisions ahead of him about how to approach this discovery with his wife.

For the next several days, he tried to put the words together. He even tried to make excuses for the find. Maybe she was holding it for a friend. He thought about how the discovery made him feel. After all, lots of people, including many of their friends, drank—responsibly. Although drinking was part of the problem, the feeling he was having the most trouble with was betrayal. She had made a concentrated effort to hide it from him. The fact that she was hiding it made him think it must be a problem for her.

A few days later, as Patricia prepared to go out for the second time that week, Robert called her into the family room to talk.

"I can't talk long—I need to meet Pam at seven."

"Patricia, I'm concerned about all the time you've been spending away from home, away from me and the kids."

"I've told you before, I need my personal time. It's tough being a stay-at-home mom. I feel so cooped up. A few nights a week, I gotta get out."

Without a lead-in or a proper segue, Robert hit her with the news. "Patricia, I found the bottle of alcohol in your drawer."

Instead of addressing the larger issue, she aimed for the easier one. "What are you doing going through my drawers?! What I have in my drawers is none of your business."

"I was putting two weeks' worth of laundry away, but that's not the issue! Are you drinking?"

"Well, what do you think I was using it for, removing nail polish?"

Robert wasn't prepared for her quick answer. He thought she would make excuses until he had to drag the truth out of her. "How long have you been drinking, Patricia?"

"I don't know. Maybe a year and a half. I started getting so caged up, so crazy and then one day, while I was over at Jill's, she offered me a glass of wine to relax me. 'I don't drink,' I said. 'It's against my religion.' She convinced me it wouldn't hurt just to have one, so I gave in. I had one glass, then another, and maybe another. I felt really relaxed, and I enjoyed it. She sent a bottle home with me and I finished the whole thing before lunch the next day while Tabbie was in school and Russell was on a play date. I slept away the afternoon."

"Wow." Robert sighed, not expecting to know so much, so soon.

"After the first day, I didn't drink as much. I tried it in moderation, thinking I could just drink a little to keep the edge off—when things got tough. One day I realized it was the alcohol buzz I was after and I didn't have to drink so much to get the buzz, so I drove to Morrilton and got a bottle of whiskey to see if I could get the same effect with less drinking."

By now, making the confession visibly shook Patricia. She wasn't crying, but as she fidgeted in her seat, Robert could tell she was uncomfortable and embarrassed about what she was saying. "Oh, I got the effect alright. I drank too much of the disgusting liquid and threw up the rest of the day. I called Mom and told her I had the stomach flu and she came and got Russell.

"I got used to the hard stuff and after a month or two, I was drinking every day. Vodka became my drink of choice, and I've had a bottle in the house ever since."

Her tone was one of confession to her husband. "I have wanted to tell you for so long, Robert. You're my husband and one of my best friends, but I couldn't bring myself to let you know. I knew you'd be so disappointed in me."

Robert always prided himself on being a good listener, but now it was his turn to talk, giving her a reprieve.

"You know my story about alcohol, babe. I fought my demons for years and it took everything I had to free myself from its clutches. I thought you were smarter than that. Why couldn't you have learned from me?"

She thought his tone was condescending, but chose to continue her story without picking a fight.

"I didn't think I had a problem for a long time. I thought I could hide it forever and just enjoy self-medicating. I started changing my schedule to accommodate drinking. I found myself forgetting where I had hidden my stash and worried about the kids finding it.

"I finally admitted to myself that I had a problem when, last summer, I made excuses not to go on the family vacation because I knew I couldn't go a week without a drink."

Knowing her pain, understanding her dependence, and the hopelessness she felt, he offered solace. "We've got to get you some help, Dear."

After her confession, he was now surprised at her response. "Who says I want help? If you didn't notice it all this time, it's obvious I'm pretty good at keeping it hidden. Just leave me alone on this, Robert. I'm fine!"

"I can't leave you alone! What if you're drunk when the kids are around and one of them gets hurt? Or worse yet, you cause one of them to get hurt? What happens when the stomach flu story doesn't work anymore? You can't just keep going on this way!"

"Just pretend you never found the bottle and things will be just fine!" At this, Patricia stood up, turned with her fist at her side, and left the room. She was both mad and ashamed.

Robert sat, not knowing his next move.

Chapter 40

Tabitha was jubilant on her birthday, just as a child turning ten should be. They held her party in the family room of Robert and Patricia's new house just north of Russellville. Tabbie actually got to have two parties: one for her friends on Friday—which Russell was not allowed to be around for—and one for the family on Saturday. At the family party, all her uncles, aunts, grandparents, and cousins attended, making it a rare family reunion.

Robert's side of the family was rambunctious and loud. They loved to have fun and were always up for a game of gin rummy that could last late into the night.

Patricia's family was quite different. Nothing like Patricia. The Potters were quiet and more dignified. They weren't snobby or unsociable, just more sophisticated in their actions.

After the cake and presents, the party moved outside. Eventually, a rousing water fight ensued. Robert, with a pail of water in his hand, mischievously came in the back door of the house with the intent of surprising the others playing on the front porch. As he scurried past the living room, he noticed something out of place. With the sounds of laughter loudly echoing outside, Patricia hadn't heard him come in. With her back to him, he could tell she was pouring herself a drink. "What do you think you're doing!?" Robert demanded. "Drinking on our daughter's birthday?"

Patricia was mad that he caught her and chastised him. "Leave me alone! I can't take all the ruckus—I want them all to go home!"

"Well, it's Tabbie's birthday! I can't ask everyone to leave."

"I just want to be left alone! I'll be in our room!"

With that, Patricia stomped out of the room, avoiding the attempts of Robert to stop her on the way. After entering their bedroom, she locked the door behind her.

Robert had to make a quick decision. Patricia was an adult, and he could deal with her later. Tabbie was an eager ten-year-old who was having an amazing birthday party. He went outside with the bucket of water in hand and pretended to be unaffected by the events inside.

After the activity settled down, some of the soaked guests asked about Patricia. He told them she had a headache and had gone to lie down. They accepted his lie.

After tucking the kids in bed, Robert went to the bedroom and found the door unlocked. He slipped into bed beside his sleeping wife. As he lay there in the dark, he dealt with his confusion—the same confusion he would have for years to come.

In the morning, Robert woke the kids up and got them ready for church. Tabbie protested at Robert's attempts to fix her hair. Daddy told Tabbie to let Mommy sleep today, as she was still not feeling well.

Church passed slowly for Robert as he tried to understand what was happening at home. He recollected the last few months and had remembered that his wife had become more and more distant. She seemed less interested in things that used to bring her joy. He had noticed that she was slipping more and more into her own world.

When Dad and the kids returned from church, Mom was awake and putting on a pleasant face for her son and daughter. After Robert prepared lunch, the kids ate and went to the family room to play video games.

Robert went outside to the porch swing and sat beside Patricia, who was slowly swinging, looking out into the yard.

The previous night had been warm and still, but today was gray and overcast, with a strong hint of rain.

After sitting quietly for a few minutes, holding her hand in his lap, Robert broke the silence. "What are we going to do?"

At this, Patricia unleashed a flood of tears. Her body quivered as she sobbed. He pulled her tight. After a while, her crying subsided and all that could be heard was the electronic sounds of the game inside.

"I don't know, Robert," she started. "I thought I could keep up the charade, but now I think I know the actual truth. I'm addicted.

"I don't feel I want to do anything, Robert. I just want to sleep all day, hoping that will make the day pass until I can have another drink. Then I'll be able to go to sleep at night and I don't want to wake up in the morning. I just want to sleep or have a buzz on all the time. I just don't want to be sober!"

Robert had compassion for her. He remembered feeling those same feelings when he was in junior high. He remembered his low point sitting on the commode with a gun in his mouth. That was in junior high when he didn't feel as if he had anything for which to live. That was during the time he was recoiling from his experiences with Ricky Goodman, a person he sometimes still anguished over.

Patricia, on the other hand, could not possibly feel those feelings. She had a family who loved her, two fun kids and a new house in the country.

"Have you thought about group meetings?"

"No, I would be too ashamed and too worried someone will find out."

"Well, it's not going to go away on its own. You need help."

They sat quietly for several minutes.

Patricia broke the silence. "I can do it, Robert! I've got to do it! I'm going to stop drinking. Tomorrow, I'm going to dump out every bottle I've got in the house. From now on, I won't drink another drop!"

"I appreciate your resolve, honey, but it's hard. You'll need help."

"No, I can do it and *will* do it!"

Although he wished her the best. He knew how hard it had been for him and quietly doubted her abilities.

A few more weeks trudged by, and Robert constantly thought of Patricia's problems. He checked with her daily and she told him all was fine.

On a Monday night, five weeks after the birthday party, Patricia met Robert at the door as he got home late. The kids were in the backyard playing. Patricia rushed past Robert.

"I've gotta go!" she said in passing.

He could see the demon in her eye, the familiar urge which drove her.

"Don't go, Patricia," he pleaded, but she almost ran for the car. He couldn't stop her.

At eleven that evening, as he sat in the front room waiting, he saw headlights from an unfamiliar car pull up in the driveway. It was Jill. She motioned to Robert now standing in the door frame.

"I know you know about her problem, Robert. I thought I'd better bring her home. She's passed out in the back seat."

Robert never liked Jill much but thanked her for her candor and kindness in protecting her friend. He carried his wife to bed.

He stayed home from work the next day. When she woke up, Robert was in the living room. He got some aspirin for her headache. He was determined not to discuss the drinking until she was completely over the previous night's bender. She slept intermittently throughout the day. At about two, she appeared at the family room doorway. "Are the kids still in school?"

Robert nodded.

"Well, I guess you want to lecture me now."

Robert shook his head. "No need to lecture. You know you have a problem."

She sat down across from him, pulling her legs up under her.

Robert stared at her and noticed for the first time how the alcohol had aged her—the wrinkles, the dark bags under her bloodshot eyes.

After a few minutes of watching Judge Judy, she broke the silence. "I need help. I can't do it by myself."

Robert replied, "I found a therapist in town who has worked with a lot of people with addiction problems. Her name is Doctor Core. Would it be ok if I set an appointment up for you?"

Patricia relented.

Although Robert had felt strongly that a couple's problems should not be shared with others, it was obvious to all who knew the Rhodes that something was wrong with Patricia. It was a tremendous source of stress for the young family. Those in the immediate circle of friends and family were told of her condition. The news surprised everyone. Most were supportive.

During these times, Robert was able to obtain a lot of solace in his conversations with his mother. Any differences he had with his mom in childhood were now distant occurrences. The two had long before shed the painful memories of his youth. She was now the epitome of a wonderful mother and grandmother. Olivia always seemed to know the right things to say and when it was right to say nothing. She was a good woman, now the honored matriarch of the Rhodes family.

Chapter 41

Patricia's visits to her psychiatrist escalated with time. She shared with Robert, the techniques Dr. Core used and the discussions they had.

Dr. Nancy Core was a large masculine woman. With her short dark hair and glasses, she resembled Janet Reno, the Attorney General in the Clinton administration. Robert had only met Dr. Core once, in a marital session with Patricia. Even though he had been the one to recommend her, he immediately did not appreciate her. She seemed to despise him without even knowing him. Robert also did not expect the level of influence Dr. Core had over Patricia. Patricia became unnaturally enamored with her doctor.

His lack of respect for her doctor escalated when she asked Patricia to try to remember things that she may have been suppressing about her childhood. Patricia tried as hard as she could and when Dr. Core was disappointed Patricia could not remember anything, Patricia considered making up some things just to please the doctor.

It became obvious to Robert that his wife was being influenced by a woman that did not have any use for men or any scruples in her procedures. On one occasion, Patricia followed her doctor's advice and wrote a letter to her dad asking him not to contact her anymore.

This upset Robert as he thought Mr. Potter was a good man and hated to see him hurt at the direction of a man-hating, self-righteous psychiatrist. Over his protest, Patricia sent the letter and severed the ties with her dad.

Patricia became obsessed with her doctor. As she ran errands, Patricia found reasons to drive by the doctor's home, hoping to catch a glimpse of her. Robert's wife was lucky not to have been arrested for stalking.

She was not drinking, as far as Robert knew, but she was being influenced by a separate threat.

After a year of Dr. Core's hundred-dollar an hour brainwashing, things came to a head. Robert came home one night to find the kids were still outside playing at ten o'clock on a school night. Robert found Patricia in the bedroom poring through a book on alcoholism and heredity.

Despite their protests, he put the children to bed and came back into the bedroom.

"Robert, Dr. Core wants me to go to a facility." Patricia announced.

With no effort to hide his frustration, Robert took a breath and exhaled. "What kind of facility?"

"It's a private facility, down around Little Rock. It's for people that are chemically dependent, like me."

Robert could almost detect a sense of pride in her condition through her desperate sadness. "We've talked about rehab before, Patricia, but you don't drink anymore."

"But I still have the desire. I need to try to be cured, so it doesn't come back."

"What does something that cost?"

Patricia hesitated. "About forty-thousand dollars," she said sheepishly.

At this, Robert raised his voice as he seldom did. "Forty-thousand dollars! We don't have that kind of money! You know our insurance doesn't cover it. The only way we could get that kind of money would be to sell the house!"

It shocked Robert when Patricia's reply was, "OK, sell the house."

Her husband did not even stop to consider it. "I am not going to sell our house just so you can go to a place that has no guarantee of working. We've already spent several thousand dollars on this man-hating quack's ideas to get you better!"

Robert knew that his words were hurtful to his wife, but he couldn't help himself. He had been keeping them bottled up for almost a year. The cork had now popped. The words poured out freely.

"It's almost a cult with her. You'll do anything she says, and she just sits there getting her hundred dollars an hour! You could get lots of people to be your friend for that kind of money. She's really like a prostitute—taking your money to give you attention!"

Robert felt a twinge of guilt for those last comments.

Patricia wasn't afraid of conflict, but this time, she wasn't ready for it. She swore at him and stormed to the family room.

Robert knew he was wrong. The truth was, he didn't know how to handle Patricia's disease. As the stereotypical man, he wanted to *fix* her. Hiring someone else to help her was an admission of failure. It embarrassed him to mention her condition to anyone outside the family circle. Cancer or diabetes could be understood, but alcoholism carried with it so many stigmas. He didn't understand the disease in himself, and definitely couldn't seem to get a handle on it with her.

The next morning, he prepared the kids for school, as was the new routine, while she slept on the couch.

Robert swung by home each day to make sure the kids arrived from school ok, then headed back to his office at the restaurant to get ready for the dinner rush.

One day, as he entered the driveway a few minutes before the kids' bus arrived, he could see the trunk of Patricia's car was open with two suitcases already loaded.

His car's gearshift was barely in park when he leaped out and bounded toward the house. He found his wife in the kitchen, slicing some apples for the trip.

"What's going on, Honey?" Robert asked.

"Dr. Core said maybe I should go away for a little while. Maybe it would help me to think—that maybe *you* are preventing me from healing. She says we shouldn't have any contact, so don't call me."

Robert felt the warmth rise in his face as his anger sought to escape. *How dare Dr. Core try to break up this family?*

"But Patricia. Where are you going? How long will you be gone?"

"I'm going to stay with some friends of Jill's down at Fort Smith. I'm thinking two weeks might do it."

"Two weeks, but what about the kids?" Robert pleaded.

"I've got to take care of me now, Robert. I hope you'll try to understand."

Without a kiss, Patricia put her apples in a baggie and headed for her car. She drove out onto the pavement just as the kids' bus turned on its flashing lights to unload in front of their house.

The next two weeks were full of emotional turmoil for Robert. While keeping a certain air of normalcy about himself for the kids' sake, he wallowed in pain internally. He tried his best to understand what was happening in his wife's life, but he couldn't. One night, as he worked in the garage, he dropped his head and prayed out loud. "God, why can't you make her better?!"

The kids were stoic about Mom's absence. Dad had told them she was off for a visit, but they held concerns about her ever coming back. She had never been a doting mother, but for the last several months, she had even been aloof to her offspring.

The family was all relieved when, in two weeks, Mom again returned. She seemed to be a little better and maybe a little better was all Robert should've hoped for.

Chapter 42

Patricia's current state became almost routine for the Rhodes family. As the children got older, they were acutely aware of it and it was no longer a hush-hush issue.

Robert's attitudes about her condition evolved. He still spent sleepless nights wondering if his wife would ever get better, but at least he didn't think it was a choice she had made. He now viewed it as a real medical condition.

The fact that Patricia had an addictive personality by nature certainly didn't help her. He always thought she could do so much better if she had better friends. When he had first met her, she had great friends. They had long since been out of touch.

A few years passed and Robert now defined himself more as a caregiver than a husband, but the vows said *for better or worse*, so this was in the contract.

Charley promoted Robert to director of operations for his company. Charley was aware of Patricia's issues but admired Robert's dedication to her and the family. The aging Charley let Robert work from a home office to oversee their seven restaurants.

Dad wrapped himself up in the lives of his kids. He wanted them to be as unaffected as they could be by Mom's state. Even Patricia's parents praised Robert for being *the mom and the dad* to the kids. They could see he performed his duties out of love for his family, and they appreciated it. They loved Patricia dearly, but couldn't understand completely what was happening.

No one, including Robert, knew when she was on or off the wagon, but there were signs that he had learned to watch for. Sometimes even pitiful signs. Robert once found an empty bottle of cough medicine in the garbage, even though no one had been sick.

In Robert's weakened state, he understood how men could stray. He didn't condone it, but he understood it. There were always romantic opportunities within the restaurants. Although he was tempted—and thought about the possibilities—he hadn't acted on them.

One evening Robert worked late loading software on one of the restaurant's computers, trying to prevent the impending Y2K disaster.

With his face staring six inches from the screen, he heard a slight knock on the open door behind him.

Leaning against the door was Alexis, a server he had known for several years. Alexis was a single mother whose serving job was her only source of income for her two children. Her ex-husband was a deadbeat who had never supported his progeny. Robert felt bad for the kids and always made sure he gave them presents on their birthdays and paid attention to them when they came in.

The single mom was in her early thirties. She wore her dresses just tight enough to maximize her tips and attract the eyes of future suitors.

"It's eleven o'clock, Robert. You sure are working late tonight," Alexis said in a soft voice.

"Yeah, I've got to get this software installed before the end of the year. They say if we don't, it could make all our computers useless." Robert replied, trying at the same time not to think about Alexis' software.

She continued, "Well, we're all closed up. It's just me and Jose left. We'll be leaving soon. Do you want someone to stay with you for safety?"

The phone in the office rang. Alexis reached across Robert to answer it. In the process of reaching for the receiver in the cramped office, her chest rubbed against Robert's cheek.

Robert took a shallow breath.

"Sure, he's right here," she said into the phone, then turned to Robert. "It's for you."

She didn't notice Robert's face was flush.

After a brief conversation, Robert hung up and turned back to Alexis. There was a sense of disappointment and frustration in his voice.

"That was my son, Russell. He's at the theater and Patricia was supposed to pick up him and his friends an hour ago. I've got to go save them," he said while picking up his keys. "Will you go ahead and lock up as usual, Alexis?"

She agreed, also with the sound of disappointment.

As Russell and Robert neared home, Dad was feeling his frustration building to anger. It was not completely unusual for Patricia to forget one of the kids or sleep through an appointment. As they approached the house, there were no lights on. Robert knew that Tabbie was out with friends and wouldn't be home for another hour or so.

Patricia's car was not in the driveway.

As they entered the house, Robert noticed headlights of a car pulling up in the driveway. He went outside and met a Sherriff's Deputy getting out of his car.

"Are you Mr. Rhodes?" the officer asked.

Russell came out of the house to see what the commotion was about.

"Mr. Rhodes, can I talk to you for a minute by yourself?"

"Russell, go back inside. I'll be in soon."

Russell reluctantly returned, but peeked out from behind a curtain.

"Mr. Rhodes," the Deputy began, "it's about your wife. She was in an accident tonight."

"What happened? Is she alright?" Robert anxiously asked.

"She's pretty banged up. It looks as though she had been drinking and missed a curve in the road. The car rolled once. Thank goodness she had the sense to have her seatbelt on. She's at the hospital right now, in the ER."

"Thanks, officer. I'll get right down there," Robert said as he headed back into the house to get Russell.

Was Robert surprised? Not especially. He had wondered if and when this would happen.

It didn't surprise the children, either. At seventeen and fourteen, her condition had given them a crash course in real life.

At the hospital, the ER doctor informed them that Patricia was ok.

"So, can we take her home?" Dad asked.

"I'm afraid not, Mr. Rhodes. We've checked her medical records and talked to her therapist. She's either got to go to rehab or jail. What will it be?"

"I guess rehab."

The doctor continued, "After consulting with our resident psychiatrist and talking to Mrs. Rhodes' doctors, we are going to send her to a chemical dependence unit at University Hospital in Little Rock. We'll send her down tonight."

The Rhodes family went home, minus one. The two teenagers didn't seem overly worried. They loved their mom, but over the last seven years, they had learned to deal with Mom's situation.

Dr. Core had finally gotten her wish to get Patricia hospitalized. Robert's insurance had changed a few years prior and now included in-patient rehab. Luckily, it would cover the majority of the costs.

After twenty-one days, her return home was awkward. Everyone was careful not to upset her. Eventually, normalness resumed.

Over time, Robert started noticing changes ... for the better. On the first day of April of the new millennium, Robert found his wife in the kitchen washing dishes and singing.

"Is it over?" Robert asked.

"Once an alcoholic, always an alcoholic, but I think I'm ok."

For the next few weeks and then months, Patricia continued to improve. She had experienced good times along the way, but this instance seemed to last longer and the family started to have genuine hope.

It couldn't really be said that the kids hoped for Mom to be the way she used to be. They had not known her any other way than distracted and aloof. This was a new mom.

Later that same week, Patricia asked Robert to meet him for lunch, something she had not done in many years.

He met her outside *Stoby's* restaurant, an old railroad car converted into a sandwich shop near downtown Russellville.

After initial small talk, they ordered food. There was a lull in the conversation, which was not unusual. The couple seldom had great conversation. Near the end of the meal, Patricia spoke in a new sober voice, "Robert, I want a divorce."

Robert stopped chewing and sat stone quiet. He hoped he hadn't heard her words, but they were clear.

"Patricia! What are you talking about? I know we've not been very close for a long time, but we made it work."

Several times over the previous seven years, the couple had gone to counseling. Each time, she had been the one to quit.

"I've come to the conclusion over the last year or so that maybe I could be better off …," Patricia answered, "… if I wasn't married to you."

Robert returned to stunned silence. After half a minute of contemplation, he responded, "I've spent the last seven or eight years taking care of you, coddling you, raising the kids. Now that you are better, you want to kick me to the curb?"

"It's not exactly that way," she said. "I just think I could be happier with just me and the kids. I've already talked to a lawyer, Robert. I hope you won't make this difficult on me. I don't need any frustration right now. I'm doing so well."

Chapter 43

Over the next few months, Robert's world fell apart.

Reflecting on his childhood by himself, he wanted nothing more in life than to be a husband and father. Those roles fit him well and were as comfortable as shorts and flip-flops. Even though it had not been easy, he enjoyed being a family. Now he would be less a part of his kid's lives. He now understood what it meant when people talked about a *broken heart*. He physically ached. The pain he felt when his dad had died a few years back was miniscule compared to the pain he was feeling at the death of his marriage.

Marriage and family had resembled a long-anticipated movie for him, and now the ushers were kicking him out halfway through, unable to see the ending.

Robert didn't fight against Patricia's lawyer on fiscal matters. He easily gave up the house, all savings, and investments. Robert knew he had a job that would allow him to build himself up again. He could start from zero and he didn't want the kids to suffer, though they would have to move. Even in their absence, Robert felt an obligation to be responsible for his kids and even to Patricia.

He would not give up the kids so easily, but in the end, her attorney painted a better picture to the courts, which left Robert with his children every other weekend and half the holidays.

A motel room, which the owners converted to a low-rent apartment, became his cave. To have more room, he had the bed moved out and bought a garage sale couch, which served as his bed at night. When the couch felt too lumpy, he rolled onto the floor. He worked from a temporary office in one of the restaurant's back rooms.

Robert had known misery through his childhood and adolescent years, but this was the first time he knew how depression felt. He couldn't imagine how those who live with these types of thoughts and feelings survive. He didn't know how it could get worse.

But it did.

On a Monday just before noon, when *Catfish Charley's* was starting to fill up with the lunch crowd, the manager knocked on the door frame of Robert's temporary office.

"Robert, there are a couple of police officers out here looking for you."

Robert quickly went to the front, hoping nothing had happened to Patricia or the kids.

As he reached the hostess podium, one officer spoke. "Robert Rhodes?"

"Yes, that's me."

"Mr. Rhodes, please turn around for me. You're being arrested for assault and battery."

There was a hush in the restaurant and a gasp from one of the employees who had gathered around.

"What are you talking about?" Robert asked desperately.

"They'll explain it all down at the courthouse, Mr. Rhodes."

As they handcuffed him and put him into the back of the patrol car, Robert was confused and humiliated. The people that respected and loved him had seen him taken away as a dangerous man.

Robert could not surmise what was happening.

They arrived at the Pope County Courthouse at 12:30. The courthouse was a three-story, tan, stone structure positioned on the corner of Main and Arkansas Streets in downtown Russellville. Most county courthouses in the South sat in the middle of a town square, but for some reason Pope County's didn't follow this pattern.

As the officers escorted Robert down the long hallway, he was glad to see most employees were away at lunch.

He was uncuffed and put into a cell by himself. Still totally confused, he sat in the cold cement chamber.

After several hours, an officer came and led him to the chambers of Judge Bennie Burdette. Robert had known Judge Burdette for several years and had voted for him each time he came up for re-election. On several occasions, the judge had sent juveniles to work for Robert when he thought they had a chance at reform.

The officer left Robert alone with Judge Burdette. The judge welcomed Robert and offered him a seat.

"Robert, I just want to talk to you for a minute." The Judge began. "This is not an interrogation, but you're welcome to have your lawyer with you if you want."

He had been Mirandized at the restaurant in front of his peers, but had not acted on it yet. "Should I?" Robert asked. "I don't even know why I'm here. I mean, they told me I was being arrested for assault, but Judge, I haven't tried to hurt anyone, ever!"

"Well, Robert," Judge Burdette said in a fatherly voice, "Patricia is the one who made the complaint."

Robert sat looking at the cuffs on his wrists, but staring beyond. Then questioned in a soft voice, "Really?"

"Yes, Robert. She claims over the course of your marriage, you threatened her several times. Do you have anything to say about that?"

Confused and shaking his head slowly from side to side, he tried to remember any incident which Patricia might be referring.

"Judge Burdette, Patricia and I were not close for a long time, but I can guarantee you with every fiber of my soul that I never lifted a hand toward her. I spent many nights in frustration and even went out and punched the brick wall a few times, but I never, *never* hit her."

"Her case is pretty weak, Robert. There are no reports of abuse or complaints against you. She even admits you never physically hurt her. She said she was just scared of you," the Judge explained.

In some ways, that statement even hurt worse. Robert wondered what kind of husband made his wife afraid of him.

Then he remembered the influence of Dr. Core and it all made sense.

"When I saw the complaint on the prosecuting attorney's desk, I asked him if I could talk to you first," Judge Burgert continued. "I hate to drag your good name through the dirt. I think I can get him to dismiss it on lack of evidence. Sorry, I'll have to send you back down to our concrete condos, but I'll talk to him this afternoon."

"Thanks so much, Judge. I am just blown away by this and embarrassed."

There was no news before everyone went home for the day, so Robert had a night in jail to think about all the potential outcomes of this situation. He also couldn't help but wonder what Patricia had to gain from this accusation. Undoubtedly fueled by her man-hating psychiatrist, Patricia must've felt this was helping her recovery.

At about ten o'clock the next morning, the guard opened the door and told Robert he was free. The officers gave him a ride back to Catfish Charley's.

It embarrassed him, but felt the best way to handle his situation was to confront the accusations with those who were aware of his arrest. He called Charley Stanley and explained what had happened. Charley knew well of the situation with Patricia over the years. He was fully supportive of his employee and business partner.

The employees at the restaurant were welcoming to him and felt they could trust the man they had known for so long.

Robert even called his former in-laws. The Potters loved and sustained Robert as if he were their own. He explained what had happened and assured them he was innocent of such behavior.

Martha Potter had been a second mother to Robert. She had seen what he had gone through with her daughter and how he had supported her. She believed Robert but told him she had already been told about the charges by Patricia.

"It gets a little worse, I'm afraid," Martha cautiously said. "I am pretty sure she has told the kids about it."

This was another blow to the gut. For some reason, he felt dirty and guilty, as if he *had* done something. He wondered how he would address it with his kids. If he weren't careful, it would appear as if he were calling their mother a liar and they would rally around her.

He wondered if he had ever left some of his journals lying around outlining his frustrations with her, which could lead them to believe he could do something as horrible as this.

Worst of all, what if they believed he was an abuser and because they had his DNA pulsing through them, they may be capable of such behavior? How could Patricia have possibly felt these accusations could benefit her children?

For the millionth time since the divorce, sitting in his hotel room, Robert cried.

Robert decided not to even talk to his children about the accusations but hoped they could sometime soon judge for themselves who their dad really was.

Chapter 44

Robert felt it would be a betrayal to his kids to get over the divorce. He couldn't just throw away the twenty-year marriage and forget about it, but he knew it wasn't healthy to wallow in his sorrow.

He learned to take one day at a time, one hour at a time, until periodically, he could feel a twinge of normalcy and happiness. The twinges became more frequent and the normalcy more constant.

He continued to nourish the relationship with his kids, and eventually they defined their father-child relationships by a new paradigm.

A year passed since the divorce and Robert buried himself in his work. Charley arrived at a point in his life where he wasn't able to work at the restaurants much. At just over eighty years old, his health was such that he didn't know how much longer he would be around. Because of this, Robert practically ran *Catfish Enterprises, Inc.*

Sixty hours of work per week ensured Robert didn't get bored. Robert bought a small house and furnished it slowly, since he was rarely there. One Sunday, some friends from church, Jan and Alan Higgins, pulled Robert aside and made a proposal.

"Robert, we've got a friend that's coming out to visit from California," Jan said. "She's been divorced for a couple of years now. Well, we were wondering if you might want to meet her. Maybe show her around?"

"Oh, I don't think I'm ready for that yet," Robert responded. "But thanks for thinking of me."

In fact, Robert had thought about dating again. He had even chatted online and joined a couple of dating sites, but couldn't bring himself to ask anyone out yet. Maybe, he thought, it was a natural progression of his returning happiness. Maybe it was time.

He called the Higgins and arranged the date. The date was uneventful, but he was glad he stuck his toe in the water. If it did anything, it broke the ice for future dates.

In the following months, Robert enjoyed periodic dating. He didn't think about getting married again, but did enjoy the company and friendships.

In May, he received notice in the mail of his upcoming twenty-fifth class reunion. Having never been to a reunion. He thought it would be nice to see some of the people he had gone to school with.

They held the first night of the reunion at the Commons in Russellville High School. He had been back to the school a few times as a parent. Tabbie had graduated two years earlier from his alma mater. Robert approached the welcome table and picked up his nametag. He was already as uncomfortable as he had been in high school. Robert preferred the small intimate groups rather than being in crowds.

He slowly worked the crowd, trying to remember people he had disliked twenty-five years earlier. It surprised him how many people remembered him. He had lost his thick head of hair many years ago and now shaved his head daily. His build was average in high school, but now he weighed forty more pounds. Even though he had been beaten up by life, he felt much more confident than he had back then.

After talking to several people, he made his way back to the welcoming table where he saw a list of *Couldn't Contact*. He glanced over the names, seeing ones he had forgotten and many he had never known. Beside that list was another list of *Couldn't Attend but with Contact Information*. Again, the list included names he had forgotten. As he ran his finger down the page, he paused on one name in particular and sighed a smile—*Carla Morton!*

Robert had lost track of Carla after her parents moved from Russellville twenty years ago. The last he heard, she was still living in Utah, but it listed her home as Denver. There was no physical address listed, but there was an email address. He borrowed a pen and paper and jotted down the information.

Slightly giddy at seeing her name, Robert's thoughts drifted back twenty-five years earlier to the best single year of his life. His senior year was a year of definition for the awkward boy. He had learned how to love and be loved. He had grown in self-worth and esteem, all because of the girl whose name was in front of him.

He always assumed she was married, but it listed her maiden name, which piqued his interest. At home that night, Robert sat at his computer, carefully crafting his email. *How do you say hello after all these years?*

Finally, he settled on something friendly but unassuming.

Carla,

I saw your name and email address listed at the RHS 25th anniversary. I am hoping that you remember me. How are you? I would really like to catch up with you. I look forward to hearing from you.

He was excited to check his email in the morning. That night, he went to sleep remembering what he could about a happy time in his life and about a girl who had saved him and spilled sunshine into his soul.

Robert had trouble concentrating on work for the next couple of days. He checked his email account several times each day. On the third day, after sending his email to Carla, he began losing hope. *For whatever reason*, he thought, *she must not want to dig up the past. She probably has moved on quite nicely.*

Four days after he sent the message to Carla, he sat staring at the inbox of his email account. She had written him back, and he was one click away from seeing her salutation:

Robert,

Of course, I remember you! How could I not? You were an important part of my life in Russellville. Sorry I didn't answer earlier. I took a long weekend with a friend and just got back.

I hear from my parents that you married a local girl. How many kids do you have? I know you wanted about a dozen! LOL.

I live in Denver. My only child is going to college in Southern California.
Please let me know what's happening in your life. Please write back and fill me in.
CM

Robert sat staring at the screen for several minutes. He read the message many times, looking for any nuances in the words which would somehow reveal hidden meaning. She didn't mention a husband, but she had been away with a friend. It could be a serious boyfriend. It could just be one of her girlfriends; she surely had many. As far as he knew, she could be gay and it could be a girlfriend. At this point, he had no way of knowing.

The next step in his thought process was how and when to answer. He certainly couldn't answer right away. Suavely, he needed to wait a couple of days, but not too long. The next email needed to be perfect. He had a couple of days to plan it, but it couldn't look planned.

Forty-eight hours later, he responded,

Carla,

I was so pleased that you responded to my email. It was good to see your name at the reunion. I had hoped you would respond.

I am still living in Russellville. How are your parents? I miss seeing them at church.

I married a girl who moved here after you left. Her name is Patricia. Sadly, we divorced a few years ago. I have two children, Tabbie and Russell. They live here in town, but I don't get to see them enough. I wish I could be with them every day.

So, you have a son? Tell me about him and all about what is going on in your life. I look forward to hearing from you.

Now, how to end?

Regards,

RR

Robert read and re-read the message. It was simple, yet shared enough information. He wanted to know more about her but didn't want to come across as anxious.

After hitting *send*, Robert leaned back in his desk chair and again thought of Carla.

She had been an amazing part of his life. Maybe it had only been a teenaged love affair, but she had corrected his course. He knew she was sincerely in love with him and was one of the few people in life which truly cared about him. It was fun to think about her now with no restraints.

He also remembered the broken heart with which she had left him. How could she have walked away so easily from something so important? Even though he was feeling giddy, he was also cautious.

A few minutes later, while still reclining in his chair, the computer dinged, and an email popped up.

Her immediate response started a procession of emails between the two.

During the next hour, Robert learned a lot about his former girlfriend. She indeed was divorced. She had been married for ten years, living in Utah. During that time, she and her husband had two children: a daughter, McKell who had died of SIDS at six months old, and a boy Devin who was now in graduate school in California. After finding out that her husband had been having an affair for two years, she divorced him. Carla finished school with a degree in accounting. After graduating, she accepted a job with a firm in Denver and had lived there since, never getting remarried.

In one of her emails, she said something that gave Robert a great deal of hope; she said, *the year in Russellville is such a distant memory, but my memories of you, Robert, have been close to me always.*

Chapter 45

Robert found it hard to work the next day, thinking about Carla. He pictured her in his mind's eye as she had looked the last time he saw her, but as he looked in the mirror, he saw how much he had aged and was a little unsure of himself.

That evening, her first email had her phone number and an invitation to call her. After rehearsing as if he were a schoolboy, he reached for his phone and dialed.

They spoke for three hours that first night. That night was the start of many nights in which they spoke. They didn't speak every night, but over the next couple of weeks, they developed a sincere long-distance relationship.

On the second or third extended call, Carla revealed a very important fact about herself, yet for something so important, she revealed it quite *matter-of-factly*. Several years earlier, they diagnosed Carla with muscular dystrophy.

"I can function pretty well now," Carla told him. "As it progresses, I may not be able to work much longer. I walk very slow and deliberate. Some days, I have to rely on a wheelchair."

"I'm sorry, Carla, why didn't you tell me earlier?" Robert asked sympathetically.

Randy Judd

"I don't want the disease to define me, that's not who I am!" she responded stoically. "I don't want people to feel sorry for me."

That attitude was the same Carla he had known before—a child which died in infancy, a broken marriage, and a debilitating disease, yet she was going to come out on top! He could certainly learn a lot from her attitude.

He also remembered how much she had loved to run as a teenager. That must have been especially hard for her.

He was excited when she finally attached a picture of herself in an email. He stared at it for quite a while. In the picture, she was sitting so he couldn't see any effects of her condition, but she looked only slightly aged from the girl he had known. Her complexion appeared to have stayed young, and her eyes were as beautiful as ever. He printed the picture and hung it on his computer.

Their conversations weren't just nostalgic; they quickly covered most of the memories. Their nightly talks were current, as if they were sitting next to a friend on the couch. It didn't take long before they ended calls with "*I love you*" and each hoped a phoenix could rise from the ashes of their former love.

Both were aware that they might be chasing a dream. It's not unusual for two people to try to rekindle a high school romance only to find that current reality is far from past fantasy. Robert was also aware of people who had married too quickly after a divorce and found the second marriage ending suddenly. He was determined not to let this happen. He had resolved to proceed cautiously.

In spring of the next year, Carla planned a trip to Arkansas to see Robert. It was easier for her to get away from work and besides; she wanted to see Arkansas again.

Robert arrived at the Little Rock airport an hour before her scheduled arrival with a bouquet of freshly picked yellow daffodils in his hand.

He watched the arrival board impatiently until the words beside the flight number said *landed.*

As he waited at the bottom of the escalator, he watched the arriving passengers and cursed the 9/11 hijackers that he could no longer meet his guest at the gate.

Realizing she would not be able to use the escalator, he found a chair near the only elevator and waited. Each time the doors opened; he quickly surveyed the passengers.

When he saw the edge of a wheelchair, his heart raced. Carla thanked the agent who had assisted her and stood on her own.

There in front of him was a woman of barely five-foot tall. She was holding herself up with a hand on the wall beside her. She walked forward stiffly, looking for him. As she walked, she dragged one foot slightly behind.

There, he thought, *is the most beautiful creature I've ever seen!*

He walked toward her and she caught his eye. Without a word being spoken, he gently put his arms around her and hugged her cautiously.

As they pulled away, her first words were, "I know I made you nervous that night in the front seat of your GTO, but it's ok to kiss me." And he did. As their lips touched for the first time in twenty-five years, it was as if nothing had changed.

Her one-week visit was a passing summer shower and soon the flowers would bloom.

They spent the week in joy, laughter, and deep conversation. In an effort to come clean with her, Robert told of his reason for not joining her church when they were dating in high school. It surprised her, but she was proud that he was able to give it up so many years ago.

He told her about Ricky Goodman and the nemesis he had been. After two decades, he explained the scars she had seen on a March day in the park. She gently wiped the tears away. First hers, then his.

She had confessions to tell him as well.

Alas, they felt as though the relationship was clean of all secrets.

She apologized profusely for her actions so long ago that had left him in such pain. Carla took full accountability for her immature actions and begged for his forgiveness.

"I was so starry-eyed with my first husband. He was about ready to graduate and from a rich family. I thought my life would be bliss. For the first couple of years, we were happy with being a married couple. We were never really close, though. Steve worked a ton of hours, and I found myself lonely. Although I shouldn't have, there were many times during my marriage when my mind drifted back to my time with you, Robert. I knew that I would not have been lonely with you. I tried to bury my yearning for you and eventually, time pushed it deep down. When I heard you had got married also, I buried those feelings.

"Thanks for resurrecting them after all these years. I love you dearly and hope you will forgive me for taking away all the years of joy we could've had together."

He easily forgave.

During the short seven days together, they visited memories all around Russellville. The town had grown substantially, but the roots were the same. She knew she could love the place that was Robert's home.

In the last few hours together, they talked in definite terms about the future. They talked about marriage. In their mid-forties, there was not much use for a creative proposal. They just agreed they could think of nothing greater than to grow old together.

"I won't be able to work much longer anyway," Carla said. "I would love to continue my life with you in these green rolling hills."

She took care of her affairs in Colorado and in a simple ceremony, the couple was married in July.

Using the money they had saved and gained from the equity in both their houses, the couple bought a house in Russellville. Knowing it needed to be easy for Carla to move around in and potentially wheelchair friendly, they purchased a red brick Tudor on the end of a cul-de-sac. It had all the living areas on the main level, with only guest bedrooms upstairs.

It was a miraculous day for the couple when Carla and her cat, Wilber, finally moved in.

Carla and Robert were together. Finally, the relationship that had started awkwardly in high school experienced resurrection. Now it flourished into a mature love affair.

The newlyweds were more than just content—they were truly happy. They were puzzle pieces for each other and their relationship was that of a long forgotten yummy beanbag chair which they fell right back into.

Carla's personality hadn't waned, and she made friends quickly. It again amazed Robert how drawn people were to her. He came to the conclusion that if anyone didn't like her—it was their issue and not hers.

He felt it was an honor to be associated with her in any manner. She felt the same about him and wished she had not forsaken him so long ago. They both realized that the events of their lives had refined and defined them even more for this moment.

Carla and Robert relaxed many evenings in the backyard, entertained solely by their companionship. He thoroughly enjoyed serving her in her illness. In some ways, the years of serving Patricia in her dependence had prepared him for compassionate service to Carla.

Tabbie married and soon announced she was pregnant with Robert's first grandchild.

Robert was in a great new place in his life, yet it amazed him that he could not feel fully actualized. There was still the same gnawing feeling that had been there all his life—the feeling that he did not deserve what he had or was not worthy of it. He kept those feelings within himself.

Chapter 46

On a sunny spring day, two years after their marriage, Charley summoned Robert to have lunch with him. Over the past quarter century, the two men had become close friends.

Only one time had there been any contention in their relationship. Robert had left his employment with Charley for a short while back in the eighties. Upon leaving, Robert got a job with a private contractor which provided the food services on military bases. That adventure lasted only a month, after which Robert came humbly back to Charley for his old job. That situation was a galvanizing event for the two men.

Today, the two friends met at the *Old South Restaurant*—where Lou had once served—on the east end of town.

"Robert," Charley said after ordering, but before the food arrived, "in case you haven't noticed, I'm getting to be an old man."

His younger friend smiled because it was easy to see. The old man used a walker most of the time and could no longer go to the kitchens of his restaurants because of his oxygen tanks. Mount Charley was now little more than an eroded hill. Nearing ninety years old, he was still as active as was possible for him.

He took a drink to his mouth with his shaking hand. After warily putting it down, he continued. "I am probably going to die pretty soon. I want to get things in order."

Robert wanted to protest his demise, but it would've probably seemed patronizing.

"You've been a superb partner for me, Robert. I never had to worry about your honesty or your work ethic." He paused for a breath. "You are the reason the *Catfish Charley Empire* has sustained itself.

"As you know, my two kids think they are too good for the restaurant business, so I know that they won't run them very well after I'm gone. I don't want to see the business go to pot."

"Robert, I am going to make provisions in my will for you to buy the business at a *very* discounted price. I want you to carry on the legacy. Do you want them? Will you do it?"

Even though Robert didn't know the details, he was flabbergasted at the thought of having the stores. He had thought for several years about what he would do when his boss died. He even talked to Charley eight years before about buying them, but the man wouldn't relinquish.

"Charley, you've been a second father to me. You've been nothing but fair to me all along. You've supported me with all my problems. It would honor me to carry on the name! Thank you."

Charley wasn't an emotional man. In all the years Robert had known him, there was only one time he had seen a tear in the eyes of his stalwart friend—at the funeral of his wife. So instead of letting this scene get too mushy, the old man changed the subject.

"Robert, do you see that old Corvette out there?"

Robert swiveled on his chair and saw a red 1962 Chevrolet Corvette in perfectly restored condition.

As Robert assured him he had seen it, the old man began his recollection. "Many, many years ago, I wanted a Corvette. Of course, I was poor at the time. As time went on, I finally made enough money to buy one. By then, it didn't seem practical. I had a family and responsibilities to take care of. What business did I have gallivantin' around in a sports car like that?"

His voice got raspy. He stopped to get another drink to quench his ancient throat. Then continued.

"Robert, as most men do, I've had a lot of regrets in my life. Believe it or not, one of my biggest regrets was not having bought that sports car. Not for the car itself, but what it represents: fun, freedom, leisure. I worked too much in my life and now I'm regretting not playing more. I couldn't even get in one of those anymore, so I've missed my opportunity."

Robert watched a couple get into the Corvette and drive it away, much as the old man's dreams. He started to say something but could tell Charley wanted to finish.

Mount Charley reached into his pocket and pulled out a company check and laid it on the table.

"Robert, I don't want you to have the same regrets. I've got a check here payable to Robert Rhodes in the amount of fifty thousand dollars. Go pick out *your* sports car!"

At first, Robert smiled as if to be amused by the old storyteller, but as he looked at the check, he could see it was just as Charley had said.

"No, Charley, I can't take this. You can't just give me this much money."

"I can … and I just did. At my age, I can do whatever I please. Consider it a bonus and don't dare spend it on anything but a sports car for you and that precious sweetheart of yours."

For the first time in their relationship, Robert hugged the older man and for the second time, Robert saw a tear in his eye.

At home, Carla would not let Robert talk about doing anything else with the money. "Charley said buy a car. He's your boss, so go buy yourself a car!"

Robert reluctantly relinquished and meticulously started shopping for a sports car.

Weeks later, he finally found a Jaguar F-Type in San Diego.

Chapter 47

It was already five o'clock in Elk City when he checked into the *Grapes of Wrath Motor Inn*. After lying on the thin, lumpy mattress for a few minutes to relieve the road fatigue, Robert decided to see the town while he still had light.

For the most part, he was underwhelmed. It seemed like a nice little town, but he had no memories to be nostalgic about. His siblings would surely have lots of recollections, but not Robert.

He saw the hospital where he was born. He drove to the old gas station where they had lived. The cement building was long since abandoned and looked quite sad as it stood alongside route sixty-six with all its windows broken out.

Robert returned to the motor inn, called Carla, and nestled in bed with thoughts of being with her the following night.

That night, the last night of his journey home, he dreamed.

In his dream, he was standing on a country road. It was a gorgeous day, probably early or late summer because the temperature was perfect, hardly noticeable. He was in the Ozarks, but in a place he'd never been before. Ahead of him, about a hundred yards, stood Carla, his kids—in their younger years—and extended family. They were all beckoning him to come.

He noticed that where they were standing was even more beautiful than where he was. They were standing on the edge of a deep blue lake, lined with lush green Arkansas hardwoods.

In the dream, he was aware that he wanted nothing more than to be with them, sharing in their joy.

He walked toward them, then walked a little faster, then jogged, then ran. Almost predictably, he could feel something behind him in the woods. As he gained speed and momentum toward his goal, he started noticing his right leg became harder and harder to move. His efforts left him feeling as though he was running in knee-high mud. As much as he tried, it was laborious to run. He began to tire. Robert looked down to see if he could determine why he had to make such an effort to move toward his aspiration. Whatever had been behind him all these years had finally caught him. Looking down, he could see his lower right leg was surrounded by a dark cloud. The cloud was the color of charcoal and was denser than fog. He tried to pull his leg from the dark gray fog, but the something *held on. The cloud slowed him like invisible mud.*

Robert looked toward his family and they were moving away, looking back at him longingly. He could hear Tabbie faintly saying, "Why isn't Daddy coming?"

He tried to move again but was once again bogged down by the murky blur.

Still in his dream, he looked again at the cloud. Gradually, where nothing had been before, a face started to appear. As it fashioned more clearly, he thought he recognized the form but couldn't tell from where. As it came more into focus, he identified it from more than thirty years earlier. The face was that of his adversary, Ricky Goodman.

After waking from his dream, Robert lay in the hotel bed for quite a while. Triumphantly, after all these years, he could discern what the dream meant. He always knew Ricky was the catalyst—if not the genesis—of many of his problems, but Robert hadn't really entertained the idea, that Ricky was holding him back, holding him back from success, holding him back from giving his all, holding him back from completely experiencing life and love.

But what was the man, Robert, to do?

After lying under the cheap polyester bedspread for a few more minutes, he made his decision. He must find Ricky Goodman and confront his nemesis.

He didn't know what he was going to do, but he felt driven by some unseen power to finally deal with his foe.

He immediately went to his phone, which was charging in the bathroom. He had heard quite a while ago that Ricky was living north of Russellville, near the town of Appleton. Searching for his name, Robert checked all the towns in the county with no success. He then checked his brothers' names. Ernie returned no matches. But there was a Joel, so Robert took down the number.

He quickly dialed the number, and a woman answered. She said Joel wasn't there, and she identified herself as his wife. Robert said he was an old friend of the family but wasn't about to give his name. He then asked if she knew the whereabouts of Ricky, and she did. He didn't have a phone though, so she gave him the address and the directions to his trailer.

After thanking the woman, Robert quickly got dressed and exited the motor inn, not sure what lay ahead.

In his new car, all he heard was the quiet roar of the road. Robert hadn't turned on the music, because he needed to hear his thoughts and feel his feelings more clearly.

Confronting Ricky was a new idea for Robert. All his life, he hoped he'd never see him again. He hated the boy ... man. How many times had Robert wished Ricky had died in the fire instead of Martha, his mother? Every time he thought of his foe, the veins in his neck filled and his heart raced. How could he control his emotions? What would he say to him?

Traveling across the red dirt plains of western Oklahoma, there was plenty of time to think. He decided that he wanted to confront Ricky before returning home, before losing his determination and before Carla could reason with him. At the rate he was going, he could get to Appleton by late afternoon.

As he drove, he pictured the event in his mind and tried to fill in the many unknowns. How would Ricky look? Does he have a family and will they be there? How will he react to the visit of someone who knows how evil he really is? And the disturbing thought, what if the confrontation turns violent? What then?

Although Robert felt he could take care of himself, there were too many unknowns about what he was approaching. He decided it would be prudent to have a weapon, just in case. He had a friend who owned a pawnshop just outside of Clarksville, Arkansas who could 'loan' him a pistol. If he purchased one, he would be subject to the waiting period. The gun would only be for protection in case he was attacked.

Just a little after two o'clock, the Jaguar pulled into *Detmar's Pawn and Gun*. Robert had known Roadie Detmar in high school. They sat together sometimes at the *loser's table*. He wasn't known by 'Roadie' then, he was Ralph. He got the name Roadie by touring with Jimmy Buffet's band—the Coral Reefers—soon after high school, and his nickname stuck. After a year of touring, Buffet broke his leg, jumping off the stage, and they canceled the tour. Now, thirty years later, the picture of him and Buffet still had an honored place on the pawnshop's wall.

After exchanging salutations and looking at the new roadster, Robert revealed the reason for his visit. Looking around and making sure none of the other people in the store could hear him, Robert spoke. "Roadie, I need to get a pistol, but I need it today."

"Well, I'd love to sell you a gun," Roadie said, "but you know there's a waiting period. What you need it that fast for, you ain't planning on robbin' a bank to pay for that car, are you?"

"No, I'm not going to rob or kill anyone. I just need it for protection." Robert responded, revealing as little as possible.

"Well, let me think." Roadie thought. "I've got a small snub-nosed thirty-eight that I've been needing to get rid of. I guess I could give it to a good friend as a gift, do the paperwork later."

"That sounds pretty good, Roadie," Robert responded, "and what kind of good friend should I be in return? Maybe a two-hundred-dollar good friend?"

"Oh, I always thought you were a better friend than that." Roadie teased.

So, the two old acquaintances settled on two-hundred and seventy-five dollars. Robert left the shop after promising not to rob a bank where the gun could be traced back to him. Robert drove on to an unplanned appointment with an unsure outcome.

Randy Judd

Chapter 48

An hour later, Robert called Carla. She was not home—he remembered that she was going to pick up their granddaughter and bring her back to their house. He left a message saying how excited he was to see her tonight and how much he loved her.

His car easily navigated the curves of the highways leading to the area around Appleton. He stopped at an intersection and read the signs.

His heart started racing. Beads of sweat started forming on his brow. *Was this necessary or even smart?* He answered himself that it may not be smart, but it was essential.

Driven by a force that he didn't recognize or even want, Robert took the highway that *could* lead him to personal redemption *or* personal destruction. He thought he was getting close to the address, but wasn't exactly sure where the road was where Ricky lived. He pulled into a convenience store to ask directions. The tattooed worker behind the counter gave clear directions toward a country road about a mile up the highway. Robert slowly drove the remaining mile, not sure what the outcome of his drive would be.

He had been rehearsing the encounter with Ricky in his mind for many hours now. Robert planned on reminding him about the hell he had put him through forty years ago. If Ricky couldn't remember, Robert was prepared to tell him—in detail—of all the abuse and humiliation he had suffered at the hands of Ricky and his brothers. Robert was worried about the possibility of the encounter turning violent, initiated by either man. He stashed the thirty-eight into his sport coat. The anger that kindled within Robert was foreign to him. It was building to a crescendo, and he didn't want to be the person he had become in the last few hours.

The sign read *Buttermilk Road,* but it might as well have read *Destiny,* because the rest of his life could well be determined by the outcome of this visit. Robert had been told that Ricky's place was the first place on the left after turning on the dirt road. About a quarter mile down the road on the left, Robert saw a driveway cut into thick trees. At the head of the driveway was a mailbox which had Ricky's name handwritten in red model airplane paint.

Robert stopped for a moment at the head of the driveway, knowing this was his last chance to back out. He didn't pause for long. As he proceeded down the dusty driveway, he soon passed pieces of furniture and abandoned car parts. The closer to the house he got, the thicker the debris became. Surveying the refuse, he quickly counted five cars which had been abandoned many years before. He couldn't help but think how much it reminded him of the junk cars he and Ricky had played in when he was little and where he was introduced to the *Sissy Circle.* Robert's Jaguar was certainly on foreign ground.

Ricky's home was now in view. It was nothing more than a travel trailer parked under some trees. Robert had known many people over the years who lived in mobile homes who took great care and pride in them. The mobile homes of his friends were nice residences, but Ricky's didn't measure up. It wasn't actually even a mobile home but a travel trailer which a family would pull behind a pickup to go camping. It had been a long time since this trailer had been suitable for camping. Rust had a prominent presence on the metal sides, and the tires were flat and rotten. It sat at the back of the property, against a line of ragged old cedar trees. The driveway entered where Robert had driven in but exited at the other end of the property, creating a kind of redneck circle drive. A mangy looking dog barked at Robert, more out of obligation than threat. He noticed that among the skeletal cars in the yard, there were none that could be working. *Ricky may not be home*, Robert thought. He hadn't really entertained this idea as he planned his visit. Robert knew he couldn't come back later. The passion that had brought him to this point could not be recreated later when he was thinking rationally.

As he approached the door of the tenement on wheels, the dog's barks subsided, and now the mutt just wanted to be petted. Robert knocked on the door and the vibration reverberated down the length of the trailer. He waited thirty seconds or so and knocked again. All he could hear was a mockingbird singing above him and the buzz of a large horsefly. It was obvious that no one was home. *Now what should he do? Should he just burn the trailer down?* That might prove to be more of a blessing than a punishment to Ricky and Robert would certainly land himself in jail. He also knew he couldn't just write a sticky note and leave it on his door saying, *I was here, but you weren't. You are a sack of crap! Be back later.*

He reached for the doorknob. It turned! With nothing much to protect, the owner had left it unlocked. Robert pulled the door open and the musty smell of old smoke came over him.

"Hello, anybody home?" No response. "Hello, Ricky?" Still nothing. Robert looked around and then back over his shoulders. There was no other house in sight and the trailer was hidden from the road except for a little clearing down Buttermilk Road. He entered Ricky's home, not exactly sure why.

Entering Ricky's abode, Robert almost choked on the horrible smell. It was a combination of tobacco smoke, body odor, and of food rotting in the sink. He wondered if the owner had even been here recently until he saw a banana peel on the counter that had not had more than a few hours of decomposition. The trailer had only one main room and a bathroom. Robert knew no one was home because—with a view of the entire house—he would have been able to see them unless they were hiding under the piles of clothes.

The trailer revealed a lot about Ricky: the garbage, the dirty clothes, the soiled dishes. It smelled of death. It took him aback, but he was not totally surprised to see some drug syringes lying on the kitchen counter. As Robert got closer, he could tell that the paraphernalia probably had been used today. He wasn't surprised at all that Ricky was an active user. Suddenly, the thought of a drug crazed Ricky coming through the door scared Robert. With his fingers, he lightly pulled back a dingy curtain and looked toward the road. He didn't see any cars. He had already ascertained that there wasn't a back door to this place. If Ricky came home, Robert was trapped. Robert didn't want to take much longer inside. He would much rather wait for him outside to kick his butt.

On the counter next to the syringes was a prescription drug bottle. Robert assumed it was some stolen prescription to support his obvious drug habit. Picking up the bottle, it had Ricky's name on the label. Robert looked at the name *Xeexum*. Holding the bottle, he thought hard. He had heard of this drug recently, but what was it for? He also saw on the counter a pamphlet titled *Making Life Bearable: The Final Stages of AIDS*. That's where he had heard of the drug! The FDA had just approved it to relieve and comfort aids patients in the last days before they died. *Ricky was dying!*

For a second, a hint of compassion came over Robert, but quickly passed.

Robert almost dropped the bottle as he heard a car on the gravel of Buttermilk Road. Putting his right hand on his jacket where the gun hid, he cautiously moved the musty red curtain again and peeked out the window. He saw a newer SUV passing the property. Robert was relieved to see that the passing vehicle was much too nice and expensive for the owner of this property—but about a half mile behind the SUV was a car that certainly could be Ricky's. It was a mid-80s Buick which generated a rumble that let everyone know the muffler was almost nonexistent.

Robert leaped out of the trailer, slamming the door behind him. Suddenly, he wasn't sure he wanted to deal with Ricky right now. He didn't know how to process this new information about his disease so quickly. He ran past the dog—who still wanted to be petted—to his F-Type. Robert jumped in, started the engine, and headed quietly out of the driveway at the back end of the property. At the same time, the Buick pulled in the front end. Robert pulled to a clearing on Buttermilk Road, where he could look back at the trailer.

By the time he stopped and looked back, the Buick had parked. As the old car door creaked open, Ricky got out. It was Robert's first look at Ricky Goodman in almost thirty-five years. The stranger was barely able to pull himself up to the car door as he got out. He was thin. His hair was long and scraggly even though he was balding. He shuffled precariously with a cane. A part of Robert wanted to feel sorry for the Gollum-like man, but the larger part of Robert didn't feel sympathy at all. As Ricky pulled himself up into the trailer, Robert knew it wouldn't be long before Robert was reading the man's obituary if anyone cared enough to write one.

Sitting on the shoulder of the road hidden by some large honeysuckle bushes, with his engine turned off and his window down, Robert suddenly noticed the perfumed smell of the tiny flowers near his car door. Contrasted with Ricky, Robert couldn't help but realize how sweet his own life was and that he didn't need to talk to Ricky anymore. He had always said *that sometimes bad things happen to good people* but—in Ricky's case—sometimes bad things happen to *bad* people. Karma had entered. Robert didn't need to pursue it anymore. Robert reached for the ignition, prepared to leave.

Chapter 49

Suddenly, the sound of the trailer door opening again interrupted the calm of the country road.

As Robert watched, he saw Ricky shuffle down the wooden steps with a bag of garbage in one hand, steadying himself with the other. He took the bag over to the metal trash can and then started pulling the can the hundred feet or so toward the road. Robert could see it was quite a struggle for the frail man as he pulled it a few feet, then stopped to rest. Robert started his car and, in a spontaneous move, drove back into Ricky's driveway.

Seeing the luxurious sports car coming down his poverty littered driveway, Ricky stopped dragging the can and waited as the car and its driver approached.

After turning the engine off, Robert opened the door and stepped out. He was dressed in jeans, a black t-shirt, and a tan tweed sports coat—housing a gun in the pocket. Even though Robert was happy with the way he looked in this outfit, he felt conspicuous—dressed in a sport coat amongst the misery. "I was driving down the road and saw that you were having trouble with the can, wondered if I could help?"

Ricky, slightly embarrassed at his weakened state, said, "Oh, I'll eventually get it. I do it every other week. It gives me something to do."

"Let me get it for you. It'll only take a minute," Robert said while hoisting the can up above his shoulder.

As Robert sat the metal trash can at the edge of the dirt road, he was aware that the garbage reeked as his trailer did, or his trailer reeked as the garbage did.

When he returned, Ricky thanked him. Looking intensely at the man, he asked, "Do I know you?"

"No, I'm pretty sure not. My name is R … Richard. I was just out for a drive when I saw you." Even though he had come to confront his adversary, suddenly, he didn't want to be recognized. Robert looked for any indication that he was identified but having a shaved head and being forty pounds overweight, he hardly resembled the ten-year-old Ricky had last seen.

"I'm Ricky. That car sure is a beauty. Is it new?" Ricky asked admiringly.

"No, it's a couple of years old." Robert said, downplaying the car.

"Would you want to sit and chat for a minute?" Ricky invited.

Not sure why he agreed, he said, "Sure, only for a minute."

The two men retired to a couple of web folding chairs under a tree in the front yard. The dog circled, then settled at Robert's feet.

Robert was able to take his first close look at his nemesis in over three decades. Ricky was very thin, probably not more than a hundred pounds, which was almost nothing for a man who had probably once stood over six feet tall. His hair was thin yet long in the back, as if it had once been styled into a mullet. His jeans were held up by a synched belt on its last notch. Rickey's t-shirt was holey and stained. His shoes were no-name tennis shoes with the sole worn out on one side from dragging his foot. The condition of his teeth was the result of years of neglect and smoke. All the teeth had yellowed. Two of them had black edges, which showed they had been rotting for years. His face had several days of stubble and was spotted with sores.

It surprised Robert at how lucid Ricky was, considering there was freshly used drug paraphernalia in the trailer. He guessed that Ricky's addiction was so far advanced that he simply used the drugs as maintenance and no longer provided a high.

"Do you live around here?" Ricky started casually.

"Naw, I live over in Russellville. I just take drives sometimes."

"If I had that car, I'd take drives too. I lived in and around Russellville most of my life … at least when I wasn't in jail or prison," the man revealed.

"Oh, really?" Robert responded, not knowing whether to act intrigued or uninterested.

"Yeah, I didn't lead a very good life," Ricky said, appearing thirty years older than he really was.

"Well, you can live well the *rest* of your life," Robert half-heartedly encouraged.

"No, I don't have much time left. They tell me less than six months. I would just as soon die now."

"I'm sorry to hear that." Robert lied and then pretended not to know the prognosis. "What have you got, if you don't mind me asking?"

"I've got the AIDS, got it in prison, I guess."

"Sorry to hear that." Another lie!

"I probably deserve it. You know, when you live alone like I do, you get a lot of time to think. I have caused a lot of people's pain in this life. Some of it I got punished for and some of it I didn't." Ricky confessed. "It wasn't until the last few years that I started to see myself as I really am. I watch some of those psychiatrist shows on the television who say I could blame my parents or my lack of education or society, but the truth is … *I* made those choices that caused my life to be the way it was."

Robert, not knowing what to say, settled on, "Oh, I'm sure it wasn't that bad."

"Oh, I can assure you it was," Ricky continued. "I spent ten years down at Tucker Prison, just outside of Pine Bluff. They sent me there for holding up a little country store. I didn't actually hurt anyone, at least not physically. I held a twelve-gauge shotgun to the face of a young mother as her little girl hung onto her mom's arm. This little girl couldn't have been more than seven or eight years old. I was so high that I really didn't care. I just needed the money for more drugs. Years later, after I came to my senses, I remembered exactly how that little girl looked, even the clothes she wore, but mostly, I could still see the terror in her eyes. I bet she still thinks about it today.

"That was one I got punished for, but there were many others I never went to trial for. I hurt a lot of people through my actions over the years. I could've just as easily chosen to do good to people, but I found it easier to do bad. Not just bad … evil."

Ricky excused himself as he went to the hose and got a drink of water. His voice had become raspy and needed refreshed. Robert petted the mutt until Ricky came back. Robert felt pretty sure humans could not contract the mange.

"Could I get you something to drink?" When Robert politely refused, Ricky continued.

"There is no way at this point in my life that I could ever make it right, but if I could reach out to even some of the people whose life I ruined, like that little girl, I would *beg* for their forgiveness."

"I'm sure most of them have forgotten it by now." Robert responded, knowing he himself hadn't.

"No, I am sure there are some people out there who still think about me and cringe. They probably hate me, *actually hate me!* You know what the bad thing about hate is, Richard? It doesn't hurt the one who it's directed to, *it only hurts the one who feels it.* It's like shooting a gun with the barrel sealed. The person you were aiming it at never felt it, but it explodes in your face and you get the pain.

"I know right now there is someone who hates me, hates my guts, and I don't even know it, yet they carry it around every day as I do this disease I have. They spend precious time they could be talking to their family or playing with their kids, hating me.

"But I don't blame them. I would hate me too."

Robert was feeling slightly uncomfortable at the wisdom Ricky was articulating. "What would you say if you could meet up with some of them?"

"First, I would tell them I was sorry. *I really am sorry.* The last few years of thinking about my life have really caused me to be racked with the pains of a damned soul. I would ask for their forgiveness, but if they didn't want to give it to me, I would understand.

"But then I would tell them to *let me go.* Let me go in their minds and in their hearts. I may have hurt them and caused them pain one day, but don't continue to let me hurt them every day. Forget me. Let the Lord above deal with me," Ricky paused, then finished, "because he will, soon."

The men sat quietly for a minute. The sound of the horsefly was, again, the only sound to be heard. The mutt stood up at Robert's feet, made a tight circle and then lay down again and licked the sore on its paw.

Robert understood what Ricky was talking about, even though he wouldn't have expected Ricky to be the one to remind him of it. Several years ago, Robert had felt great peace in forgiving his mom for the times of his childhood when he felt beaten, neglected, or pushed aside. Mother and son had shared a great hug, and their relationship today was everything he would hope.

But forgiving Ricky? That might take a little longer.

"Well, I'd better go so I can get back to my family," Robert said, feeling slightly guilty when he thought about Carla and his granddaughter waiting at home.

"Thanks for coming by and thanks for helping with the garbage," Ricky said, walking with Robert to the car.

As Robert started the car and put the stick shift in gear, Ricky supported himself on the driver's side door. Speaking just above the hum of the engine, he said, "I hope something I've said today helped you, Robert."

As he exited the driveway, the car's tires spit gravel behind it down the road. The frail man watched till the car was out of sight. As Robert pulled out onto the main highway, he was reflecting on what he had just been taught. He then realized, when Ricky was saying goodbye, *He Called Me Robert,* his real name he hadn't revealed!

Chapter 50

Robert wasn't paying much attention as he drove down the winding road toward Russellville.

Ricky's words echoed in his ears and questions penetrated his soul.

How much life had he wasted thinking about Ricky? How much energy had it sucked from positive things and relinquished to thoughts of the older boy? How many times had Robert excused his failures because of the memories of Ricky? Instead of being accountable for his own actions, had he sometimes used Ricky as a crutch?

Of course, the things Ricky did to the young Robert were horrible. There is no doubt these things could haunt any person, but had he handled them well? Did he need to take them into future relationships? Was there a way to make it through his teens without resorting to alcohol? When life got so good, why did he resist its heights by being anchored by distant memories?

For over three decades, the memories of his childhood had stalked Robert; being poor, not having many friends, his parents were never around, but most of all … Ricky. He suddenly felt he had been a whiner throughout life. Whining about how these things affected him. The memories were always there, behind him. Leering around corners. Staying just far enough back to haunt him, but not cause any immediate danger. The memory was stalking him.

If he had it all to do again …?

He doubted whether he could get rid of the memories all together, but maybe he could change it from being crashing cymbals in his ears to a tinkling bell.

While approaching a bridge over the Illinois Bayou, Robert checked his rear-view mirror for other cars—there were none. As he neared the middle of the bridge, he reached into his jacket pocket for the recently purchased pistol and then slung the gun into the depths of the current below. Along with the gun, he discarded at least part of the hate that had held him back for over thirty-five years. Tears formed in his eyes and slightly blurred his vision. While he was not sure if he could forgive Ricky completely, and he certainly would never *like* him, he thought he could finally—as Ricky had said—*let him go*.

Turning into the driveway of his red brick Tudor, no beach at sunset ever looked as inviting as the sight of Carla in the driveway playing with their toddling granddaughter. Today was a good day for her. She didn't need the wheelchair. His sweetheart's face beamed as she saw him in his new car. She had no way of knowing that his journey halfway across the country had really been a different type of journey for Robert. A journey of renaissance that now would lead to a brilliant future freed from the past.

As he turned the ignition off, he exited the car, a new man unfettered and worthy of all that was his.

EPILOGUE

After an hour or so of catching up with Carla, she broke away to return their granddaughter home and get some groceries. Robert smiled as she *conveniently* took the new Jaguar because it was blocking the driveway. Robert walked through the garage and out onto the deck.

As he was passing through the garage, he stopped and picked up his dad's coffee can full of nails. He clearly remembered his father's words from that day. Robert thought about how he himself had been a rusty, misshapen nail, but with the help of many hands—both seen and unseen—he had been slowly turned and hammered until he had had been beautifully reshaped and polished.

He then took the steps down to the lower patio near the garden. He loved the smells of the plant life that he had carefully arranged in the backyard. It had taken him four seasons to get the smells and colors to a point where it satisfied him. The relaxation he found in the garden was certainly zen-like.

In the awaking he had experienced in the last few hours, there was one enlightenment he still wanted to have.

During his life, Robert had many occasions that led him to believe that he was being saved for something special. As a little boy, he survived being bitten by a poisonous snake. The doctor had alluded to the fact that his recovery was a miracle. Later in his young life, stampeding horses trampled him and he fell out of a tree within inches of a nail in his head. Two strange men picked up Robert, but released him unharmed. Aside from the cruelty heaped upon him by the Goodman boys, he had also been spared from taking his own life with his father's gun. Moreover, he had been saved from alcohol and had survived a head on collision with a truck.

He had come to believe he was being spared for something great, something magnanimous. Now that he was almost fifty, *was it still to come?*

Throughout his life, Robert had generally felt he had something to live up to—something to prove to others. He somehow thought that proving himself to others would be a way of reaching his potential. Now he began to think of the meaning of life a little differently. He thought life to be more of a journey to reconcile who we are with who we want to be. Hopefully—*who we want to be*—stretches us and, in the stretching, makes us better. As the gap between who we actually are and our expectations of who we want to be becomes smaller, we feel more fulfilled, more actualized.

He strolled out in the middle of the vegetation to a small waterfall he had built to give the backyard a constant sound of falling water. He sat on the bench near the water.

His thoughts again turned philosophical. Because of the day's events, he had already come to realize that many of the failures and shortcomings in his life were not about Ricky Goodman—but about Robert Rhodes and his own decisions. After forty-eight years of life, he was finally accepting accountability for his own choices. Now, being loosened from the bands of his past, he felt he could accomplish anything. It was finally all up to him! It always had been, but as the foursome who traveled the yellow brick road, he just didn't know it. With maybe thirty years left in his life, there was plenty of time for magnificent accomplishments.

Maybe he had been spared to see this day. What a shame it would have been for him to leave this life at any time earlier than his realization of his own power.

The sound of the garage door opening signaled Carla returning from the store. He stood up from the bench, excited to help his sweetheart with the groceries.

THE END

Thank you for reading my novel. I'm happy to share it with you.

Please consider reading my other novels:

Forging Nails

A Prequel/Sequel to This Book

&

The Listening Bench

Both are available at randyjuddauthor.com

Is your book club reading one of my books? If I'm available, I would be happy to join your club one time via Zoom..

Just email me: randy.judd@randyjuddauthor.com

Printed in the USA
CPSIA information can be obtained
at www.ICGtesting.com
LVHW092015030124
768073LV00008B/65